12

DEATH IN HER FACE

A LAUREN ATWILL MYSTERY

DEATH IN HER FACE

SHEILA YORK

FIVE STAR
A part of Gale, Cengage Learning

GALE
CENGAGE Learning®

Detroit • New York • San Francisco • New Haven, Conn • Waterville, Maine • London

Copyright © 2012 by Sheila York.
Five Star™ Publishing, a part of Gale, Cengage Learning.

LIBRARY OF CONGRESS CATALOGING-IN-PUBLICATION DATA

York, Sheila.
   Death in her face : a Lauren Atwill mystery / Sheila York. — 1st ed.
     p. cm.
     ISBN 978-1-4328-2620-8 (hardcover) — ISBN 1-4328-2620-4 (hardcover) 1. Women screenwriters—Fiction. 2. Motion picture industry—Fiction. 3. Hollywood (Los Angeles, Calif.)—Fiction. I. Title.
   PS3625.O755D43 2012
   813'.6—dc23   2012015338

First Edition. First Printing: September 2012.
Published in conjunction with Tekno Books and Ed Gorman.
Find us on Facebook– https://www.facebook.com/FiveStarCengage
Visit our Web site– http://www.gale.cengage.com/fivestar/
Contact Five Star™ Publishing at FiveStar@cengage.com

Printed in Mexico
1 2 3 4 5 6 7 16 15 14 13 12

For David

ACKNOWLEDGMENTS

I'd like to thank those who helped me travel to the past and stay sane in the present: My husband, David Nighbert, Kathy Metzger, Linda and Scott Warnasch, Patrick Oliver, Jane Cleland, John Billheimer, Mark Lentz, Mariann Moery, Paul Vasquez, Julia Al-Nawal, Jeanne Marshall, Fawzi Al-Nawal, Barbara and David Wesner, Alan and Winnie Dolderer, Steve Viola, Michael Johnson, Rebecca Roe, Deni Dietz, Bob Lange, David Salper, Woody Haut, D'Arcy Carr, Andy McCann, Julie Farrington, Chris Cooper, Wing Ng, Naveen Chaudhary, and the librarians at the Los Angeles and New York City public libraries and the Academy of Motion Picture Arts and Sciences.

CHAPTER 1

New York City
December 1946

Helen said, "You have to come back to Los Angeles." And that was all it took.

I figured I was better off in Los Angeles, where I'd been shot at, than in New York, where I'd been shot.

As it turned out, going back would put me face to face with another killer with a gun. But of course I didn't know that when my best friend, Helen Ross, marched past me and tossed her handbag onto the sofa of my hotel suite.

"You don't belong in New York," she said. "It's cold, it's dirty, it's no place to recuperate."

I closed the door. "It's nice to see you again, too."

"Oh, honey, I'm sorry." She hurried back over, took both my hands in her gloved ones, and planted a kiss near my cheek. She held on to my hands. "How are you?"

"Fine." I was two weeks out of the hospital, five weeks and four days after being shot.

"I figured if you weren't doing as well as your letters said, Mr. Winslow would have told me."

"The doctor says I'm a miracle."

"Well, you look good. A lot better than you did last time I saw you."

That would not have been hard to achieve. When she last saw me I was lying in a hospital bed.

I'd come to New York in September to hide out from the publicity of a scandalous murder case back in Hollywood. Peter Winslow, the private detective who'd helped solve the case—and with whom I'd fallen head over heels—had come with me as my "bodyguard." We ended up in the middle of another murder. And I ended up getting shot.

Peter called Helen, and she'd jumped on an airplane (despite being terrified of them) and sat at my hospital bedside with him, neither of them talking about how close I'd come to leaving them both.

Finally, the doctor declared I'd live, and after a few days convincing herself he knew what he was talking about, she'd gone home to Los Angeles. Now, she'd flown back, for a quick bit of Christmas shopping and a visit.

She let go of my hands and stripped off her gauntlet gloves. "In fact," she said, "you look damn good. Where is Mr. Winslow?"

"Working. His agency had a job for him to do here." And thank God. Peter was bored to death. He didn't know New York well enough to do much work as a private investigator. He was in New York because of me. I didn't want him to get confused and start thinking he was bored with me. Another reason to go home. "Let me take your coat," I said.

As always, Helen Ross was perfectly turned out: an impeccable navy traveling suit piped with silver-gray at the edges of the lapels and pockets; a dark-gray velvet hat with an arc of rolled brim framing her blonde head. Her makeup was flawless, if perhaps a touch heavy, the sort that made her still look thirty-five from thirty feet away. I wasn't sure how old Helen actually was, somewhere in her early forties, I supposed, six or seven years older than me. I'd never asked, of course.

She held her hands out to the merry hiss of the radiator.

"I'll make some coffee," I said. "You're not used to New York winters."

I went off into the tiny space the hotel with considerable optimism called a kitchen. But then guests at the Marquette didn't cook. They ordered up from the restaurant. The kitchen was for parties, during which the maid could use the oven to warm up hors d'oeuvres. It was just wide enough to accommodate a baking sheet.

I removed the percolator's basket, poured in four cups of water, and replaced the basket on the rod. I took the coffee canister off the shelf.

"When you're ready to get rid of the scar," Helen called to me, "let me know. I've got the doctor for you."

"It doesn't show."

"To whom?"

"How's Sam?" Sam Ross was her husband, a producer at Marathon Studios, for which I'd done most of my screenwriting in my career.

"Fine. He sends his love."

"He could send some work my way."

"Are you well enough to work?"

"Of course."

"And travel?"

"Sure."

"Soon?"

I set down the measuring spoon and went back into the living room. "What's going on?"

"What?"

"When you said you were getting on an airplane again, I should have known it wasn't just Christmas shopping and a visit."

She dropped onto the sofa. "Why don't you make that a whiskey?"

I poured her a short Scotch from the sideboard. She said, "I'd have made a rotten spy." She took a healthy sip and crossed her ex-showgirl legs. "Mala Demara's missing."

"Missing?"

"No one has any idea where she is. She went away for the weekend and hasn't come back."

Mala Demara was a gold strike for Marathon. She'd appeared practically out of nowhere after the war ended, a beautiful Hungarian refugee, at least that was what the studio publicity said. She'd got a job singing at a local nightclub—the publicity left out the part about it belonging to Ramon Elizondo, who used to be a gangster and probably still was. Studio bosses saw her, gave her a screen test, then a contract. Her first film, in which she'd played the second female lead, had done far better at the box office than expected, largely because of her. Marathon had pulled her out of her next scheduled project, and gave her a lead. The film had been a smash, making over a million dollars in profit.

She had that European glamour audiences craved, having heard and read so much about Europe over the last years from war correspondents and returning soldiers. Of course, much of Europe was in ruins now, but maybe that only enhanced the allure. Her smoldering eyes pulled men into the theater in droves. Yet women liked her; she wasn't a man-trap. She wouldn't steal your husband.

Of course, "Mala Demara" was an image the studio had scrupulously crafted. And movie reporters had been willing collaborators. If Hollywood thrived, so did they. And Hollywood was thriving. Americans flocked to theaters. They were still flush with wartime salaries and didn't have much to spend the money on. Factories were catching up on consumer production after years of being retooled for war matériel. This year was going to be the biggest box-office year in movie history.

Still, for all the canny work Marathon had done, there was no disputing she was magnetic on screen. No one can explain why some actresses have it and some, equally beautiful—and sometimes far more talented—don't. You couldn't take your eyes off her. And that's what the studio paid for, what the audiences paid for.

She was Marathon's new golden princess. And she was gone.

I said, "Does it have anything to do with that Mickey Triton?"

"We think she might have killed him."

CHAPTER 2

"I thought Mr. Winslow would be here." Helen never called him Peter. Not that long ago, he'd saved her from a scandal. The formality helped her deal with how much she owed him. How much he knew.

Helen hadn't had that high an opinion of private detectives before she met Peter. Neither had I. I'd written fictional ones and given them guts, conscience and no small amount of intelligence. I hadn't thought any like that actually existed.

I heard the key in the lock and met Peter at the door. As he closed it with one hand, the other slid around my waist. "Helen's here," I said. His hand moved quickly, though smoothly, off my body. Peter was downright prudish about my reputation. As if Helen hadn't figured out he wasn't sleeping in the suite's second bedroom.

"Mrs. Ross," he said and took off his hat.

"She needs to talk to you." I put his hat and coat away while he poured himself a bourbon. He was wearing his smaller gun, so it didn't show when he unbuttoned his suit jacket and sat down in the armchair. I took a place at the other end of the sofa.

Helen told him as much as she'd told me. Then she said, "Do you know who Mickey Triton is?"

"Yes," Peter said. From long habit interviewing witnesses, he was cautious about telling people more than they might tell him. He waited for her to continue.

She said, "Mala's been seeing him, on the quiet, since she came to the States. Their picture got in the papers a few times, so the studio told her they couldn't go out in public anymore. The studio's worked hard on her career, and one bad move could be fatal. You never know how the public will react."

Peter said, "Especially to a foreigner."

"Yes, exactly. So the studio arranged for her to be escorted by other men, actors who have good reputations with the public. But she never stopped seeing Mickey Triton. Do you know much about him?"

"Good boxer in his time, welterweight champ for a year," Peter said. "Started out as a 'mooch' with Jack Dragna's mob. That's a kid who hangs out with them, runs errands, laughs at their jokes. Later, he did some enforcement for Julie Scarza, Dragna's lieutenant, till he made a name fighting. When that was over, Scarza bought him a gym out on Sunset and set him up as a trainer. It gave Scarza a place to put the dirty money in and bring it out clean. Triton got drafted and spent a couple of years in the Pacific, then came back to his gym. He trains mostly welterweights now, some light-heavies. He's pretty good at it. And he doesn't make his boys take more dives than they have to. He gets his picture in the papers sometimes, because he's an ex-champ and a trainer. But he's also good friends with Scarza and that means there are a lot of people he can't be photographed with—baseball players, politicians and starlets like Mala Demara whose images are being controlled by the studio."

Sometimes, Peter likes to show off a little.

Helen said, "Mala's not the first actress to find men like that attractive."

She was right about that. Gangsters appealed to plenty of Hollywood women. I was in no position to judge them. I was in love with a man who probably started out pretty much like Mickey Triton had.

Helen went on. "Mickey rented a cabin out somewhere past Malibu under a phony name, and they used that for whatever they wanted to get up to, and never went out in public. This weekend it burned down. They found a body in it."

Helen opened her handbag, pulled out a fold of newspaper clippings and handed it to Peter. I perched on the arm of his chair. They were clippings from several editions of all the Los Angeles papers. He scanned them, and I tried to keep up. He'd had a lot more practice pulling important details out of newspaper stories.

From the pictures, it was impossible to tell what the cabin had looked like. Last Friday, it had burned to the ground. The only thing left standing was the stone fireplace and chimney. Everything else had collapsed to a scorched black heap of blistered rubble. According to the stories, the fire had fortunately been contained because of light winds and the ground being soaked from the recent unusually heavy rains. By the time the fire trucks arrived, though, the cabin was engulfed. It had taken three hours to put the fire out, and another day for it to cool sufficiently for a search. In the debris, they found a man's body, so badly burned, the articles said, as to be not immediately identifiable.

I thought about what the body must have looked like after that inferno. Once, for a script, I'd done some research about the effects of fire. Quickly I'd discovered it was so horrific I would never be able to put anything about it into a screenplay and get it past the censors.

When he finished reading, Peter asked Helen, "Are you sure the body's Triton's?"

"Who else could it be?"

"The arsonist, caught in his own crime. It took three hours to put the fire out, it says here. If that's accurate, it's arson. It wasn't a gas explosion. The chimney's intact. The owner might

16

have burned it down for the insurance and set himself on fire doing it. It happens. Triton and Miss Demara could be in Tijuana on a bender."

"The man's skull had a bullet hole in it."

"Where did you hear that?"

"Mack Pace told Sam. Mack's the studio's chief of security. He has police contacts."

"He better be careful who he talks to. Some cops can be bought, but not all the time. One of them might tip the investigators the studio's asking questions. Are you sure the cops haven't identified the body yet?"

"Yes. I called Sam from my hotel before I came over here. There's nothing new."

"Triton must have done a good job concealing his identity from the owner. But if the cops don't know it's his cabin, how did the studio find out?"

"Mala's cousin called Sam when she saw the papers. She knew about the cabin, recognized the address. She and Mala live together. She said Mala packed a bag Friday and went away for the weekend, but didn't say where she was going. Then she didn't come home. The cousin calls herself a spiritualist, but apparently she can't see into her crystal ball well enough to tell where Mala's gone."

"There's the possibility Miss Demara's dead, too. Whoever killed Triton took her."

"That's too awful to think about."

"But if she's still alive, why hasn't she come home?"

"If the papers find out they were using that place as a love nest, that he's dead and she's missing, it will look like she did it. Her career will never recover."

"Who else knows what's going on, besides your husband, the cousin and the security chief?"

"Sam had to tell the head of the studio, Sol Noble. And

Alastair Bishop, who's directing Mala's new picture. That's all, as far as I know."

"You want to keep that number as low as possible." Peter laid the clippings on the side table. "Mrs. Ross, why did you come all the way to New York?"

"I'm sorry?"

"The studio's security chief could have told your husband everything I just did, probably already has."

"Sam wants you to find her. Can you, before the police?"

"Your husband could have asked me to do that over the phone, and he could have told me things I'm now getting secondhand. Yet you flew here, and you hate airplanes."

"Sam doesn't know you that well." Helen glanced at me.

"This isn't up to Mrs. Atwill," Peter said. "I have a job here, as her bodyguard, and you and your husband know that."

Helen said, "I know you're worried about Lauren. Sam knows that. But it's all over, that other thing. There hasn't been anything in the papers for weeks."

After all the delays, the killer who'd started the avalanche of publicity that had driven me out of Los Angeles had made a deal with the DA. Pled guilty to one count of manslaughter. Five years in prison. The DA didn't want the blackmail and police corruption that lay behind the other crimes to end up in the courtroom, and the killer's lawyers knew it. Five years. One count. Four people dead. And if Peter and I hadn't stopped it, two more would have died.

Peter said, "Why's your husband looking for an outsider? Does he want someone not on the Marathon payroll to find her, then hide her from the cops?"

"Of course not."

"Or fix her up with an alibi?"

"Peter," I said. But I said it quietly. I knew the real reason he was angry.

18

I stood up and said to Helen, "Why don't you let us talk about this, then I'll call you at your hotel later." She was at the Plaza. The Marquette was a fine hotel if you're hiding out from the press, but she wasn't.

"Sure." She snatched up her handbag and marched to the door, briskly tugging her gloves on. I retrieved her coat. When I'd closed the door after her, Peter was pouring himself more bourbon.

He said, "I'm not going to fight about this. She's using you, and you know it."

"She's presuming on our friendship, and maybe she shouldn't have done it, but she loves Sam, and his picture will be in big trouble if the press gets hold of this. He doesn't know you that well, so she offered to come here and use our friendship to talk you into it." I laid my hand on his arm. "But she thinks the only danger to me is from publicity. You still think about how somebody out in Los Angeles might want to exact a little revenge. Helen would never ask me to come back if she thought she was putting me in that kind of danger. Make me a drink."

I sat down on the sofa. He took the lid off the ice bucket, shot some cubes into a glass and poured me a gin and tonic.

I said, "Part of the DA's deal was that no witnesses—by which he meant me—would ever be touched."

"A deal he couldn't enforce, and everybody knew it."

"We also know you made it personally very plain to the defense that if anything at all ever happened to me, the killer would die a painful death. I'm not saying take the job. But you're bored out of your mind here."

He handed me the drink. "You know anything about this girl?"

"Not much. The studio says she's Hungarian, maybe she is. I heard she'd had a screen test with Marathon over in Europe before the war, when she was just a kid. They told her to improve her English and get in touch. Then the war came. Last summer, she turns up, gets a job as a singer out at Elizondo's. She got a screen test, a contract. Every young girl's Hollywood dream. Of course, most young girls don't look like Mala. She did two movies fast, and they were hits. She's beautiful, she's popular. Alastair Bishop is directing her new picture. I can't imagine why she'd disappear, and I don't know anything that would help you find her."

"Would a lot of people know she was seeing Triton?"

"You can't keep something like that quiet in Hollywood. But plenty of actresses see men they shouldn't, and the press generally cooperates."

"Until it's a story that'll sell a lot of papers, like a murder. Why does Sam Ross want me?"

"He doesn't want you to get her an alibi if that's what you mean. He needs somebody who knows how to get information without making things worse. Asking around, if it's not done right, could make her look like she did something, when she could be completely innocent. Studio security's good at hushing things up. But they're not—and don't take this the wrong way—delicate."

He laughed and sat down beside me. I crossed my legs and pressed them against him. He slipped his hand beneath my skirt with a touch that was gentle but not what you'd call delicate.

"It won't be long before the cops find out whose body that is," he said. "And as soon as it's public, somebody will tell them he was seeing Miss Demara. If she wants to stay missing, I'd have practically no chance of finding her before they start looking for her. It's an impossible job, and Ross has to know that. Yet he wants me to come back. Didn't ask me to recommend other men who are already out there, men who could do as much as I could. He wants me. Something's not right here."

"What do you say we go back home, and you can find out what it is."

CHAPTER 3

Juanita, my housekeeper, shooed me up the stairs of my house, her hands flapping below my rear end as she followed me up and into my bedroom.

"First, bath," she declared, "then bed."

"Yes, it was a rough trip."

"Airplanes," she sniffed and went off through the dressing room to the bathroom. She turned on the taps and poured salts under the cascade.

I took off my hat, kicked off my shoes and sat down on my bed with a sigh.

I was home.

Well, sort of.

My house in Pasadena was home in the sense that I lived there. It had been part of a considerable inheritance from my maternal uncle, Bennett Lauren, the oil magnate. When my husband and I separated, it had been in between tenants, so I'd moved in. It was a Mediterranean style in brick—complete with a loggia across the front—in a neighborhood that prized Arts and Crafts mansions built with what passed for old money in California and owned by folks not inclined to like "Hollywood people."

Juanita deposited a brandy on the stool beside the bathtub, unplugged the bedroom telephone extension, closed the drapes, and left me alone. I slipped into the tub and after a few minutes, my knotted nerves began to relax. Juanita was right. Airplanes.

Helen wasn't alone in being reluctant to climb aboard one. The last time I'd flown, before the war, it had been in a plane with pontoons. It had skimmed across the water on takeoff and landing, and bobbed gently to the pier at Long Beach. I'd hated it. I certainly didn't feel any safer when a plane landed on concrete.

Helen had stayed on in New York, to finish her Christmas shopping and recover from her flight. She said she'd come back in a week or so, on a train. Peter called Sam Ross and took the job. He leveled with Sam about how hard finding Mala Demara would be if she wanted to stay missing. Sam said Peter had more experience than his security staff at chasing missing people. Peter told him he'd be better off with a man already out there. Sam still wanted him to run the search. I agreed with Peter: something was off. But it was a job.

More importantly, the fat fee would get him back on Ed Paxton's good side. Paxton owned the agency. Unlike fictional detectives, Peter didn't work solo out of a dingy office. Paxton had been furious because Peter let the New York City police walk away with all the credit in the case we'd just solved. Peter had pointed out that his job was not to get the agency publicity. His job had been to protect me, and he'd failed at that, so if Paxton wanted to fire him, he damned well could. Of course, Paxton wasn't going to fire him—and it wasn't true he'd failed to protect me, although he felt that way for a long time, perhaps still did. Nevertheless, Paxton could have tried to teach him a lesson by giving him lousy jobs for a while, making him follow war-bride floozies to see if they were cheating on their ex-soldier husbands with sugar daddies who sat out the war getting rich on airplane parts.

But now Peter wouldn't be punished. He had something to do, and on his own terms.

Our plane took six hours to Kansas City, followed by a two-hour layover for refueling and lunch, then another six to Los

Angeles. We made good time, they tell me. Which is very different from having a good time.

On the way, Peter let me read the file Marathon security kept on Mala Demara. Sam had sent it with Helen, sealed, in case Peter took the job. Reading it gave me something to do with my hands instead of digging my fingernails into his arm.

Studio security's job was ostensibly to protect the studio's property. Most of the staff were night watchmen, guards on the gates, and men who investigated when something went missing, like the petty cash or the costume of a top star.

But protecting a studio also meant making sure that, if a star crashed his car into somebody, the police didn't file a report and the victim's silence was purchased.

There were rumors that some studios would go much, much further, if the star was big enough, the potential publicity bad enough. Alibis could be provided if a prostitute got herself beaten to death in a shabby hotel, the body moved if she turned up dead in the star's house.

Each studio's security chief made it his business to get to know the local division cops. And top brass could depend on being treated very well—tickets to premiers, invitations to Hollywood parties and cruises on producers' yachts.

It helped ensure that any trouble that could be made to go away, would go away.

I knew of course that the studio kept personnel files, but it had never occurred to me security kept files too. Did they have one on me?

The file contained four typewritten pages. The first was a typical form, with personal information in the appropriate blanks. Address. Phone number. General description: five-three, dark-brown hair, brown eyes. Weight: 105. Birth date: October 21, 1924 (I assumed the studio took a woman's word on that one). Birthplace: Linz, Austria. Mala Demara had been born after the breakup of the Austro-Hungarian Empire at the end of World War I. Yet the studio would call her Hungarian. Hitler had been Austrian.

There were also spaces on the form for her publicist and her agent. Under next of kin, there was her cousin, Zorka Karoly, at the same address as Mala. Below that, a space for "Associates." Five women's names, only one of them I'd ever met. Kitty Sharp Dunning, the Sharp's Grocery Stores heiress. The men listed included the actors I'd seen her photographed with from time to time as her escorts; Ramon Elizondo, at whose club she'd sung while trying to get her contract; and Mickey Triton. Someone had put a red circle around Triton's name, I presumed because he was trouble, not because he was a Red.

His was the only picture in the file, a recent one of him at the weigh-in of one of his fighters. Even though he hadn't been the focus of the shot, he stood out. Italian tough-guy good looks, with a bit of scarring above his right eye and a strong high-bridged nose that had managed to stay mostly straight despite his former profession. Even under the loose sports jacket, the shoulders were impressive.

The other pages were typed reports of incidents the studio had cleaned up.

Two were for drunk driving, against Mala's cousin. Given that Los Angeles drivers killed each other at a rate that would top 1,000 this year, she would have had plenty of company on the roads. Another was a complaint to the vice cops, which boiled down to a man being angry that his wife was spending too much of his money going to Zorka Karoly's séances to talk to her dead mother. According to notes in the file, Mala had agreed not to mention her cousin to reporters, and not allow séances at the house they shared.

The rest involved Triton, a half dozen incidents, all from last year—before they stopped going out in public. Triton had regularly roughed up men who tried to get too close to Mala, men who claimed they were old friends. Mala hadn't been in this country long enough to have old friends. She'd been in Europe, occupied Europe. I wondered if she'd earned the money to get to America by making "old friends" with soldiers.

There were cryptic notes at the bottom of each incident's description—names and dollar amounts. Probably not the victims, the amounts weren't large enough. Probably cops, paid off by the studio to keep anything about Mala out of the official record.

What struck me most about the file was that the studio had gone to great lengths to sweep this stuff under the carpet, yet committed it all to written record.

People could be very odd.

I finished my bath and the brandy, dried off and climbed into bed, the space beside me empty for the first time in months.

I was back home. I was safe. I'd be escorted when I left the house, and the house would be watched overnight until Peter was sure nobody intended to bother me. But Peter wouldn't be here. He had a job. There would be no time for side trips to Pasadena.

I pulled the other pillow against me, but it's hard to pretend it's a man when the damned thing smells like lavender.

The brandy and hot bath worked. I slept till late the next morning. I staggered upright, scratchy eyed from my heavy sleep, found the sleeves of my bathrobe and the openings in my slippers, padded down to the kitchen and poured myself a cup of coffee.

"You want breakfast now?" Juanita asked. She held open the refrigerator door hopefully. It was full.

"Maybe some toast in a bit. I missed you, too."

She closed the door. "We hung the picture."

"I'm sorry?"

"The picture you shipped last month from New York." She made a strong effort not to wrinkle her nose. "I had it unpacked and hung up like you said."

"Not to your taste?"

"I only have to look at it when I dust it."

I picked up the paper from the hall table, shuffled into the study and tossed it on the desk.

My new painting had been hung perfectly, in the space between the bookcases. I'd bought it while I was working on the New York case, having seen it at a party thrown by the artist, Zack Eisler. A party where I thought I might learn something. A party where I got spotted by someone who shouldn't have seen me there. Never take the size of New York City as a promise of anonymity. In my admittedly limited experience, it was a very large small town.

The painting was the modern world in sharp angles, jangling, exhausting, exhilarating, but here and there, something else: pentimento. The golden shimmer of a meticulously recreated Renaissance religious painting pushed through so subtly you had to look closely. Gradually, you realized it was a woman in rapturous adoration of something unseen, something the modern world could never resist. Or was trying to obliterate. You couldn't tell.

And that was what I loved about it.

On the table under the painting sat a crystal bowl of stunning white gardenias, fragile, lush and exotic. There was a small vellum envelope beside them, its corner tucked under the vase. I opened it.

Glad to have you back.

Sam

Of course they would be from Sam, probably reminded by Helen. Who had I thought they'd be from? Peter? Franklin, my husband, from whom I'd been separated for almost two years and who didn't even know I was back in LA? Who was up to God knows what with God knows who on vacation in Cuba?

My parents? Who likewise didn't know where I was, and unlike Franklin, hadn't called New York regularly to see how I was. If they hadn't bothered when I was dying, they probably wouldn't send flowers now.

I sat down at the desk and sorted through the stack of mail on the blotter, everything Juanita had been preparing to forward to New York. I dumped the catalogs and advertisements into the wastebasket. Then I stacked the letters into two piles, business and personal. The latter was embarrassingly small. I told myself it was because acquaintances knew I was away, allegedly in Cuba with my estranged husband, avoiding publicity. Not because I didn't have many friends.

I found a few invitations, all to holiday high-society events. Five years ago, I never would have received any of these: they were all from Old Money names. Then I inherited a lot of money from Uncle Bennett Lauren, and within a month, I was on everyone's socially acceptable list.

The phone rang. I picked it up. "Hello."

"Hey. Bluepoint Vance."

It was Sam Ross. He'd picked Bluepoint Vance out of a Dashiell Hammett novel and used it as his code name so whomever answered my phone would know it was him, and not some reporter pretending to be him.

"Did you find Mala?" I asked right off.

"No, no, your boyfriend's still looking. You free?"

"Yes."

"Then get over here. I got a job for you."

Fifty yards past Marathon Studios' tall, arched wrought-iron front gate, squatting on what otherwise would have been a perfectly lovely expanse of lawn, was the main office building—commonly referred to, without any affection, as the Ice House. Other buildings on the sprawling lot were Spanish: creamy stucco, red tile roofs and narrow wrought-iron balconies. So naturally, a former studio head had decided a decade ago that what Marathon really needed was something modern. A square of blinding white relieved only by a wall of glass down its center. And inside, white marble on white marble.

The lobby made you want to get back to work really fast.

Sam's appointment was running a little late, his secretary told me. I sat down on one of the high-fashion but rock-hard armchairs and picked up a November copy of *Look*. On the cover, a close-up of a girl in a silver-sequined blouse, a Thanksgiving holiday story: "Why I'm Grateful to Be in America."

Mala Demara.

Sam's door opened and the man who'd probably arranged for the magazine story came out.

Morty Engler had enjoyed too much of everything that wasn't good for him: rich food, straight gin and bad temper from his bosses. Despite those indulgences, he still had the moist, small-pored skin of a baby. He wasn't short, but it wasn't easy to tell: he was perpetually bent forward, ready for the next crisis.

Another man appeared, with broad shoulders, thinning hair, and a lot of chin. He headed straight out with purpose, erect, important. More particularly, he walked like a man who wanted to show he was important.

Mack Pace, head of studio security.

Morty saw me and grinned. "Hey, when'd you get back?"

"Yesterday."

"You working on this?"

"On what?"

"Sam's picture."

I felt like an idiot, what else would he think I was working

29

on? Finding Mala Demara?

I said, "Sam asked me to come in."

"Now you're back, if any reporters bother you, let me know, I'll call their editors. We can toss them a few things, they'll leave you alone. Studio owes you a lot."

"Thanks, I appreciate it."

"Mr. Ross will see you now," his secretary said.

"Get in here, come on over here." Sam came around his desk smoothing his jacket over his short, barrel-chested frame. He pumped my hand. I didn't have to say anything yet. You could count on Sam Ross to do all the talking for a while.

"How you doing? How are you? You look good, you put on a little weight. That's a good thing, on you. Sit down, sit down. Have a seat." Sam was maybe fifty, with short, coarse, dark hair in orderly retreat on the top of his head and victorious elsewhere. His five-o'clock shadow showed up about twelve-thirty. He went back to his desk and dropped into his chair. "I shouldn't even be speaking to you, you know that? Helen almost divorced me when she found out I helped get you hurt."

"You told a few people in New York I was someone else. You helped solve a murder. I don't blame you for my getting shot."

"You say. Tell Helen."

"We caught the killer. We wouldn't have without you."

He grumped a few more times, took out his handkerchief and polished his glasses. "Well, you're lucky I'm talking to you."

"Thank you for the flowers."

"Sure, sure."

"I saw Morty and Mack Pace leaving. Is there anything new?"

"Morty's working on what we're going to say if Mala doesn't show up. By the way, Mack's not too happy I brought your boyfriend in."

"Can we call him by his name?"

"What? Oh, yeah, sure. But Mr. Winslow's out there getting

things done. He's talked to her agent, her publicist, sent some men out to the hotels she's stayed at. Her cousin, you met her? Don't be fooled by that fruitcake fortune-teller act, she's the one managing Mala's career. She's the one got her that job singing out at Elizondo's, got the studios to come out and take a look. Hired her vocal coach, her acting teachers. Pain in the rear, but you can't argue with the result.

"Your boyfriend—I mean, Mr. Winslow—has got the cousin calling all of Mala's friends, with him telling her what to say, see if any of them know where Mala might be, she just needs to reach Mala about some business, can't recall where she said she was going. She can't make it sound serious. Otherwise, people start asking their own questions. For all we know, it could turn out Mala's run off to marry some Mexican playboy. First time I'd pray for something like that." He shoved the handkerchief back into his pocket.

"Look, we got to be prepared," he went on. "We need you to take a look at the script, in case we got to rewrite it for another actress. Officially, we just say Alastair Bishop might want some last-minute revisions."

I was a script doctor. A few years ago, I'd cut back my screen-writing assignments to try to save my marriage, relegating myself mostly to rewriting the work of others, often for no credit. I turned out to be very good at it, but what was wrong with the marriage couldn't be fixed as easily as a script.

I said, "Won't people wonder why Bill Linden isn't doing the rewrites? Didn't he write the script?"

"He's working on something else."

"Sam."

"Okay, him and Alastair had a falling out. I'm sure Bill'll be glad to fill you in."

Alastair Bishop had been wooed away from Harbour Studios in England back in thirty-eight, before the war broke out in

Europe. He had a solid reputation for suspense pictures in Europe, and had not disappointed his new employer. But in the press, he'd been overshadowed by another English suspense director who'd arrived a bit later: Alfred Hitchcock. Bishop had dealt with this disappointment by confusing script suggestions with actual writing, and insisting his name appear on screenplays. Apparently, he wanted to be Hitchcock *and* Preston Sturges.

Sam sat forward. "I told Helen I was thinking about asking you in, and she says it's good for you to get back to work. But that's as far as it goes. You're not getting mixed up in this, you understand? You're here to write. And I know you can get along with Alastair. You get along with people. When you're not putting them in jail.

"We got a military consultant for the picture, humor him. Alastair wanted one, everybody wants a military guy hanging around the set these days. Guy's showing up today of all days. We couldn't tell him not to come; we can't act like anything's wrong. Oh, call Alastair 'Mr. Bishop' till he tells you otherwise, all right? You sign on, we'll get you a bungalow, twenty-five hundred a week."

"You do feel guilty about New York."

"You'd have talked me into it anyway. Why don't you get an agent? It would save me money."

CHAPTER 4

"Please come this way?"

Betty Guinness met me at the door to Bishop's bungalow. She was maybe thirty-five, with dark hair smoothed back precisely. She wore a blue serge suit and a white cotton blouse, buttoned up. If there'd been any more starch in the collar, she'd have cut her own throat.

She'd been Bishop's secretary since he came to the States. I'd heard rumors Betty was more than his secretary, more like his perpetual secret mistress, while publicly, he went out with society divorcées. I didn't give much credence to the rumors. People will say anything about a woman who works for a man. And I didn't think Betty was the sort who'd settle for back-alley humiliation.

Betty led the way to Bishop's office, which required our crossing ten feet of foyer. She rapped briskly on the door, then opened it.

Bishop's office had been decorated in British country-house style, complete with floral slipcovers and Turkish carpets. Heavy drapes, although tied back with braided, tassled cords, still did their best to block the California light streaming in through the French doors overlooking the English garden that had been created in the small fenced space behind the bungalow.

Alastair Bishop nearly filled an armchair, but he did it in an impeccably cut three-piece suit of navy wool. At the moment, his full lips were pressed forward as he concentrated on a letter he held at arm's length. His plump fingers tapered delicately to the fingertips.

"Mrs. Atwill," Betty announced.

Bishop kept reading. We waited. His eyes didn't leave the page. He continued reading, his lips pursed, then finally he laid the letter down on the side table.

"Betty, please do not show in my guests until I am prepared to greet them properly," he said in a British accent that managed to sound clipped and drawling at the same time. "Won't you sit down? Bring the tea, Betty."

"What a lovely garden," I said.

"I'm fond of gardening. Are you?"

"I'm fond of a nice garden."

The tea arrived. It must have been waiting just across the hall. Betty set the japanned tray on the low table in front of Bishop. "Shall I call the set?" she asked.

"No, this won't take long."

Betty went out. Bishop poured, asked about milk and sugar, and handed me the cup. Then he said, "If we must replace Miss Demara and if we are to meet our shooting schedule, I won't have time to do any more work on the script."

I'd been right. He was trying to cadge writing credit.

"I understand Bill Linden's moved on to another project," I said.

"Yes, he's not involved anymore."

"Who did you have in mind to replace Mala? It will make a difference, of course, for the rewrites. Each woman would have her own strengths."

"My dear girl," he said and dropped his chins so he was looking at me from the tops of his eyes. "In my films, it is the peril the lady is in, not what she says while she's in it."

"Then you must be relieved not to have to write any more words for her."

"I beg your pardon?"

I smiled, full of sunshine. "I'll be glad to take the task of writing the words off your hands, Mr. Bishop." I sipped and he sipped. I said, "Is there a copy of the script I can have?"

He motioned with his tapered fingertips to his desk, but I didn't jump up and get it. "The other actresses," I said. "I'd like to see some of their latest pictures."

"If you must. You give actors too much credit. But if you must, we can arrange that."

"And something from Mala as well, in case we need to make changes for her."

"Very well. We'll meet again, here, ten o'clock tomorrow and discuss the script. We should have the censor's revisions soon. Would you ring the bell?"

Behind the desk was an actual bell cord. When I pulled, the bell rang on the other side of the bungalow, which was the room next door.

Betty appeared.

"The cart is waiting, Mr. Bishop."

We could have walked. The soundstage on which they were shooting was less than a hundred yards from Bishop's front door. But the three of us took one of the small carts that ferried the famous—and those the famous deemed worthy—to their destinations.

I was lucky Bishop still wanted me to go with him after that crack I made about his not having to write anymore. And Sam said I got along with people. It was a good thing I hadn't said the first thing that popped into my head: "Well, gosh, Alastair, if you don't care about the words, why do you keep stealing credit for them?"

Soundstage 14 was among the first built in Hollywood after the advent of sound recording. Before that, movies were shot on wooden structures, simply called "stages." After sound, wooden floors were impossible and solid walls and substantial roofs essential. That meant a concrete foundation and steel support beams, because you had to be able to insulate the walls and ceiling if you wanted to record sound. And you had to be able to close the doors and control when people went in and out with lighted signs announcing when the stage was in use.

The crew was rehearsing, not shooting, so we didn't have to wait to get in.

"You're welcome to look around," Betty said, "but you must stay out of the way. It's a very important shot."

"Sure," I said, amiably. I didn't point out how many sets I'd been on in my career. I was back to getting along with people.

A street scene filled the far half of the soundstage, a European town, I guessed, given the cobblestones and mansard roofs. Two sets of townhouse facades faced me, divided by a cobbled street, also lined with housefronts and streetlamps, that curved away out of view. As I crossed the floor, I could see deeper and deeper into the curve, to the point where it broke away into a narrow side street designed and constructed to appear to be a full block away.

The crew was practicing a tracking shot. The camera, with the director of photography seated behind it, was on a crane, although the camera platform was now at ground level. First, the crane moved on tracks from left to right till it reached the cobbled street, then the platform soared above the roofline. As it did, crew moved in rapidly and rolled that section of houses away, just far enough that the camera could appear to be diving over the roofs into the curving street. Another crew whipped away sheets of fake cobbles that had covered other tracks and the crane continued into the labyrinth, the camera dropping back toward the ground.

"It's a pursuit shot," Betty said. "Mr. Bishop wants it in continuity. You may sit here," she said and indicated a canvas-backed chair among a scattered group well out of the crew's way. One of them had Bishop's name on the back.

A wiry, tightly wound young man in a yellow sweater, clipboard in hand, came over to Bishop and escorted him to the crane.

I sat down in my assigned chair, flipped open my script and found the scene they appeared to be rehearsing. Mala, searching for a house number, is suddenly afraid she's being followed. She passes the house she's looking for because she cannot endanger the man she's come to meet. She flees deeper and deeper into the neighborhood.

The camera's diving pursuit would establish the villain as a swooping bird of prey and shudder the audience's stomachs. The Alastair Bishop touch. If they could get it to work.

Briefly, I wondered why they weren't shooting on the back lot, then remembered how much rain had soaked the area in the last weeks. They couldn't rely on being able to rehearse or shoot and meet schedule. If a scene was supposed to take place at night, it was much easier to shoot it indoors.

The crane rolled back on the tracks, and the platform descended to the stage floor. The man behind the camera relinquished his chair to Bishop, taking the one beside it. They went back up for another set of run-throughs with Bishop behind the lens.

The wiry young man zipped past me and around the far end of the housefronts. "Little stick," he called out. "How we doing?"

"I'm almost ready," a girl's voice called back.

He zipped back and claimed a place near the base of the crane, paying no attention to me. I got up and wandered in the direction of the girl's voice. I found a dressing room of sorts: four Chinese screens set in a rough square, vibrantly colored, the kind you get in a tourist trap in Chinatown.

Inside was a short clothing rack, with two costumes, and a small dressing table. A girl in a rose-colored dressing gown combed her thick dark hair carefully. She bore a striking resemblance to Mala.

In the corner, laid back against the pillows of a frayed armchair was another woman, in a tight russet jersey dress, her long legs crossed, reading a magazine. She was considerably older, maybe forty. The mouth was hard, but she had the girl's eyes.

I knocked lightly on the screen's frame.

I said. "Hi, I'm Lauren Atwill. I—"

"Really?" the girl cried happily. "Are you really?"

"Not everyone gets excited about meeting a writer. It could go to my head," I said. The girl giggled. The woman didn't. She eyed me with new interest.

I was sure the girl recognized my name from the newspapers, not my movie career, but her interest didn't seem lurid. She turned in her chair, giving me her full attention, smiling radiantly. It made me want to go on. And I did, telling myself I wasn't really sticking my nose in when I'd been told not to.

"You must be Miss Demara's stand-in."

"Yes. Jane Graham. This is my mother."

"Are you working on the picture?" the mother asked. She had a voice she must have practiced. It's hard to get that husky without working on it. Or smoking a couple of packs of cigarettes a day.

"Maybe a few last-minute things. Bill Linden's tied up right now."

"Whatever they need Jane to do, she's ready. If you need anyone to read lines for you, Jane will be glad to help."

The young man with the clipboard appeared in the doorway space. "Little stick," he said. "We're almost ready."

"Don't call her that," the woman said. "She's a young lady."

"And I didn't say she wasn't." He grinned affably, leaned in, tapped the back of Jane's chair with his clipboard and winked. Then he turned to the woman, still grinning. "It's the way we talk, and you just might have to get used to that. Five minutes, okay, hon?" The girl nodded and he went off. A costume assistant edged in around me, carrying a hat.

"You have to change," I said. "I'll be on my way."

As I moved out, the girl's mother said, "Don't run when they call you. Act like a professional, like you belong."

I returned to my assigned seat and my script reading. Quickly, I found a scene the Hays Office censors were certain to object to. Mala and the hero, full of sexual undercurrents. In her bedroom. It didn't matter that nothing happened and they stood up the whole time. They weren't married. And they were in her bedroom. How like Bill Linden to put something like that in there, just to twist the censors' noses.

It—and I was sure, plenty more, knowing Bill—would have to be fixed, and there would be no choice. Every movie—the script and final film—had to get approval from the Production Code Administration, often called the Hays Office after the man who'd been in charge of the studios' efforts to impose some sort of censorship on themselves back in the twenties and during the early thirties when the code was being put together. But he'd never administered the final version of the code. That was Mr. Breen, and an unpopular fellow he was.

The code did have some benefit. It had reduced the number of state censorship boards that could cut a film to pieces, rendering it incomprehensible to audiences. And it saved the studios money. They didn't have to ship separate versions of films to different states. But fear of those state boards had driven the code enforcers to strive to satisfy the most conservative view of what was acceptable for other people to see.

The crew began rehearsing with the nighttime light levels, so it was harder to see the pages now. I lifted my behind to scoot my chair closer to a small work light.

"What are you doing here?" a voice whispered angrily. I jumped and whipped around. Peter stood behind my chair. I hadn't heard him approach.

"Working. Jeez, you scared me. Sam Ross wants me to take a look at the script, in case they need to replace Mala. He's already warned me to keep my nose out. What are you doing here?"

"Waiting to talk to Bishop, brief him. Ross is on his way over. The body's been identified. It's Triton."

"Is it murder?"

"Yes. You hear anything around here, while you weren't sticking your nose in?"

"Well, I met Mala's little stand-in, just saying hello. Her mother won't be sorry if Mala's out of the way. She's angling to get—"

"Pete!"

The little stand-in dashed past me and flung herself into Peter's arms.

CHAPTER 5

I didn't often see Peter shocked. Actually, when I thought about it, I'd never seen Peter look shocked. He did now.

For a moment, he froze, then slowly folded his arms around her. "Hey, kid."

"Where have you been? I—" Abruptly, she pulled away. "I got makeup on you. Did I get makeup on you?"

"No. It's all right, Janie."

"Jane," she corrected him, happily. "But we might change it." She twirled for him. "I'm Mala's stand-in. Isn't it wonderful? They saw a hundred girls. But I looked the most like her. And it helped that Momma knows her. Where have you been? Momma says she hasn't seen you in months."

"I was out of town. Someplace I couldn't tell anybody."

"Little stick!" The wiry young man with the clipboard called. "Come on, hon, we're ready."

"Coming! I'm coming!" She scurried off, completely forgetting what her mother said about making them wait.

I said, "I take it you've met."

"What? Yeah. Yeah, I've known her for years."

"She seems like a sweet kid."

"I could tell you were thinking that when she threw her arms around me."

"She's a little young for you."

"And short. And brunette. I prefer tall blondes who never do what they're told."

"Then you must be a happy man."

"I heard she was doing some bit parts, Central Casting stuff. You said her mother's here?"

"Around the corner, they've got a dressing room."

"They used to work together, Lily and Miss Demara, out at the club."

"Elizondo's?"

"Lily runs the coat check and the cigarette girls. Let me go talk to her, see what I can find out," he said before he disappeared around the corner. I picked up my script and sat back down in the canvas chair.

Another rehearsal began, and Jane appeared, following her marks and pretending to search the house numbers. She reached the curving street and disappeared. The crane rose, the crew jumped in, pushed away the housefronts, snatched aside the cobbles.

"Who's that?" The wiry young man appeared at my side, pointing his clipboard in the direction Peter had gone.

"It's okay. He has permission to be here."

"A lot of characters get permission. You know him?"

"If you're worried about Jane, he's not her boyfriend or anything. It's not like that. Lauren Atwill." I offered my hand.

"Glenn Watkins."

"No! No! No! Damn it!" Bishop, high up in his crane seat, began shouting. "Do you think you could possibly be bothered to find your mark, Miss Featherbrain? Could we have a little less acting, and a little more accuracy? You are not Mala Demara! Look at the damn ground if you have to! Or we can find someone who can walk without thinking about it! Get out of there! Go on! Get out!"

The young man dashed into the labyrinth. "Okay, hon, come on out of there." He slipped his hand beneath Jane's arm.

"If you would like to be of some help, Mr. Watkins," Bishop

said, "perhaps you could find me someone who can walk and think simultaneously."

Her head tucked, Jane pulled her arm away and ran off toward her dressing room.

"Shall we take ten?" Watkins suggested.

Bishop grunted.

"Let's take ten," Watkins called out. He pulled out a pack of cigarettes and offered them around. The crew stretched and wandered toward the stage door.

I followed Jane and found her in the armchair, weeping into Peter's handkerchief. Her mother sat in the hard chair, comforting her daughter by telling her to stop crying.

"They can't test the lights if your face is all red. And he won't like to wait while you fix yourself up."

I said, "I'm sorry to disturb you, but I just wanted to say he's mad about the shot, not at you. It's not working like he hoped, and hasn't been."

Jane smiled weakly, but she stopped crying.

"Go ahead," Peter said to her, "blow your nose on it, it's all right."

Jane did, and began to gently blot the mascara from under her eyes, trying not to dislodge the false eyelashes.

"Here, clean yourself up," her mother said to Jane and they switched chairs. "You got a cigarette?" she asked Peter.

He pulled out his case and she took one. He lit it for her. She laid her fingers on his as she guided the lighter.

"So what the hell is going on with Mala?" she said to him.

"Miss Demara?" Peter asked, and looked believably puzzled. If he'd wanted a career as an actor, he could have had it.

"I thought maybe that's why you're here."

"I'm doing some work for the studio. I needed to talk to Mr. Bishop. Is something up?"

"We had a costume fitting yesterday. Mala didn't show. It's

not like her. She's serious about her career. And her battle-ax of a cousin wouldn't let her ditch anything anyway. Before we left, the head of security showed up. He asked us if we knew where she was. Acting like he's a cop."

"Mack Pace?" I said.

"Big guy, real important to himself?"

"That's him. What did you tell him?"

"I *didn't* tell him he should talk to Mickey Triton."

"The boxer?" Peter asked.

"The studio doesn't like people talking about all that, so don't say anything. They think it's such a secret. The two of them, all that was supposed to be on the QT, but most of us out at the club knew it was still going on. He's got it bad for her. The first time he saw her, her cousin brought her over to audition for a singing job. Mickey was hanging around that day, talking to Ray. Ray Elizondo," she said to me. I knew who she meant and nodded. She went on, "She came out, told Ray her name, little bit about herself, and started to sing. Meanwhile, Mickey's coming straight up out of his chair, can't take his eyes off her. And that was it. Why's a guy from security asking me where Mala is?"

Peter agreed it sounded odd. I was sure that, inside, he was calculating how much damage Mack Pace's bulling around might have done to the secrecy of his own search for Mala.

Watkins appeared in the doorway to see how Janie was and if she'd be ready to go.

"Of course she will," Lily said.

We left them to it. Jane made Peter promise to visit the set again.

On the way back to my chair, he said, "Thanks, you made her feel better."

"She's nice."

"Lily's all right too. She's had it hard. Her husband died.

Jane turned into a looker, so she started taking her around to auditions. A job like this means a lot to them. The kid must get fifty, sixty a week. That's a lot of money to them."

"I didn't say it wasn't. And I didn't say anything against her mother."

I'd got rich through no greater accomplishment than being born Bennett Lauren's niece. It rubbed on Peter from time to time, when he thought I didn't fully appreciate the hardships of others.

"You. Who are you?" Alastair Bishop demanded. He shoved some papers at Betty, left her standing with a group of men by the camera crane and descended on us. "Nobody comes on my set without my approval."

"It's all right, Alastair." Sam Ross had arrived and hurried up behind Bishop. "This is the Mr. Winslow I was telling you about."

"He does nothing on this set without asking me first."

Peter looked at him. Not hard, just looked at him. Then he said, "I apologize, Mr. Bishop. I should have waited for you and Mr. Ross."

Sam said, "Why don't I introduce you around?" He led us over to the crane where Morty Engler, from publicity, was talking amiably with a tall, slim, handsome young man in an army officer's uniform of olive drab, his hat tucked beneath his arm. Of course, most people were amiable to servicemen these days, especially officers.

Up close, he wasn't as young as I'd thought. Maybe mid-thirties. With close-cut but still wavy red-blonde hair and a slight ruddiness to his cheeks that made him look younger.

Sam said, "This is Major McCann, he'll be our military consultant on the picture. Lauren Atwill, one of our writers. Mr. Winslow, one of our guests."

"We've met before," I said, brightly.

"I'm sorry," the major said. "Forgive me, I don't remember."

"I'm sure we have. You weren't in uniform, though. I can't remember where it was. We were talking, I remember you handing me a drink."

"This is my first time in California. Before that, I was stationed in Washington."

"I've never been there."

"I was stationed in Europe during the war."

"No."

"Then I must have a doppelganger," he said. "I hope whoever he was, he behaved himself. I'd hate to have someone ruin my reputation out here before I've had a chance to."

We all laughed. And yet I couldn't shake the absolute conviction that I had in fact met him before.

"Betty, why don't you show the major around the set," Sam said. "We have some business to discuss."

"Good to meet all of you," the major said. Betty took him off down the fake cobbled street.

"Why don't I leave you all to it," I said. Hanging around would make Peter think I was sticking my nose into his search for Mala. I went back to my chair and my script.

The crew returned from their break, carrying the smell of cigarettes back in with them. The meeting by the crane broke up. I kept reading. Then Betty Guinness's high heels came clicking across the concrete to me.

"Mr. Bishop won't be able to discuss the script today. We'll arrange a bungalow for you near him."

Given the pecking order in Hollywood, "near" Bishop probably only meant somewhere within cart-driving distance.

"I'll arrange any meetings with Mr. Bishop," Betty continued. "You know you'll be working only with him. Mr. Linden is no longer involved."

"Yes, Mr. Bishop told me that."

"I'll call you at your home this afternoon with the details." She tripped off.

I frowned after her for a couple of minutes, thinking, then dug a nickel out of my handbag and made a call from the pay telephone by the stage door. As I finished, Glenn Watkins, the young man with the clipboard, began gathering the crew for the next rehearsal. Sam and Bishop consulted over a sheet of paper Morty had given them, no doubt the press statement Morty had prepared in case it became necessary. As the script doctor, I was completely superfluous. For the moment, so was Peter.

"When did Ross call you to work on this?" he asked.

"First thing this morning."

"What happened to the other writer?"

"He and Bishop had a falling out. It's odd. I've been warned off talking to the other writer, twice. First Bishop, then just now his secretary. It's nothing to do with Mala, just odd."

"Who is it?"

"I'm sorry?"

"The writer, who is it?"

"It's not important."

"Who is it?"

"Bill Linden."

"You didn't mention he wrote the script."

"It's not important."

"So you're headed right over."

"What?"

"She warned you off. You got right on the phone. That's who you just called, isn't it?"

"Peter."

"You're headed straight over to see him."

"For heaven's sake, he's a friend, I want to tell him face to face that I'm on the picture. Are you still thinking about that? Peter, I was sedated."

47

I admit it's a poor excuse for calling out another man's name in your sleep.

CHAPTER 6

I still didn't know exactly what I'd said. Helen, who'd been at my hospital bedside with Peter, told me I'd called out Bill's name several times, quite clearly, then sobbed something about being sorry. She'd tried to convince Peter it was just the morphine talking. He'd told her I might die, and if there was somebody I wanted to see before I did, I was going to see him. So she'd called Bill, who'd hopped the first plane to New York. By the time he got there, my fever had dropped and I was out of danger. The danger of dying anyway. What it would end up meaning to Peter and me I wasn't sure.

Sam motioned Peter to rejoin them, and he did. I gathered my things and left.

Johnny Winslow sat waiting for me in the visitors' lot behind the wheel of his Olds, a younger version of his brother, except that he had lighter hair and kinder eyes.

He got out and opened the passenger door for me, swinging a stiff left leg as he walked. In the last days of the war, during a routine escort of a supply convoy in Germany, the jeep in which he was riding hit a land mine. It was easier for him to drive an Olds. They were the only cars with the new hydra-matic drive, which meant he didn't have to use a clutch.

"I need to go to Malibu," I said.

"Sure. You okay?"

"I'm fine." I wasn't. He knew it, but he left it alone.

Outside Marathon's gates, a smattering of union pickets lazed their way along the pavement. It was another warm day, too warm for early December, even in Los Angeles. And they had no serious squabble with Marathon. Only one police squad car sat at the curb, and its passenger door was open so the picketers could listen to the music on the radio.

This was the second long strike of the major studios in the last two years, once again triggered by jurisdictional disputes among the different unions, disputes that had been going on for at least a decade. To the general public, the question of who built a bar for the saloon scene might seem ridiculous. Was it a set piece? Or a prop because actors used it? To people whose jobs depended on it, it was serious.

Some union members had refused to work on the disputed—or "hot"—sets, and a couple of the studios, displaying a remarkable talent for taking a bad situation and making it worse, demoted or fired them. Other union members walked out in sympathy, and now picketed all the major studios and the companies that developed Technicolor films, delaying movies' releases.

My instinct is to side with labor. Despite how glamorous a Hollywood studio job sounded, plenty of them didn't pay that well. But I didn't think these men and women had much hope in this strike. The national leadership of the AFL had told its members not to honor the picket lines. The Screen Actors Guild had done the same. What hope did these strikers have, especially these days, when everyone was sure trade unions were rife with communists? The House committee investigating communist infiltration of the country had declared Hollywood a haven for "foreign thought" and last week announced their intention to return in February and expose all communists and their sympathizers.

They hadn't meant only in the trade unions.

★ ★ ★ ★ ★

The Malibu Colony curved along the oceanfront off the Theodore Roosevelt Highway, which not that long ago—back when all the land out here was privately owned—had been nothing but a dirt road cut into the slope of land that swept up from the coast to the hills. Now it was paved and graded, and it divided the sun-weathered, salt-cured tourist hotels and restaurants from the estates along the pristine beach—a beach the public could reach only if they knew how to find the well-hidden path.

These were the Malibu versions of estates. Mansions that were careful to hide themselves from the hoi polloi with a high wall that faced the highway, but many of the houses had only enough land on either side to decently separate them from their neighbors.

We were waved through the colony's entry gate, the guard having been told to expect us, and continued down the sun-baked strip of pavement that ran behind the homes.

Stars lived here. And other wealthy citizens who didn't mind having movie stars for neighbors. One of them was Kitty Sharp Dunning, the Sharp's Grocery Stores heiress. Bill Linden had lived for most of his Hollywood career in the guest cottage of her mansion, which she had shared, since the death of her husband, Tommy Dunning, at Dunkirk, with a succession of handsome, lightly talented actors under contract to studios that, like Kitty, were more interested in the handsome than the talent. Then she'd toss the latest one out when she discovered he was just as big a bounder as the last one.

The arrangement suited Bill. He loved the ocean, and although he'd come into quite a bit of money a few years ago, he'd kept his convenient, comfortable arrangement with Kitty. She never expected him to police her men, just provide a shoulder and a drinking companion when she needed one. She also liked having a man on the property when she was in between bounders.

The wrought-iron gates at the back of the property were closed, so Johnny tucked the car against the wall and I got out and rang the bell labeled "B Linden." After a minute, Bill appeared at a light run. He swung open the door by the gates and took my hand. He held it up to his handsome, sun-seamed face and kissed the palm. Johnny probably saw it. But Bill didn't see him. He was concentrating on me.

"I'm glad you decided to live," Bill said. "You scared me, baby, you know that?" Except he said it like Bogart. "You shcared me, baby." I laughed and he pulled me inside and shut the door.

The estate was laid out in three tiers that stepped down to the ocean. The first, where we were standing, was a courtyard of well-tended paving stones surrounded by garages and outbuildings of immaculate stucco and sparkling red tile roofs. Kitty's Packard touring limousine sat in the middle of the courtyard. In comparison, the Buick convertible beside it looked like the country cousin.

The second tier was a rectangle of vibrant rolled lawn bordered by raked gravel paths, flowering bushes and lime trees. The guest cottage, Bill's home, sat at one end, two stories of cream stucco and black shutters.

Inside, Bill's decorating tended to writer-comfort. Slouchy striped slipcovers, ancient carpets overlapping each other, bookcases, a scuffed leather chair by the green-painted fireplace.

"Want something to drink?" Bill asked.

"Anything with a lot of gin in it." I tossed my handbag and gloves into the chair.

"Not a Manhattan?" he asked as he disappeared into his small, yellow-tiled kitchen.

"Ha. Ha. I think I'm through with all things New York for a while."

"Go on outside, get some sun on that East Coast pallor."

I picked my way through his cluttered study where piles of papers cascaded across the tables, and towers of books teetered on the floor. As I reached the patio door, it flew open. Immediately, I was sure I was looking at Kitty's latest bounder-in-residence. Slim, wavy brown hair, good looks uncomplicated by character.

"Oh, uh," he said. "Hello, there. So sorry. Looking for Bill. He about?" A British accent, very upper class.

"In the kitchen."

He went off, without introduction. I heard their voices, at first so low I couldn't tell what they were saying, then, "You must help me out," rather desperately from the bounder.

I went out to the patio. The heat from the chair massaged my back and thighs. I sighed. California.

Above the tiled roof of the main house, down on the third tier, I could see the stunning sweep of the Pacific. It beat the hell out of any view from any skyscraper. In my humble but perfectly correct opinion.

After a minute, the front door slammed and the boyfriend appeared, striding across the lawn and down the wide stone steps to the mansion's garden. After another minute, Bill came out the patio door, carrying a tray with a tall pitcher of citrus-colored liquid. He poured me a cocktail glass of it. "Here you go. I call it the 'Back Home in Hollywood.' "

I swallowed a grateful mouthful. "Tastes like a gimlet."

He snapped a leafy sprig from a lime tree and dropped it in my glass. "There. Now, it's a 'Back Home in Hollywood.' "

I plucked the sprig out, shook off a few drops on Bill, then gestured with it in the direction the man had gone. "I don't want to run anybody off."

"You would if you knew him." He sat down.

"Kitty's new actor?"

"Brother-in-law. That's Charlie Dunning. Lord Dunning,

actually. Very old family, practically bankrupt. Kitty's father bought her a title you may recall, but then Tommy died and Charlie inherited it. He shows up from time to time when his money runs out." He poured himself a drink. "I shouldn't be so hard on him. He wasn't brought up to earn a living. And it's not his fault he has to let some Americans live over in Sussex in the family seat because he can't afford the upkeep. He makes some money from time to time teaching actors how to act British. Tries to take the crude American out of how they talk, walk, hold a cigar." He sat back. "So when's Mr. Winslow coming out here to punch me in the face?"

"I had a fever, I was full of morphine. I didn't know what I was saying."

"What have you told him?"

"That we're not having an affair, we're friends."

"And he could see you were lying."

"I didn't lie."

"Okay, he could see you weren't telling the whole truth, then."

"We're not having an affair. That's all he needs to know."

"Lauren—"

"I didn't come out here to talk about this." I stared stubbornly out over the ocean. "Is Charlie living out here?"

"Kitty's taken him in, but she's mad at him today and locked herself in her bedroom. He wanted me to tell her he was out here last night playing poker with me and the guys and not really off screwing whoever it was he was off screwing."

"Why would he think you'd lie to Kitty?"

"He figures any man would naturally lie for another about that sort of thing."

"Is she going to marry him?"

"I think she likes him too much. Speaking of bounders, how's your husband?"

"Franklin's fine, thank you very much. He's in Cuba,

vacationing after his movie wrapped."

"Yes, I know, and according to the columns, you're supposed to be out there with him. How are you going to explain being back in town?"

"The studio will take care of it."

"Let's see. You both tried hard to make it work. You love each other and you think he's terrific and you'll support him in whatever he does."

"He was a bad husband, but he's not a bad man. Nothing that happened last summer was his fault." My estranged husband had got himself into some trouble mostly not of his making as a result of the murder case last summer, the one that sent me temporarily to New York.

"He'll be all right; he always lands on his feet," Bill said. "The studio'll put him foursquare on the side of justice in his next picture. And he'll have you by his side whenever he needs you. How does Mr. Winslow feel about that?"

"I didn't come to talk about this, either."

"But I like to insult men I envy. All right," he said and refilled our glasses. "Why *did* you come out here?"

"To see you, idiot. I almost died. I realized how little time I take to see my friends. And to tell you in person I'm working on your Bishop script."

"Asshole."

I knew he didn't mean me. "What happened?"

"Maybe I'd had one too many drinks. The whole time I was writing the script, he'd send me pages of notes—all of them crap. To make him happy, I used a few, or made it look like I did. Then I get the word he's expecting to share writing credit. I stormed over to his bungalow, told him I'd take him to the Guild, called him a few things, up to and including a thief. Unfortunately, he had guests in the other room who heard everything. Bishop called Sol Noble, went straight over Sam to the studio head, wanted me fired. Not just off the picture, off the lot. Sam calmed him down, said he'd take me off the picture and get somebody in to do the final polish. Look, don't pay any attention to me. You can handle Bishop. You've got more patience than I do, and you don't drink on the job. Mala'll be glad to have you in her corner. Actresses love you."

"What?" I asked sharply, momentarily distracted from what I'd been about to tell him. "Are you saying I'm a woman's writer? Is that how people see me?"

"You write great dialogue for women, everybody knows that. Nothing wrong with it."

Except that nobody wanted to be called a woman's writer or a woman's director. So that was why Sam hired me. If he had to convince another star to step into Mala's role, he could say he'd got a woman's writer for her.

Bill refreshed my drink.

I said, "Bishop's got himself a military consultant. A Major McCann."

"Surprised he didn't hold out for a general."

"How much attention will I have to pay to his suggestions?"

"None. Nod and smile. Don't let him bully you."

"He doesn't seem the type. Funny thing, I'm sure I've met him before, but he says it's his first time in Hollywood. What were you thinking, by the way, when you wrote that script? Making Mala—who happens to be a foreigner—a married woman and then putting her and the hero in her bedroom, for God's sake."

He threw himself back in the chair and laughed with great enjoyment.

"You are an idiot," I said. But I laughed too. "God, I missed you."

"I don't suppose you heard anything from Martin and Cornelia. Or should I shut up?"

Martin and Cornelia Tanner. My parents. "Peter called them from New York to tell them I was in the hospital. They thanked him and that was it."

"What does he think about that?"

"He had some idea we didn't get along. He hasn't spoken to his own father since he threw him out of the house."

"His old man threw him out?"

"He threw his father out. He never talks about it; I got the story from someone else. His father lost his job after the crash, and he was drinking, slapping Peter's stepmother around and some of the kids. Finally one night, Peter picked him up and tossed him out the door. He dropped out of high school and supported all of them. Four sisters and a brother."

"In the Depression? How the hell did he do that?"

"Rum-running for Ramon Elizondo. After Prohibition ended, Mr. Elizondo sent him over to Ed Paxton's agency."

"So now I have to admire him for something in addition to his taste in women."

"Thank you, sir."

He topped off my drink, and I let him.

I said, "What are you up to next?"

"Headed over to the office later to work through some story lines they sent over. What's up? Something's on your mind. You're not upset because I said you can write for women, are you?"

"Look, I'm not on the picture just to do some polishing. We might need to do a heavy rewrite with another actress. Mala's missing."

"Anyone checked Mickey Triton's bed?"

"I'm serious. She's disappeared. No one's seen her since Friday. And Mickey Triton's dead."

"Good Christ. How?"

"That fire last weekend, the body in the cabin was his. The

police just identified him. It wasn't an accident. Don't tell anybody I told you that. The police will find out they were lovers and will want to talk to Mala. If she's still missing, they'll think she did it. The studio's hired Peter to look for her, but he has to be careful how he does it, or it'll look like the studio thinks she's guilty. He might want to talk to you."

"I'm looking forward to *that*. He should talk to Kitty. She and Mala are friends. I don't know Mala much at all. I think she and her cousin are a little nervous around me."

"Why?"

"I'm one of the few people who know she's probably older than she claims to be. Keep that to yourself. I saw her screen test, her first one, over in London before the war. Marathon was seeing some European actresses; I got asked to sit in. You remember Dickie Lucas?"

"God, yes, whatever happened to him?"

"He went back to living off his daddy in Boston. He was over there scouting, looking for new faces. We got drunk one night; he asked me to sit in. She was one of the girls they'd put on film. She was head and shoulders better than the rest of them, but her English wasn't that good. I made Dickie promise to give her another shot if she improved her English, but the war came along. She ended up stuck in Austria the whole time. Maybe another reason she's nervous around me. I know she's not Hungarian. We wrote a few letters back and forth, me trying to keep her chin up. I still have them, asked if she wanted to take a look at them, but I got booted off the picture and haven't seen her since. She says she's twenty-two. I think she must be at least twenty-six. I say more power to her if she can pull it off."

His brow knitted. "You say Mr. Winslow's father lost his job after the stock market crashed?"

"Yes."

"So, say, maybe nineteen-thirty. He never got to finish high school, so he was maybe seventeen when he tossed the old man out. So, let me see, the oldest he can be is . . . ?" He stood up, chortling happily. "This is wonderful. Now we have an excuse to go talk to Kitty. You two can swap stories about your adventures with younger men."

CHAPTER 7

"What are you doing?" I scrambled after Bill's long strides.

"It's okay, I don't need a key," Bill said.

"You know that's not what I mean."

"Kitty knows Mala. Maybe we can get something to give Mr. Winslow, and make him less inclined to punch me."

"You can't talk about this, any of this."

"How long before the police start looking for Mala? As soon as that makes the papers, her career's dead. We drop in, we chat. See what happens."

Bill trotted down the sand-swept steps, through the garden, and sailed through an unlocked door.

"We can't say anything, anything about Mickey Triton," I said.

"What if she brings him up?"

"We let her talk. Nothing about that cabin."

I chased him down the corridor, which was wide and cool, the floor covered in ocean-blue tiles, the walls painted in vivid blues, greens and yellows in Romanesque designs. Gilded pilasters led to the main hall, which soared two stories to a vaulted ceiling like a Renaissance cathedral.

"It's not much," Bill said, "but she calls it home."

Somewhere not far away, someone was vacuuming.

"Hey, Martha, that you?" Bill called out.

"Hello, Mr. Linden," a voice called back above the vacuum whirr. "They're upstairs."

"She and Charlie made up?"

"No, the madam's here."

"She is? This is even better."

"The madam?" I said.

"It's not what you think," he said and laughed. He took the stairs two at a time.

"Bill, she has company!"

"Right."

"Then why are we still climbing the stairs?"

The second floor was as opulent as the first. He knocked lightly on a door. No response. He turned the knob.

"She's locked herself in," I said. "Let's go."

"There's locked and there's locked." He felt around the top of the pilaster and retrieved a silver key. "She once locked herself in for two days. After that, I made myself a copy of the key."

"Bill! It's her bedroom!"

"God, you're beautiful when you're a prude."

The door swung open into an Arabian dream: A bed canopied in yard upon yard of glowing silk, wall panels painted in shimmering frescos of peacocks among golden leaves and topped with delicate Moorish arches.

While I gaped, Bill eased the draperies closed, throwing dusk across the room. Then he pressed his lips to my ear. "Let's see what the old girl's telling Kitty." He cat-stepped to another door. I followed him. I figured I wasn't going to stop him.

He slipped the other door open a few silent inches. Incense enveloped us. The room beyond was nearly black, lit by a solitary taper on a small round table in the center of the room. Over his shoulder, I saw two women at the table, holding hands across it. One had her back to us. The other was Kitty Dunning, her head tilted back, her eyes closed.

Bill opened the door another inch.

"No men!" the other woman cried. "No men!"

Kitty's chin snapped down, her eyes flew open.

Bill stuck his head into the room. "Sorry, Kitty. I saw Charlie. Just wanted to make sure you were all right."

"I tell you no men can be here," the other woman complained, in a thick accent. "Where does he come from? You say you lock doors."

I said, "Maybe the key wasn't turned all the way."

"I can hardly see," Kitty said. "Who's that with you?"

"Hi," I said. "Lauren Atwill. We've met a few times. I'm so sorry. Bill has no manners at all."

"You're right about that. Come on in. Let me get some light in here."

"Yes, come, come," the other woman said wearily, motioning us in with a dramatic wave of her chubby, jeweled hand. "Is gone now. Is gone. Too late."

"I'm so sorry," I said.

"That's okay," Kitty said. "We were having some trouble finding Choppers anyway."

"You should respect," the woman admonished.

"You're right." She tossed back the thick draperies, and light splashed across the room. She said to me, "Charlie's brother, my late husband, Tommy, also known as Choppers. He had a pretty remarkable set and they used to click and clack like mad in moments of passion. Sit down, let me get you something."

We assured her we were fine. If I hadn't already had two and a half gimlets, I wouldn't have let Bill talk me into breaking into her house in the first place. We sat down on the silk tapestry sofa. Kitty poured a couple of brandies from the bar in the corner.

She was maybe forty, a bit too slender, with blonde hair, overbleached, cut short and curled around her head. She had a good tan, but her face looked strained, with puffiness beneath the eyes, possibly the result of too much dieting, too much booze, or too much bad luck with men.

She handed one of the snifters to the other woman, who took half of it in a swallow.

"Oh, Lord, how rude of me," Kitty said. "I haven't introduced you. I just assume everybody knows Madame." She said mah-*dahm*, not *mad*-uhm. "This is Lauren Atwill. Lauren, Madame Karoly."

Madame nodded regally. She was thin of limb and stout of middle. It was hard to tell her age. I would have guessed late thirties, but maybe the heavy makeup and dark shadowing around her large brown eyes made her look older than she was. The thick penciled brows and rather aggressive widow's peak didn't help either. Her hat looked like a chocolate meringue, a chocolate meringue with sprays of tulle shooting out of one side and a couple of long feathers cutting across her scowling brow.

I didn't have a lot of patience with these so-called spiritualists. What I usually called them was quacks. Los Angeles had been full of them for decades, ever since they realized how much new money there was out here just waiting to be taken from its owners. They could contact your beloved departed, guide your future, redirect mortal danger, even make someone love you. For enough money.

Still I was curious how Madame had known a man had entered the room behind her. She must have heard the door open, guessed it was Charlie. There hadn't been enough light in the room for her to have seen a reflection in anything.

I certainly didn't believe she'd sensed Bill with magical powers.

Madame picked up a bracelet from the table and handed it to Kitty. "Here. Do not forget where you leave this."

"Oh, yes. Thanks. It's all right, then?"

"Yes. Much love when worn, when given, much happiness. Sorrow at end. Perhaps touched by those who loved this woman after she died."

"Tommy's grandmother," Kitty said to me. She laid the bracelet in my hand, a cuff band about three inches wide, an art-deco design, quite popular in the late twenties and thirties. A base of white gold, and on top, laid with random precision, stars of various sizes, charged with diamonds.

"It would be hard not to be happy wearing that," I said, and gave it back.

Kitty sailed off into the bedroom and returned without the bracelet. "I like to have Madame Karoly's opinion on my jewelry before I wear it, the aura is so important."

And then it hit me.

"You're Mala's cousin," I blurted. Damn those gimlets, I'd read Mala's studio file on the plane, and this very morning, Sam had reminded me Mala's cousin was a fortune-teller. And damn those gimlets, I couldn't keep the astonishment out of my voice. Damn Bill for not telling me who she was when we were downstairs.

Madame drew herself up. "You think is not possible I am cousin?"

"Not at all. I meant I should have recognized you."

"Yes, Madame is quite famous," Kitty said and snuggled happily into an armchair. "Lauren is Frank Atwill's wife." Then she said to me, "I think I first met you with him, at one of our parties before the war."

"Oh, God, I remember those parties," Bill said fondly and laid back against the sofa pillows. "Which one was it? The Lady Godiva party?"

"Bill, they'd just raised taxes again, we were protesting, and we were all wearing leotards. Well, most of us were. And we raised a lot of money for that hospital."

"Maybe the Roman Orgy party?"

"It was not! We were Roman gods and goddesses."

"Having their way with the ordinary citizens. Then there was the Scheherazade party, the tents, the wine, the near-naked slave girls."

"It was a charity auction. We raised a lot of money for that charity."

"The name of which you can't even remember."

"It was something for refugees from Europe. Tommy hired some dancers to dress up like harem girls to tell stories and serve the drinks. That was all they did."

"Not all. I seem to recall Lauren caught Frank letting one of the girls show him just how small her costume was."

"Bill!" Kitty and I said in unison.

"You make the party sound horrible," Kitty said. "It was all meant in fun. And we were trying to help people."

"To disport themselves." He turned to me. "I think you'd already gone home in high dudgeon. But later Charlie, Tommy, and a few of the other expatriate Brits induced the harem girls into naked ocean bathing. Alas, the Brits took their clothes off too. Even Alastair Bishop, though I do believe Betty tried to stop him. It's the ghastly memories that stick with you."

"Bill, that's not funny," Kitty said.

"You're damned right."

"I mean it."

Madame held up a hand, her eyes closed. "Something bad happened. Something very bad that night. But, I think, not here."

"Yes," Kitty said, "two of our guests were killed later." She said to Bill, "Mickey Triton brought some people over with him that night, a couple. They were nice enough, maybe not polished. Mickey was the welterweight champion then, headed over to box in England, to defend his title, so of course we wanted him to come. We said yes, he could bring them. They bought a nice little painting, too, I remember, at the auction.

But they were ambushed in their car on the way home. The papers hushed up where they'd been because it didn't have anything to do with us. Apparently, the husband was a gangster."

"Why didn't I know about this?" Bill said.

"Because you're a self-centered bastard."

"True enough."

"And you left for Europe right after. Tommy and I decided never to talk about it. It was too awful."

There was a sharp rapping on the door.

"I am not speaking to you, Charlie," Kitty called out.

"I have to talk to you. Something's happened. It's important. Please."

Kitty got up and flung the door open. "I told you I didn't want to talk to you. Madame, look at him. He's been up to no good, hasn't he?"

"I haven't," Charlie protested, venturing a foot across the threshold. "I met some friends last night, had some drinks. Just friends."

"Whose aftershave smelled like perfume. What do you want?"

Charlie said, "I just heard on the wireless. Mickey Triton's dead."

"What? What are you talking about?"

"That fire, that body they found. It was him. It was Mickey. I just heard it."

"Dear God." Kitty hurried over to Madame and took her hand. "I can't believe it."

Charlie said, "If you don't have your car, I can drive you home, Madame. You'll want to be with Mala."

"Maybe it's a mistake," Kitty said.

"I heard it on the wireless," Charlie declared.

"Is not mistake," Madame said, then turned to me. "And you know is not mistake."

Kitty dropped Madame's hand and stepped back. "What?"

It was useless to deny it. I'm not the best of liars sober, and I'd had gimlets.

"I know who you are," Madame went on. "I remember I see you in the newspapers. This man who comes to see me, who comes from the studio, this Mr. Winslow. He is same man you hired last summer."

"What is she talking about?" Charlie said.

"Oh, shut up, Charlie," Kitty said. "And if you ever open your mouth about anything you're going to hear in this room, I'll never speak to you again as long as you live. Sit down."

Charlie did as he was told.

Madame said to me, "What do you know?"

"Pretty much everything," I said, "but not because Mr. Winslow was indiscreet. We were in New York, Mr. Winslow and I. The studio asked him to come back and help. They trust him."

She regarded me with those piercing dark eyes. Then she said, "Would you give to me my handbag?"

I took it off the side table and handed it over. She opened it and took out a card. She gave it to Kitty. "You must call this man. He is trying to find Mala. We have known for many days that Mickey was probably dead."

"When you called me Monday," Kitty said, "and asked if I'd seen her? You knew then?"

I said, "Madame couldn't tell you the truth. She had to be careful. It was very important that no one knew how serious it might be." I turned to Charlie. "Mala went away on Friday, and no one knows where she is. She has to be found before the police discover she knew Mickey, before they find out she's gone."

"They couldn't possibly think she'd ever hurt him," Kitty said.

Madame said, "People will see in the papers that he is dead

and she disappeared. It could ruin her. Even though she does nothing wrong."

"Good God," Charlie said. "What can we do to help?"

I said, "Talk to Mr. Winslow. And don't tell anyone else anything. It would help if you made a list of all the people Mala knew well, especially those she might know well enough to go stay with. Anything you can think of."

"Bill, stay. Help me," Kitty said. "You've got a better memory. I'll call this man as soon as we finish the list."

"Shall I drive you home?" Charlie asked Madame. "Glad to."

"I have car. I have other appointment, at studio. I must go. No one can know is anything wrong."

"Why don't I leave you to the list," I said to Kitty. "I should be going anyway."

Madame rose, and the women exchanged cheek kisses. Kitty slipped some bills into Madame's hand to pay for the session.

Madame and I went out into the hallway.

"I hope I was not rude to Mr. Linden," Madame said. "He has been good friend to Mala, and so to me."

I wasn't sure what he'd done to qualify as Mala's friend except to say nice things about her acting in a letter years ago. And write her a good movie. Maybe that was it. Sam had indicated Madame was the force behind Mala's career. "You weren't rude. And we should never have intruded."

"You love Mr. Linden," she said.

"I'm sorry?"

"Mr. Linden. You love him."

"I do, but not like you mean."

"Ah, then it is Mr. Winslow. He has much light. But pressed in. There was confusion from you. Mr. Linden. Mr. Winslow. Love. And confusion. And much regret."

CHAPTER 8

Johnny Winslow held the car door for me. Was I imagining it, or did he close it a little harder than normal? He'd seen Bill kiss me—well, kiss my hand—but surely, he couldn't think I'd ask him to drive me out here so I could spend an hour in Bill's bed?

"Mala Demara's cousin's in there, with Kitty Dunning," I said. "Madame Karoly. She's a spiritualist."

He started the car.

"Kitty's going to call Peter, see if she can help. She knows the body was identified. Her brother-in-law heard it on the radio."

He pulled away, kept his eyes on the road.

"Bill's the screenwriter on the movie. He gave me a lot of help when I was getting started. He's a good friend."

I was making it worse.

But it was true.

When I was twenty-two, my uncle Bennett's connections got me a job at Marathon. I'd spent my college summers working for *Brindell's* magazine in New York, answering phones, doing the odd research assignment, and writing a few articles on my own. I wanted to be a magazine writer. The women who did that seemed so glamorous, or at any rate independent, which in my youth was the same thing. The magazine liked my research. They even liked my articles and published a dozen of them. As a reward, *Brindell's* gave me a full-time job after I graduated from Vassar, as a researcher for some men whose work habits could most generously be described as loose. "Here, honey," they'd say, "why don't you try your hand at this? Good practice for you." They'd toss their rough drafts at me and head to the bar. I'd take the drafts home to my five-story-walkup, bathtub-in-the-kitchen flat and rewrite them.

I turned out to be very good at rewriting.

Along the way, I realized a few things. Despite all the women's bylines I'd noticed, most of the writers were men. And they—and their editors—weren't all that interested in women with ambition. They were even less interested in women with ambition who'd been born west of Pennsylvania.

Undaunted—well, daunted, but still game—at the end of the year, I went to see my boss, showed him my work, my rewrites, my articles, made my case.

He was impressed. He gave me a dollar-a-week raise. I looked for another job at other magazines. But the country was in the full grip of the Depression. Writers with far more reputation than I had were lined up in front of me.

My uncle wrote me: quit. Come home. Work in Hollywood. And almost just like that, I had a job at Marathon. Of course, it helped that Uncle Bennett owned ten percent of the studio.

In my new job, I read novels and created synopses. I learned fast that what the studio needed wasn't a synopsis. They needed to know what was in the book that might make a good movie. So that's how I wrote my synopses. And along the way, I read every screenplay I could get my hands on. In my spare time, I took the books I thought could be movies and wrote scripts. Nobody would read them, but I kept writing them.

Something beyond my inexperience was going to get in my way: novelists. When pictures had begun to talk, just a few years before my arrival, producers needed writers who could come up with more than story lines and inter-title, or title, cards. Talkies needed dialogue. So the studios had hired novelists and playwrights. But it was the novelists who really stood in my way. The studios kept them around for the prestige, even if most of them turned out to be not very good at script writing. They got handed the projects that might otherwise go to a beginner.

William Linden's two novels had sold modestly but had been very well received by the East Coast reviewers, who were what really mattered to the studios. Marathon had lured him west with a salary that would pay him more in two months than he'd made off two books. He moved to Hollywood and never looked back.

The first time I ever spoke to Bill, he was lounging on his office sofa in the Tate Building, which housed most of the writers, and was ancient by Hollywood standards, having been built in 1910. The glare of sunlight was held at bay by dark-green awnings over every window. All the better, given the proportion of hangovers among the writers.

Bill had one leg slung up onto the sofa's back and was writing on a tablet resting on that knee. I'd been told to go drop off a half dozen of my synopses with him. He could see if any of them interested him.

"Yeah, thanks," he said, "put it on the desk. Wait a minute, wait a minute. Who are you? Do I know you?"

I told him who I was.

"Are you really? How'd you like to go to a party tonight? You look like you know how to dress, for a writer."

"I'm not a writer."

"Hell you're not. I actually do read the slop people put on my desk, you know. I'm working on *Garden of Shadows*. You wrote the synopsis, right?"

"Yes."

"Dear God, I hope you have more to say for yourself at a party. I'm stealing all your ideas, by the way, hope you don't mind. Glad to see you didn't get the job just because your uncle owns half the studio."

"My uncle owns ten percent of the studio."

"Writer's license."

"Is that the rumor, I only got the job because of him?"

"No. A rumor has a chance of being wrong. Sit down, take a load off your umbrage."

I did. He pulled a bottle of rye out of his desk and poured me a clean glass of it, then dropped into his chair and threw his legs up on the desk. "If your feelings get hurt, kid, this is the wrong town for you. I only got this job because some guy whose old man sold pots off a cart wanted to boss a college boy around. My writing gets called crap twice a week, sometimes twice a day. So, you want to go to the party with me or not?"

"Somebody's following us," Johnny said, yanking me back to the present.

"What? I'm sorry, what?" I'd been so deep in my thoughts, I'd forgotten where I was.

"We're being followed. Studebaker, couple of cars back. Dark blue."

I didn't ask if he was sure. If Johnny said we were being followed, we were. And I was curiously proud he felt he didn't have to tell me not to turn around.

He drove on, his eyes—and only his eyes—shifting to the rearview mirror. "Nobody followed me to your house this morning when I picked you up," he said, "and nobody tailed us to the studio. I spotted him on the way out here."

"Pull over, let him go by, we'll get the license number."

"Even an amateur could figure out what we were up to, we just pull off the road."

"I have an idea." I told him what I had in mind, and we caught Wilshire when we reached Santa Monica and headed back to town.

Beginning at Hancock Park, the Miracle Mile was decked out

for Christmas. Dozens of evergreen trees had been chopped down in the mountains and now lined the shopping boulevard, potted, flocked white and pruned to match, sparkling in the eighty-degree sun. *Holiday Inn* imported for Los Angeles.

Fortunately, the Mile was designed for automobile, not foot, traffic, so even with the holiday-shopping crowd, we found a parking space in a lot on Fairfax.

The entrance to the May Department Store faced the corner of Wilshire and Fairfax, the building's angle softened by a wide gold-banded tower in moderne style that ran to the roof. Johnny held one of the doors for me and a few other women, who thanked him. He touched his hat and smiled, but he wasn't looking at them. He was looking over their shoulders.

Inside, I headed for the glove counter. Johnny tucked himself by the doors, where he could see traffic passing and remain concealed. I bought a pair of gloves, which I needed, and a large envelope handbag, which I didn't, but which gave me a big, neatly tied bandbox to show anyone watching us that I had an innocent reason to stop.

We got back in the car.

"Nothing," he said. "They might have figured out they were spotted. But let's see if they pick us up again. Who knew you were going out to Malibu?"

"Nobody. Well, Peter and Bill. No one else. I called Bill from the soundstage. No one overheard me. And it was a pay phone, no switchboard operator."

"Who knew you were going to be at the studio today?"

"Sam Ross. Alastair Bishop. Bishop's assistant, Betty Guinness. And anyone they told. I wasn't supposed to go out to Malibu. Bishop told me twice not to contact Bill."

"So you think Alastair Bishop's having you followed in case you went to see a writer?"

"You sound like your brother."

Johnny took me to Peter's office at the Paxton Agency, which was downtown, on Fourth at Hill. Unfortunately, Peter wasn't there.

Johnny said, "Use his desk, write down everything that happened at the studio, even stuff Pete was there to see, and everything out in Malibu, and I'll pass it along."

"Why doesn't he come over to my house tonight, I can fill in details."

"If he has time, but write it down now so you don't forget." He left, and I rolled some paper into the typewriter, then called Juanita to tell her there might be company for dinner. She thought a pork roast with pears. Peter liked her roast. She liked Peter. To the extent she liked any man.

I had a message, she said, from Mr. Bishop. His secretary, Betty Guinness, had called to say she'd arranged for a bungalow for me to work in. I asked Juanita what time the call came in. A half hour ago. It must have been the gimlets still clouding my brain because after I hung up, I actually considered whether that meant anything. If Alastair Bishop still wanted to get me a bungalow a half hour ago, did it mean he didn't know I'd seen Bill so he wasn't the one having me followed? I should never drink in the middle of the day.

I called Betty back. She gave me the details about my bungalow, its location, its phone number. She said Mr. Bishop would like me to come in right away and start working on ideas since, now that Mickey Triton's body had been identified, it seemed more likely some significant changes would have to be made to the script. Bishop had three actresses to whom Mala's role would first be offered if that became necessary. Mr. Bishop wanted me to determine how much rewriting would be required for each one. She'd arrange for dinner to be sent to me.

Okay, I said, sure. I'd be at Bishop's bungalow in an hour. I hung up, then snarled at the phone. I called Juanita and told her not to bother with the roast.

I wrote my report for Peter and included everything I'd done and heard that day. Even the part about Mickey Triton having brought two people to a society party seven years ago, two people who ended up dead in a gangster ambush later that night, even though it was unlikely to have anything to do with his death all these years later.

I read the report over, then laid it in the middle of Peter's blotter. I noticed a file sitting in the in-box. The tab said "Triton, Mickey." I slipped it out of the shallow wooden box and opened it.

There were two pictures, one in his boxing days, posed with gloves raised, his well-muscled torso shining; the second, a casual photo of him at the racetrack, in a plaid sport coat, binoculars around his neck.

Also in the file was a brief personal history. Where he was born, raised, known family, known associates. Promoters, boxers, trainers, gamblers, Jack Dragna and Julius "Julie" Scarza, Dragna's chief lieutenant. Mala Demara's name had been penciled into the list.

"Enjoying yourself?" Johnny said from the doorway.

"Sorry, couldn't resist. You already had a file on Mickey Triton?"

"We keep information on lots of people. We need to know what we might be up against when we take on a job. Be crazy not to. You finished with your report?"

I handed it over. "I have to go over to the studio and work for a while, maybe most of the evening."

"One of the men will take you. He'll keep an eye out for that Studebaker. You call when you're ready to go home, and someone will come get you."

"Would you ask Peter to call me? Here's the number at the bungalow I'll be using. Tell him we can get him dinner sent over there, and I could fill in any blanks in my report." And I could see him again. And make it clear I hadn't gone to Malibu to jump into Bill Linden's bed even if I wasn't ready yet to tell him anything more.

It was past six, and dark, by the time I reached Bishop's office. He was still there, his Packard tucked up against the building. But Betty didn't invite me inside. She handed me a sealed envelope, with CONFIDENTIAL printed on it. "This is everything you need to get started. There's a key in there."

I heard a voice coming from behind the closed sitting-room door, a woman's voice, low, deep, although I couldn't make out the words. Then I smelled incense. Madame Karoly said she had appointments at the studio. One of them apparently was Alastair Bishop.

I thanked Betty and climbed back into the motorized cart that had brought me over from visitors' parking.

The prestige bungalows lined this end of Marathon's lot, a street running between them with just enough room on either side to parallel-park a car. Then the street narrowed to an alley, the parking spaces disappeared as did any bit of front lawn, and the bungalows grew smaller, plainer. Mine wasn't as close to the back of the lot as I'd expected, nor as neglected. In the inadequate light thrown from the streetlamps, the paint on the stucco looked fairly fresh and the awnings not too frayed. No one had left any lights on for me, though. The street was deserted.

The driver gave me a card with the dispatch number so I could call for a ride when I was through, then waited while I climbed the cracked wooden steps and unlocked the door. I flipped on the porch light and the one in the small foyer, waved to the driver and he drove off.

The foyer had nothing in it but a set of coat pegs and an iron-framed mirror. I knew the layout of most of the smaller bungalows; from time to time over the years I'd had to use one of them. A small room on each side: one a sitting room with a tiny kitchen area; the other the office, with a postage stamp of a bathroom. I flipped on the sitting-room light and stuck my head in. Bamboo furniture, cushions with large purple gardenias. The kitchen had a small refrigerator with a growling motor. The legs of the dining table had been the victim of an unhappy, strong-jawed dog.

I hung up my suit jacket in the foyer, opened the office door, and flipped on the light.

And saw the body.

CHAPTER 9

Major McCann lay on his back at the base of the open bathroom door, his head tilted against it, his face pushed down toward his chest. The upper half of his body lay on the tiles, the lower half on the wood floor of the office. His heels had caught in the edge of the hooked rug, so his knees were bunched up and the legs collapsed to one side. He wore a gray suit, not his uniform. His fedora had come off and lay on its crown in the crook of his right elbow.

His jacket had fallen open, revealing a blood-soaked shirt and a gun he never got to touch.

It took two seconds for me to see it all. In the next second, I whipped around, my arms thrust in front of me, warding off some unseen attack, my eyes madly searching the empty room, my breathing so hard I could hear it. But then there wasn't anything else to hear.

It took another five seconds to start reasoning again.

"All right," I said to myself—and I said it out loud, "there's no one here. No. One. Here."

No. One. Here.

The killer's gone. He was not looking for me. Or he would have waited, and I'd be dead by now.

Get help. There's a phone on the desk. Walk over to the desk. Pick up the phone.

I laid my hand on it.

It rang.

I jumped and cried out, somewhere between a scream and a sob.

It rang again. I picked it up, then suddenly I was afraid to say anything.

"Hello," Peter said.

"Peter. Oh, God. Peter. Major McCann. The military advisor on the picture. He's dead. I turned on the light and there he was."

"Where? Inside the bungalow?"

"He's been shot."

"Get out of there. Go outside and scream your head off."

"I'm scared to leave. It's dark out. Nobody's—"

"Can you call studio security from there?"

"I can call the switchboard."

"When I hang up, do it. First, tell me exactly where you are. I'll be there in ten minutes."

I told him. Then I said, "If I call security, they'll close the gates. You can't get in."

"Lauren, call them. And make someone stay on the phone with you till they get there. I'm on my way."

It was a good thing I only had to dial one number for the switchboard, my hand was shaking so badly. It took a while for someone to answer. While I waited, I pictured Peter dashing for his car, racing toward me, and calmed down. He couldn't have been at his house or office. That would take longer than ten minutes. But if he said he'd be here in ten, he would be.

I had to give him time to get inside the gates.

After a dozen rings, a bored switchboard girl answered. Instead of security, I asked for the front gate. I told the guard a Mr. Winslow was coming and to let him in. The guard said sure.

I hung up, but couldn't let go of the phone. I stared at it. I couldn't look at the body.

What was Major McCann doing here? Why was he wearing a gun?

How much longer till I could call security?

Maybe if I said I'd found a man on the floor, collapsed, they'd send someone over, without closing the gates. Three minutes to get here. As soon as they saw he was dead, they'd close the gates. I had to give Peter time.

I walked, stiff-legged, to the other side of the desk. There was a clock. I could watch it. Count the minutes.

One of the desk drawers gaped, pulled out much farther than you normally would, unless you'd lost something way at the back. The chair had been pushed away, into the curtains.

I waited seven minutes and called security.

Peter got inside just before they closed the gates, and made it to the bungalow ahead of the first prowl cars. Because the union strikers had quit picketing at dusk, there had been no patrol cars stationed in front of Marathon.

I pretended to be even more upset than I was, so nobody would think about separating us. An officer took my handbag and my story and didn't see anything in the bungalow to contradict it, so he put us out on the front steps of the bungalow opposite, watched over by a square-shouldered, laconic officer named DiSalvo. Any other questions would wait for the detectives.

Security staff, in suits, and night watchmen, in uniforms, lingered on the other side of the alley, as close as possible to more action than they usually got to see.

In a few minutes, a dull gray Ford eased its way between the prowl cars. Two detectives got out and looked around before they closed their doors. Peter always did the same thing. He'd get out, look around, then close the door. A habit, in his line of work, that could come in handy.

One of the detectives made his way through the knot of officers and security and went inside. The driver spotted us, shoved a matchstick between his teeth and strolled over. He was pushing fifty, with heavy, untamed brows and the kind of heft that might make you think he was going soft. You'd be wrong.

"Sergeant Barty," I said.

"Mrs. Atwill." He pulled out the matchstick. "How long you been back in town?"

"Two days."

"You couldn't wait a week to turn up another body?"

Peter said, "All she did was find the guy, Phil."

"You with her when she did?"

"No."

"Then you don't have much to say right now, do you?"

Barty introduced himself to DiSalvo, then asked, "You been with them the whole time?"

"No. He was already here before the first car. One of us been with them since, though. Guard said he came in a couple of minutes before they closed the gates."

"He have a gun?"

"We got it. He told us about it, handed it over. We searched him. Nothing else."

"What about security? Night watchmen? Were they searched?"

"Sergeant Gillsby's over there, he'd know. Security said only one of their men went inside."

Peter said, "I saw four of them coming out when I got here, two night watchmen and two security men in suits." Peter pointed those four men out to Barty.

"Christ," Barty said. He signaled sharply to another officer and ordered him to corral those four men and make sure everybody from security had been searched. Then he asked Peter, "How'd you get here so fast?"

"I called Mrs. Atwill, to see if she wanted to get some dinner before she started work. She'd just walked in and found the body. I wasn't ten minutes from here."

Barty had heard stories from us before that were fairly ripe with coincidence. He'd decide whether he believed this one. "Tell me what happened," he said to me.

I did, although I left out the part about waiting to call security. Then I said, "The dead man's named McCann, Major McCann. I don't know his first name. He's the military advisor on the movie I'm working on."

"What was he doing in there?"

"I don't know."

"I want everything that happened and what you saw."

I gave him what he wanted, then he said, "Come on inside, see if it looks the same." Apparently, he trusted my memory more than he did studio security's ability to resist touching anything.

"Not you," he said to Peter, who'd started to stand.

Barty's partner was crouched beside the body, looking at the wound and the undrawn gun, his hands in his suit jacket pockets, maybe to remind him not to touch anything.

Barty said, "Take a look. He look any different than he did a half hour ago?"

"Somebody might have lifted his coat because his hat's a little further away from his body."

Barty jerked a look at the officer by the door. The man spread his hands to say, we didn't touch him.

"What about the stuff on the desk?"

"I don't think anything's been moved." I walked around it and looked at the drawer. "This looks the same. It was already pulled all the way out like this."

He signaled his partner over and told him security had lied about how many men had come into the room. They decided it was a good idea to find out why. The partner stalked off. I didn't doubt he'd get the job done. He looked like someone who wouldn't worry overmuch about what Emily Post might think.

Barty guided me across the foyer to the sitting room. Nothing there looked any different to me and I told him. I also told him I hadn't noticed before the small broken pane of glass in the back door above the knob.

He sat me down at the dog-chewed table. "You want some water?"

"I'm all right, thank you. But there's something you should know." I confessed to delaying my call to security. "I was scared, I didn't know what the police would think, maybe that I'd done it. I didn't want to face them without Peter. I didn't know it would be you."

He grunted. "Lucky for both of us, huh?"

I didn't tell him I was sorry. It wouldn't make any difference. There was a lot I could never say to him, mostly about how grateful I was for what he'd done last summer. He'd gone out on a limb for us. We'd been right, but it had made him unpopular with some other cops. Peter'd told me never to mention it to Barty: he didn't need to be reminded.

We went out. The night had turned misty. A thin haze hung above us under scudding clouds that were tinged in deep lavender in the spectral moonlight. A hot, damp wind pushed an acrid smell up the alley, something like burned leaves but rawer on the tongue. Who knew what it was? Los Angeles sat beneath a layer of industrial smog most days, thick enough that the city had ordered studies done. No one could agree on what caused it.

With a good wind, it disappeared to the ocean. This wasn't that wind.

At the end of the parade line of prowl cars, a dark sedan pulled up. Two men, hats pulled low, got out.

"Who's that?" Barty asked me. "You know?"

"The driver's Mack Pace, the head of studio security. I don't know the other man."

Barty shoved his matchstick between his teeth and headed for them. I scurried back to Peter, and filled him in.

The man with Pace was taller and quite a bit thinner, wearing a topcoat even in the warm night. He had a long, pale face, but I couldn't make out much detail at that distance with his hat brim low.

Pace said something to Barty, then the taller man strode off toward the bungalow. Barty got in front of him in a hurry. Pace tried to interject, and whatever Barty said to him shut him up fast.

The tall man gestured Barty to follow him, back down the row of cars, out of the light, out of anyone else's earshot. All I could see were dark shapes in the settling mist. Finally, they returned, Barty leading the way to the crime scene, grimmer than before. Pace trailed them, but was left at the bottom of the steps. He wasn't going to see anything else. With the curtains closed, neither were we.

Peter said, "What would you say, Officer DiSalvo? Not state police."

"Nope. State boys got manners."

"Feds maybe, but not local."

"Why's that?"

"The coat, the suit, too heavy for an LA winter."

"Looks like we got more of them, whoever they are," DiSalvo observed, and jerked his chin toward a car that had stopped behind the dark sedan. A man got out.

I said, "That one's harmless, relatively. It's Sam Ross. He's a producer here."

"Why are they always short?"

"He's a friend. Could I just run over and tell him I'm all right? I'll come right back."

Before DiSalvo could think about it too hard, Peter pulled out his cigarette case and offered him a Chesterfield. "Come right back, though," DiSalvo said and took a smoke.

I intercepted Sam. "I don't have much time. I'm only supposed to be telling you I'm all right."

"What are you doing here?"

They must have reached him at home. His suit looked like it had been thrown back on; his tie was badly knotted. He hadn't taken time to shave: his cheeks were gray-blue with the shadow of his thick beard.

I said, "I was supposed to be working in there tonight. I found the body. It's Major McCann. Did you know?"

"Yeah, Pace called me. You okay?"

"I'm fine. Peter's here. We think there's a government man inside with Sergeant Barty. What's going on?"

"I wish to hell I knew. Wait, did you say Mr. Winslow's here?"

"Over on the steps. He—"

"Look, I can't talk here. Take Mr. Winslow to my house. Don't let anybody see you."

"It might be a while before the police let us go."

"Call my study, you know the number? I'll be up. Bring him."

I returned to my perch. Pace collected Sam, and after a while, Barty came out and spoke to him for a couple of minutes, but he didn't let him in.

Sam spent another few minutes talking to Pace, then left. Probably to make sure Morty Engler and the publicity staff were on the job. A man had been murdered at Marathon.

We waited for two more hours. Peter seemed content to smoke and talk sports with DiSalvo, including the rumors that surfaced from time to time that a major-league baseball team might move to Los Angeles. Last summer, it had been the Pirates. The Pirates denied it, but that never stopped a rumor that people wanted to believe. I thought it was all guff. We had the Pacific Coast League. We didn't need anything else. Besides, it would take any East Coast team two days on the train just to get here to play.

Nobody in their right mind would put a team on an airplane.

Barty never came back. Finally an officer marched over and barked at DiSalvo that we could go, but don't leave town. He never even looked at us while he was doing it.

CHAPTER 10

Peter put me in his car, which he had parked at the top of the alley. As soon as we'd turned a corner, he jerked on the hand brake.

"Why the hell didn't you call security when I told you to?" he snapped.

I snapped right back, "Because I couldn't face the police! I couldn't stand the thought of going through all that again without you! The way they'd look at me, what they'd think!" In the next second, he pulled me against him, raked my hat off, pin and all, flung it into the backseat, and buried his lips in my hair.

"You could have been killed."

"Please don't yell at me. Just hold me."

And he did. I lay gratefully in his arms, relishing the solid drumming of his heart against my breasts and the soft brush of his lips in my hair. For a long time, we were silent there in the dark. Finally, he whispered, "And you never thought once about how this could be connected to Mala Demara's disappearance and Mickey Triton's killing, and whether maybe I could get a look in that bungalow before the cops got there."

I smoothed his lapel, then snuggled my cheek against it. I snuggled my breasts back against him, too.

"Lauren."

"All right, maybe, yes. I thought maybe you could get inside. And I knew the killer was gone."

"How? How could you know that?"

"He'd shot somebody. He certainly didn't want to get caught. He'd be listening for anyone coming. The cart made noise. I made noise climbing the steps, using the key. If he was still inside, he would have heard me and run out the back door, which is how he got in. A panel of glass was broken. If he'd been there to kill me, I never would have made it to the phone."

I snuggled again, and he didn't chastise me for it.

"You told Phil Barty a drawer was open," he said.

"Major McCann had been searching the desk."

"And the back door, the glass was broken?"

"Yes. Why? What is it?"

"He gets killed and within an hour the Feds show up. It looks like McCann was working for them. And if he was, he'd have better ways to get inside than leaving broken glass behind. You told Barty it looked like he slid down the bathroom door."

"He was lying against it." I described again the position of the body.

"He wouldn't want to risk being seen picking a lock, so he'd come around the back way. But if that glass had already been broken, I don't think he would just walk in with his gun in his holster."

"But even if he were inside first, when he heard the glass break, wouldn't he have pulled his gun?"

"He could have hidden in the bathroom, waited to see what was going on, then stepped out to confront the guy and got himself shot. That would account for him sliding down the door."

"But why wouldn't he pull his gun when he came out?"

"Yes, why didn't he pull his gun? Come on, sit up, get your hat. It's time we found out more about this Major McCann."

We called Sam's study phone from an all-night drugstore. He was still up, as he said he would be. Sam said not to let anyone see us, so Peter made sure we weren't followed. We parked behind the house, out of sight. Sam was waiting at the back door, in a cashmere dressing gown over striped pajamas. His deep-red slippers padded ahead of us through the still, silent house. He closed the study door softly and offered us chairs and drinks.

"You hungry? I made a few sandwiches, over there on the coffee table. I hope you don't mind corned beef."

I didn't. I hadn't had any dinner. I put a half sandwich on a napkin and sat down.

Sam handed Peter a bourbon and sat behind his desk, his fists in the pockets of his robe, thrust into his lap. "I probably shouldn't be talking to you at all."

But he wanted to talk to us. He'd had time to think it over, yet he'd invited us inside.

"The detective who was there tonight, the big guy," Sam said.

"Barty, Phil Barty," Peter said.

"You know him?"

"Not well enough he'll tell me anything he doesn't want to. Are you asking me to get information from him? Or asking if he's likely to tell me something you should've told me already? Mr. Ross, that man in the sedan with Mack Pace was a Fed. He shows up with your head of security less than an hour after the body's found. McCann was working for him. And I think you knew it."

"I swear to God I didn't think there was any connection between that and asking you to find Mala. I still don't know there is. But after tonight, I couldn't let you keep looking for her without knowing there could be."

Peter kept his eyes on Sam, whose own eyes suddenly looked much older, pouchy and creased.

"All right," Peter said, "I'm willing to believe you wouldn't deliberately put me in the middle of a federal investigation and you wouldn't bring Mrs. Atwill onto that movie if you thought she'd be in danger."

"God, no. Lauren."

Peter went on. "You're off the hook there. So don't get yourself into trouble with the Feds by telling me things they told you not to."

"McCann was working for them and got killed on our lot doing it. We're already in trouble, wouldn't you say? As much trouble as they want to make if they need to blame someone for their screwup."

"Don't talk to me because you're mad at them."

"I'm trying to protect the goddamn studio!" Sam snapped. "Congress is crawling up our asses. Every breath we take's a commie plot. I'd rather Marathon wasn't the name plastered all over the headlines when some asshole in Washington starts looking for a studio to make an example out of."

"Get yourself a drink, take a minute, think it over."

"If I'm going to betray my country, I better stay sober."

"If we're going that far, we better both get drunk."

Sam barked a laugh, then yanked his hands from his pockets. "What the hell." He poured himself a stiff brandy, then sat back down heavily and swirled it around the snifter globe. He had wide, blunt hands, with thick dark hair on the backs. Workingman's hands, even though they were manicured.

"I'll start at the beginning," he said. "If you don't want to hear any more, you can stop me."

Peter said, "First, you and I have to agree on something. Mrs. Atwill wasn't here. We left her in the living room."

"It's okay if she waits in there."

"If you want her out of the room, you can give it a try. You'll probably have to lock her in a closet."

Sam glanced at me. I kept a straight face. Then he said,

"Okay. All right." He sat back, cupped the snifter to his chest and took a breath. "All right. Two weeks ago Sunday, Sol Noble, the head of the studio, called me over to his house. I knew it had to be important. Sol spends every Sunday of his life on his boat. Mack Pace was already there and two other men. One of them was a studio lawyer. The other was the man you saw tonight, the guy that looks like an undertaker. His name's Bitterston." He spelled it for us. "Though it might not be his real name."

"Probably is, the way he looks," Peter said. "The Feds don't have that kind of sense of humor. Go on."

"So, we're there at Sol's, and the lawyer didn't say ten words, just sat there like a lump, while this Bitterston laid everything out. The FBI needed the studio's cooperation to wrap some things up. The FBI would appreciate it and remember our help. They needed a few records, and they needed to get a man on the lot. My movie could use a military advisor, and they had someone with military experience. All we had to do was give him the job. He made it sound simple. And you don't refuse the FBI anything these days. I thought hiring him was just to get him on the lot. They said it didn't have anything to do with my picture."

I interrupted my chewing to say, "So I guess we have to consider the FBI might have lied to you."

Sam snorted. "I thought they were lying about why they were there, but I thought they were telling the truth about my movie. What a fucking mess. Sorry, Lauren," he said, apologizing for the language, not what he'd got me into by extension.

I said, "What reason did they give you?"

"They were closing the books on their search for collaborators." When I stared at him, he said, "Nazi collaborators in Hollywood during the war. They made it sound like a mop-up job, cross their t's, fill out some paperwork, close the files. They said they were doing it at all the studios, all hush-hush, so the studios wouldn't have to worry about the newspapers. *Now* they're looking for Nazis," he said with disgust. "You remember, seven, eight years ago, Lauren."

"I do." I turned to Peter and explained, "Back then, the government didn't want to offend Hitler. The censors wouldn't let us write bad things about the Nazis."

Sam said, "McCann showed up in my office this morning, we talked. He seemed like a nice guy. Said we'd talk later about any help he might need from me. But he asked if I remembered who was organizing propaganda parties, back before Pearl Harbor. You remember those? There'd be some special guest, some German official or some aristocrat trying to keep us out of the war. McCann asked me if any of the people who ran those parties spent a lot of time later volunteering at the Hollywood Canteen after we got into the war, places they might get information from soldiers, sailors. I told him, look, I'm a Jew, nobody talked to me about how much they loved Hitler. I repeated some rumors I'd heard, but it was old stuff."

Peter said, "What did you think he was really up to?"

"I was afraid they were looking for commies, of course."

"Did McCann mention communists? Or Bitterston that day you met with him?"

"No. That's what made me think they were looking for them."

Peter said, "Do you have any idea what McCann could have been doing in that bungalow?"

"No. He never asked me about it. But Mack Pace gave Bitterston all kinds of information. A map of the entire lot, all the buildings, what they're for, who works where. Which bungalows belong to which director, producer, actor. That bungalow's been assigned to Alastair Bishop a couple of years, it's been his to loan out. Before he took it over, we had it cleaned out, spic and span. Any stuff still in there belongs to him and whoever else worked in there the last two years."

"Who uses it?" Peter asked.

"His writers."

"What?" I said, sharply.

Peter said, "Anyone who's been a writer for Bishop in the last two years would have used it?"

Sam said, "Alastair's got a reputation for wanting credit for more writing than he actually does. He likes to get his writers out of their offices, keep them isolated while the script's coming together. He's not fooling anybody, but we let him think he is."

"Mr. Ross," Peter said, "this is a federal investigation now. I need to know why you hired me. Finding Miss Demara before the cops wanted to talk to her was always a long shot. But you wanted me to try and you wanted me to run it, even though there were good men already out here, men I work with, who could have done it. You wanted me. I need to know why."

Sam set down his drink and rubbed the lower part of his face hard. "Oh, hell, you know the score. There's a lot of stuff goes on the studios fix, fix up. A star gets a girl pregnant, we pay her off, keep it from the press, from his wife. A party gets out of hand, somebody falls in the pool and drowns. The cops agree to keep our actors' names out of the official record. An actor's too fond of other men, we pay to keep it quiet.

"After we found out it was Triton's cabin, and there was a body in it, we were in Sol Noble's office—me, Sol, Morty Engler and Mack Pace—talking about what happens if the body's Triton's, and the public finds out Mala was sleeping with him and somebody burned him up in their love nest. Morty's good at what he does, but even Morty couldn't figure out how to make that come out right. If it makes the papers, it could destroy her even if the cops decide later she didn't do anything except sleep with the guy. Sol thanks Morty, tells him to keep working on it, and sends him away. Then he says to me and Mack it looks like the only way to make sure we save what the studio's got invested in her is for somebody else to get caught and soon. He says it was probably some lowlife with a record of arson. He says Mack knows a lot of cops, maybe they'll find some guy with a history of arson.

"There's plenty I've gone along with, don't think I haven't. But sitting there, listening to the head of the studio say we ought to think about framing some poor bastard for a murder. I wanted you here in case they ended up trying it. I needed someone who knew how to make them stop."

Peter said, "If it helps you any, your security chief probably isn't crazy enough to risk trouble with Julie Scarza. He has to know Triton was Scarza's friend."

"I guess I should have told you all this before, take a load off my mind. Of course, now I've got a military hero murdered while he's working for the Feds, on my movie. Not much chance it was a burglar who climbed over the wall, I guess."

"No," Peter said, "and it's probably not a thief who happens to work for the studio. They'd know it was unlikely they'd find anything valuable in there. Tell me about how people get in and out of that lot."

Sam said, "The crews have to clock in and out, and use the back gate. Guards keep an eye on them, what with the strike. If you're a visitor, you use the front gate, and your name's on a list. People who belong on the lot, if the guard knows you, he just waves you in. The guards are too busy to notice too much when people leave."

"Chances are McCann was killed after dark," Peter said. "The killer broke in, and wouldn't want to risk being seen. Mrs. Atwill found the body about six. It gets dark before five. The police will want to talk to anyone who might have been on the lot about that time."

"It means Mala couldn't have done it."

"Till we know where she's been, we don't know that."

"Will you keep looking for her?"

"Unless the Feds tell me to stop. I talked to Kitty Dunning today; she called me. She's a good friend of Miss Demara's and she gave me some more names. I'm going over to her house tomorrow, to be with her when she calls them, tell her what to say. We might turn up a lead. But Mickey Triton's name will be all over the papers tomorrow. After that, if Miss Demara doesn't show up or call her cousin, you should plan for the worst. She's dead or she's guilty."

We didn't get back to Pasadena until after midnight. Peter kept a spare set of clothes at my house, along with some pajamas and a toiletry kit in the guest room at the end of the second-floor hallway. It was a large room, with a comfortable mattress and its own bathroom.

He didn't catch up with his spare clothes until early the next morning.

CHAPTER 11

By the time the phone jangled me awake at eight, I was alone.

I fumbled for the receiver and answered before Juanita did downstairs. I was groggy from short sleep, and I guess I thought it might be Peter, even though it was hardly likely.

It was Betty Guinness, Alastair Bishop's secretary, reminding me I had an appointment with him at ten. I reminded her I'd been with the police most of the night because I found a dead man. She didn't seem to think that event, unfortunate as it might be, should get in the way of Bishop's schedule.

I got up and smoothed the bed covers. It really wasn't necessary. Peter had already made sure his side of the bed looked as if no one had been there. The whole time we'd been in New York, in that two-bedroom suite, he'd done the same. And made sure the other room's bed looked slept in. No hotel maid would ever be able to swear in divorce court that we were more than employer and bodyguard. And Juanita would never have to lie under oath for me. It didn't matter that I told Peter my husband wouldn't contest a divorce. He'd been a private detective a long time, and had worked his share of divorces. He wasn't taking any chances, in case my husband's lawyer decided one day that some of the small fortune my uncle Bennett left me would sleep better at night if it was resting in Franklin's bank account.

Peter had slipped out of my bed about two, while I was drifting happily toward sleep, but not until we'd talked about my going back to the studio.

"You need to rest," he said. "It's not that long since you were in the hospital."

"I also need a job. If I turn down work, I don't get work." I stretched my body alongside his. "Besides, it's a chance to spot that Studebaker that was following me and Johnny. I could drive my own car, Johnny could follow me and get a look at the plates."

"Somebody got killed out there last night."

"They weren't after me."

"The cops will be over there. They might want to talk to you again. They know how to question people. Don't answer any more than what they ask. And remember you don't leave the lot unless you've got one of my men with you."

"Yes, sir."

"I mean it."

"I have a gun, maybe I should take it with me."

"Only if you won't shoot your foot off. Or mine."

He was joking. I was serious.

He left. He might have had another three hours of sleep. He had plenty to do before going out to Malibu to see Kitty Dunning. He'd talk to Bill while he was out there. But only about Mala. Not about anything else. Like me and Bill, for instance.

I bathed and dressed. It was going to be another unusually warm day, far above even seasonal averages. If I were working at home, I'd have chosen linen slacks. But for the studio, I'd have to wear a dress, so I pulled out a lightweight jersey of pale blue. Like so many clothes tailored since the war started, it was made of a synthetic fiber, cotton and wool being hard to come by. I hoped it wouldn't be too hot. I decided against stockings. I'd be cooler, and stockings were still hard to get while the factories fully retooled from the wartime work.

I grabbed a large envelope bag and gloves from the dressing-room shelves, and despite its being December, a straw hat with a wide brim.

Juanita whipped me up an omelet, stuffed with cheese, also a stack of pancakes as I'd mentioned I'd only had half a sandwich for dinner.

The Mickey Triton story took up several columns on the front page. EX-CHAMP SHOT TO DEATH. The police weren't labeling it murder yet, leaving open the possibility of suicide. There was nothing in the story I didn't already know.

But his death was now on the front pages. Peter was right. If Mala didn't show herself, she was either dead or guilty.

In the study, I collected a few things to take to the studio, things I liked to work with, having found routine was not the antithesis of creative inspiration: my notebook on which I scribbled random ideas; my fountain pen, even though I rarely wrote in ink; a silver paperweight; a pack of index cards. In the sideboard behind the desk, I found my collection of recipe boxes. Most of them had labels pasted on to them for the movies I'd worked on; these were what I carried my index cards around in when I had to work both at home and the studio. I grabbed an unlabeled one.

I opened a desk drawer and took out a small chamois bag. Inside were three lock picks. Years ago I'd asked a retired locksmith about lock picking for a detective picture I was writing. He'd given me a set as a gift, as a sort of joke, really. He figured I wasn't going to become a notorious jewel thief. The producer had been scandalized however, and pointed out the censors didn't even allow movie characters to warn each other to wear gloves to avoid fingerprints, let alone mention there were such things as lock picks. As if criminals hadn't figured out these things by now.

I usually took the picks with me if I had to write at the studio. I'd found the borrowed offices too often had file cabinets and desk drawers with missing keys.

My safe was not very cleverly concealed behind a tooled leather set of Shakespeare. I opened it, felt past the stacks of velvet jewelry boxes and pulled out a much larger chamois bag that held the .38 snub-nosed revolver my uncle Bennett had given me. I hadn't used the gun in years, hadn't practiced, hadn't cleaned it. I'd been a fair shot when I was younger, much younger. I took the gun out, carried it over to the window and examined the empty cylinder and the barrel. Plenty of dust. I should get the gun checked out by an expert to make sure it was all right to use after all this time. I put it back in the bag, then returned the jewelry boxes and locked the safe.

When I had the chance, I also had to get better lighting for my new painting. It had replaced a smaller landscape, which of course had no pentimento, no hints of gold shining through, and so the single rectangular fixture above had been adequate. Now I could see I needed an expert to balance illuminating the gold without giving it prominence, which would betray the artist's intention. You were not supposed to know whether the artist was commenting on the past's right to intrude upon the present. Too much light would render the gold a lie.

"What is it?" Juanita asked. She stood in the doorway with a canvas bag in her hand, just large enough to carry my writer's talismans.

"I don't know. Something about the painting. Something the painting made me think of. Something in the wrong place. I had a thought."

"I'm sorry. I made you lose it."

"No. It's still there, in the back of my head. I just can't drag it forward."

"Important?"

"I don't know."

"About the movie?"

"No."

"I was afraid of that."

It was the first time I'd driven my Lincoln Continental cabriolet in four months. I'd missed it. While I was in New York, Helen Ross had arranged to have it repainted, its having ended up fire-engine red last summer through no fault of its own. It was back to its original glossy cream—no mean feat, I was sure, considering the depth of the red.

I settled under the steering wheel, into the soft leather seat. I kept the top up, much as I would have loved to drive with it down. Johnny tucked his car in behind me, and stayed there down the Pasadena Parkway. Then, as he'd said he would, he fell back a bit. By the time we reached the studio, anyone watching the gate for my arrival wouldn't know I had another companion. No dark-blue Studebaker showed itself.

I followed Betty's stiff back out to the garden. Alastair Bishop, in cotton trousers, a gardening smock and gloves, and slouchy straw hat, was weeding a strip of earth beneath a radiant hydrangea, still blooming in December. He sat on a contraption like a short bench, with wheels that allowed him to push himself from spot to spot across the paving without getting up. The bench was just wide enough for his girth. Sprouting from its back was a small canvas umbrella, shielding his pale English skin.

"You're early," Bishop said.

"I expected more traffic. I can wait inside if you'd like."

"That won't be necessary, if you don't mind sitting in the sun. At least you had the good sense to put on the right sort of hat. I cannot understand women, summer hats like candy dishes."

I took a patio chair nearby, set my canvas bag and pocketbook on the pavement. He kept working, surgically removing the offending shoots with a narrow trowel.

"Mr. Triton is dead," he said. "I would of course prefer to do this picture with Miss Demara. But we must plan. I have reserved a viewing room for you, to see the actresses we will consider if we must recast. You may go over there when we have finished. This Mr. Winslow—the man the studio hired to try to find Mala—I understand you know him."

"Yes."

"Can he find her?"

"Time is very short. It depends on how much cooperation he can get. It's possible Mala just decided to stay somewhere a bit longer, somewhere without newspapers or radios."

"Humph. Mala Demara is a limited actress, but a limited actress with ambition. She keeps her appointments, and she missed a costume fitting. Betty tells me you found Major Mc-Cann's body. I should have thought of that when I heard the news, as you were supposed to be working there, but I confess I did not. That must have been upsetting."

"Thank you. Yes, it was. I'll need to get another copy of whatever was in the envelope Betty gave me last night. The police took everything but my handbag."

"She's thought of that already. The police have been here this morning. They asked why he might have been in that bungalow. I have no idea. I haven't set foot inside for months. I have some old scripts stored there, old correspondence. I told them they should talk to Bill Linden."

Betty appeared in the French doors to the sitting room. "There are two gentlemen wishing to see you, sir. Mr. Pace is with them."

"I've already spoken to the police," Bishop said.

On cue, three men appeared behind her. One was Bitterston, the federal agent I'd seen last night. One was the chief of security, Mack Pace. The other man, I'd never seen before.

"Please," Betty said to them, her mouth pursed, "if you would wait in the hall."

"These men are from the FBI," Pace announced.

Bitterston pulled out identification, swept past the nonplussed Betty, and showed it to Bishop for perhaps two seconds, then shoved it back into his jacket.

"I am Alastair Bishop. Forgive me, but I did not have the opportunity to read your name."

"Agent Bitterston. This is Agent Larkin." He used his tough voice, and he had a good one, efficient, staccato, intimidating. And his eyes fixed you.

"Mr. Pace, my staff must have made a mistake and neglected to relay that you had called to say these gentlemen wished to speak with me. Agent Bitterston, Agent Larkin. You are welcome of course, nonetheless. This is Mrs. Atwill. Would you like tea? Betty will ice it for you, if you wish. I have learned American tastes."

"No, thanks," Bitterston said.

"Then what may I do for you?" Bishop stripped off his gloves and laid them on his chubby knee.

"Why don't we start with Miss Atwill."

"*Mrs.* Atwill," Bishop corrected. "She's married to Frank Atwill, one of our stars."

"May I ask what you're doing here," Bitterston said to me.

Bishop said, "We were discussing a script. She's a talented scriptwriter."

"She can speak for herself."

"But I couldn't have said it better," I remarked.

"We'll start with her, since she's here. We'll talk to you after. You can finish with your flowers."

"These are hydrangea, not flowers, but a flowering bush. A common misunderstanding. I know this must be about poor Major McCann, but neither Mrs. Atwill nor I knew him. She only found the body. And I'm the one who assigned that bungalow to her."

"We'll talk to anybody we need to, Mr. Bishop. And if they don't cooperate fully here, we can take them to our offices and let them think about changing their minds."

"That was hardly necessary, sir. No one is refusing to co-operate."

"It's all right," I said to Bishop. "May we use your sitting room?"

"Of course," he said. "Will you be with them, Mr. Pace?"

"No, sir."

"Then get out of my bungalow right now."

CHAPTER 12

Bishop's sitting room was a lot nicer than the one in the writers' bungalow: curtains of heavy celery-colored polished cotton with cabbage roses; a sofa in a satiny gold-stripe; armchairs covered in pale-green leaves. The kitchen had a silent refrigerator, and the legs of the dining table hadn't been chewed by dogs.

"Have a seat," Bitterston said and gestured to one of the hard chairs at the table.

If I sat there, I'd feel like I was in the homicide interrogation room at Central Division, where I'd once come close to being put in jail.

Instead, I sat down in one of the armchairs, placed my canvas bag on the floor, and tucked my envelope handbag with my gun in it down beside me, giving him the opportunity to lower his hand.

When he did, he walked over, his hard eyes on me. He remained standing, silent. Remembering what Peter had said about only answering the questions I was asked, I resisted the strong temptation to say something, break the ice, ingratiate myself. If I started off chatty, then shut up, I might look like I knew something, which I didn't.

Agent Larkin planted himself at the table and took a notebook out of his jacket. He didn't say anything. His job was to look like he knew you had secrets.

Finally, Bitterston sat in the armchair opposite me. "Most

professional women don't change their names when they marry."

"That's true," I said. That was all. There were plenty of decisions I'd made in my near-consuming passion for my husband. Changing my name had been one of the few with no painful results.

"You understand we're not at liberty to discuss why we're involved in this investigation."

"Of course."

"What are you doing for Mr. Bishop?"

"Maybe some rewrites." It was hard not to say more, harder than I ever would have imagined. It went against every instinct. First, it's in the nature of human beings to take advantage of our ability to speak. Then there was the matter of self-protection. These men had the power to make my life hell if they chose to. And finally, whatever their attitude, they were investigating the killing of a man they probably knew well. I wanted to help. It wasn't a combination that encouraged a person to just sit there.

"Doesn't this movie already have a writer?" he asked.

"Sometimes the original writer's tied up."

"Is that what happened on this one?"

"I'm not sure exactly. Mr. Bishop could tell you."

"Not Mr. Linden?"

"And of course, Mr. Linden."

"Do you know him well?"

"Yes, I do."

Silence. He waited. Then he said, "Is there some reason you don't want to talk about him?"

"Not at all."

"So tell me about him."

"He was a novelist before he came to Hollywood. Unlike a lot of novelists, he's an excellent screenwriter. He was kind to me, showed me the ropes when I first came to Hollywood. In some ways, I owe him my career."

"You know that bungalow belonged to him."

"I think it was loaned to him by Mr. Bishop," I said.

"He was the last person who had it."

"Not necessarily the last person in it."

"Are you lovers?"

"None of your business."

"You don't get to choose what to answer, Mrs. Atwill. A man's been murdered."

"If you can show me what it has to do with the murder, I'll answer the question."

"You're a little touchy about him."

I bit back a retort. He was goading me, although it seemed a foolish strategy to annoy me right off the bat. But maybe in his experience, it made people spill things in their anger they didn't mean to.

"You and Mr. Linden have known each other a long time, then."

"Fourteen years."

"You must have been very young when you started working here."

Now flattery. It's been known to work on women, especially women over thirty-five. "I was two years out of college."

"Your uncle was Bennett Lauren. Are you named after him?"

"Yes. My middle name is Lauren, my mother's maiden name. My first name is Mabel, but I preferred Lauren as a professional name."

"He left you a lot of money."

"He was generous in his will. I don't know what this has to do with Major McCann's murder."

"Some of the money he left you came from the Nazis."

"I beg your pardon? My uncle was in the oil business. Germany doesn't have much oil. Before the war, they bought oil from his company, from dozens of companies. The German government had money, and this country was in a depression. I never heard my uncle say one nice thing about the Nazis."

"And yet he did business with them."

"So did the United States government, Agent Bitterston. Major McCann served his country in the war, and apparently he was still doing that. And while he was doing it, someone killed him. If I can help you find who did it, I will, but it's a waste of your time to slander my uncle. I'm on your side."

"What side is that?"

"Justice." I said it the way I would have said it a dozen years ago, when I admired the FBI, when they caught bank thieves and killers and kidnappers of babies. Before I knew how much of their time they spent spying on ordinary citizens.

"Is that why you made sure a private detective got there last night before the police?"

"Yes."

"Are you trying to be smart?"

"Mr. Winslow was ten minutes away. I wanted him there so he could make sure the police didn't waste their time thinking I had anything to do with the killing. And make sure security didn't trample the crime scene before the police arrived. But he was too late for that. Several of them went into the bungalow, they didn't wait for the patrol cars, and they lied about it to the police. Mr. Winslow saw them, and told Sergeant Barty about it. You might want to ask Mr. Pace what his men were up to."

"Are you accusing Mr. Pace?"

"No, but his men shouldn't have gone in."

"The first thing you did was call a private detective."

"You've talked to Sergeant Barty. You know how Mr. Winslow got there."

"You and Mr. Winslow are very friendly."

"He saved my life, twice. I'll be glad to tell you all about that, if you think it can help. And if you need more recommendation on him than Sergeant Barty, you could talk to the assistant DA out here—his name is Betts."

"Major McCann told us you thought you recognized him, that you mistook him for someone else."

"I thought he looked familiar, yes."

"I'm interested in who you thought he was. There's the possibility the killer made the same mistake."

"I don't know what it is I'm remembering, except that he looked familiar. I'm sure I've seen him before. I see him handing me a drink, but we're not in a bar. Sometimes the room has books in it, sometimes a piano. But the room's not familiar. That's all I recall. If I remember anything else, I'll let you know."

"We'll probably need to talk to you again. You live in Pasadena?"

"I'll be on the lot most days. It will be easier to talk here. I'm sorry about Major McCann."

I stood up. He didn't stop me.

I went straight outside, into the bright midday light, pulling in air and puffing it out. My hands started to shake. Why was he goading me with Uncle Bennett? Did he really think Bill could have had anything to do with this? Yesterday, Bill told me he planned to come in to work on story ideas. But he wouldn't have gone to the bungalow. He would have gone to his office.

I'd walked all the way across the street before I realized what I'd seen tucked into the parking spaces beside the bungalow: Alastair Bishop's Packard and a dark-blue 1940 Studebaker Champion.

I couldn't stare at it, couldn't be seen staring at it. I took off smartly. I had to find a phone now, one Bitterston couldn't see me use.

I walked, fast, over to the Clark Building, where Marathon housed its editing facilities and screening rooms. I jumped into the phone booth in its lobby and shut the door. Peter wasn't in the office, of course. Neither was his brother, Johnny, so I left a message: Agent Bitterston had a dark-blue Studebaker. There were plenty of Studebakers. There was always a chance this wasn't the same car that had followed me to Bill's yesterday. Sure.

Screening rooms were generally used for watching "rushes," a movie's recently shot scenes, still unedited. It allowed the director, director of photography, and producer a chance to see the lighting, angles and performances. Other than looking through the camera during a rehearsal, the director had no idea what his movie would look like on screen till he saw rushes.

Marathon had three viewing rooms used for exclusive screenings of movies for special guests: soft seats, mahogany paneling, and a bartender on hand.

All three were over in the Ice House.

I was in one of the others, with scuffed walls and rows of hard chairs. I was there to watch portions of recent performances by the three candidates to take over for Mala, should that become necessary. All three were Americans, so first off, if I had to rewrite, the heroine would have to be changed to an American. Even if one of the candidates could do a phoneme-perfect Hungarian accent, American audiences wouldn't like it, so the studio wouldn't allow it. American audiences didn't like their leading actresses to do foreign accents, not in a drama, rarely in comedy.

I pulled out my notebook and a pencil, and called out to the projectionist I was ready. The first actress I knew fairly well, Kim Wagner, who'd starred opposite my husband in his last picture, which was still making a bundle at the box office and was going to help save his career. I thought Kim was the wrong actress to take over Mala's role, not because she wasn't attractive, but she wasn't attractive in the sensual way this heroine needed to be. I doubted Bishop had put her on the list. More likely, the studio had decided they might give her another important vehicle, with the popularity of her current release. But she was wrong for it, and I thought it wouldn't make anybody happy, least of all her. All these years, and I still didn't understand why studios made some of their casting decisions.

"Thank you. Ready for the next reel."

Immediately, the brisk whirring of the second projector began, and underneath, the efficient clicking of high heels. Betty Guinness marched into my row, sat down in the hard chair beside me and whipped out a steno pad.

"I would have been glad to order a cart for you," she said briskly.

"Thanks, but I decided to walk. I needed one, after that."

"Agent Bitterston asked me what time you picked up the key last night. I told him. So I don't think they believe you killed him."

"Thanks, that's good to hear."

"I brought you a copy of what I gave you last night. We understand the police took everything."

"For all they knew, it was evidence."

"Run that back to the beginning," she ordered the projectionist, and he took the second reel back to its start.

I wanted to ask her what other questions Bitterston had asked her. She didn't seem to have been in any way disconcerted by them, whatever they were. But then she probably wouldn't be disconcerted by a Panzer division.

We watched the other two actresses on Bishop's list. They both had the right look, but they weren't up to Kim's acting standard. If Bishop saw either of these reels up against Kim's, maybe he'd change his mind about whether acting talent really mattered.

A fourth reel rolled, a few seconds of the fluttering grays of the film leader, then the scene began. "That is the wrong reel," Betty pronounced loudly, sounding like the schoolmarm who fervently believes her mission in life is to make you feel as stupid as possible for your error. "That's Mala Demara."

The projectionist called back, unperturbed, "What can I tell you, she's on my list."

"It's fine, thank you," I called up to him, then lowered my voice so he couldn't hear. "I asked to see her. If she ends up doing the movie but I have to modify her role because of publicity from all this, I need to know her strengths."

"Looking beautiful," Betty said with a sour tightening to her lips. She went back to her own notes.

Well, Betty was right about it being a distinction. Mala Demara was beautiful by anyone's standard. On screen, she had a rare luminous quality—her skin, her eyes, her hair. And even conservative costuming could not conceal her spectacular figure.

But I was here for the acting. And despite Bill's opinion of her very first screen test he'd seen years ago in London, this was not a varied performance, but then what I was watching had been her first film, and the script hadn't been exactly challenging. Still, she had timing; she could deliver a snappy line with charm. That could prove very useful if I needed to rewrite for her.

I realized Betty was watching me, more precisely watching me write. I'd taken fully as many notes on Mala as I had on any of the others.

"Thanks," I sang out to the projectionist. "That's all I need."

The projector died and the lights went up in the room.

Betty said, "Mr. Bishop will want your report as soon as possible."

"I'll give it to him in the morning."

"Tomorrow is Saturday," she reminded me. "We will send it to his home." She snapped her steno pad shut. "The police say you should be able to use the other bungalow within a few days."

Oh, yes, I was looking forward to working in the same room where Major McCann had died. Just clean up the blood, I'll be fine.

"Until then," she went on, "I've arranged an office for you over in the Tate Building, beginning Monday. Tonight, you may use the sitting room in Mr. Bishop's bungalow. As Mr. Bishop would like the report tomorrow, we can also arrange a stenographer and typist."

"Thanks, but I do my best work when I'm not watched."

"Leave the report in his office, and I'll arrange to deliver it to him."

Agent Bitterston, Agent Larkin and their blue Studebaker were gone. So was Bishop's Packard.

A Corona Streamline portable typewriter had been set up on the sitting room's dining table, a stack of paper beside it and a cup of sharpened pencils. Betty was efficient.

"The commissary closes early on Fridays," she reminded me.

"I can order dinner from Madison's," I said. Madison's was the de facto studio bar and grill and watering hole, across from the front gate.

It was now one o'clock. I used Bishop's phone to order lunch from the commissary. They were glad to bring it over. I let them assume it was for Bishop.

Betty shut herself in the office. I shut myself in the sitting room and set to work.

The first thing I had to do was read the script again. I'd only had a chance to read it through once, while I was on the set yesterday. As I read, I made notes in the margins. I ate my soup, a rather watery vegetable, then read the script again.

By four o'clock, Betty was gone, and I began tackling the

rough draft of my report on the script changes that would be necessary for each of the other three actresses. It wasn't my job to comment on their talent, at least not directly. But you don't suggest a rewrite the actress can't pull off. At least I didn't.

By six, I needed coffee.

It turned out Betty wasn't perfect after all. There was a percolator in the cabinet, but no coffee. There was plenty of tea, and all the accompanying paraphernalia to make it. But I hadn't been invited to help myself to Alastair Bishop's imported tea leaves. And what I really needed was strong coffee.

I called Madison's and spoke to Anthony, the titular head bartender. Anthony was in fact co-owner of Madison's, along with Jimmy Madison. But Anthony was Negro, so his partnership was kept something of a secret.

I ordered one of their famous hot-roast-beef sandwiches and a large pot of coffee. The gravy would come piping hot in a separate covered dish, so the sandwich would only be as scrumptiously soggy as you wanted it to be. Anthony said they were already pretty busy on a Friday evening, but he'd make sure one of the delivery boys brought it over to me before seven. Maybe some pie with that? They had a nice Southern pecan, fresh from the oven, his mama's recipe. I thanked him for his efforts to make me big as a house, gave him Bishop's bungalow address and phone number, and hung up.

I had an hour. I sat down in one of the armchairs and started going through my notes, flipping through the script, deciding if every change I'd suggested was necessary. Given Bill wrote it— and he'd written a good script—I'd like to keep as much as possible.

It was warm in the room, but the breeze through the open windows fingered aside the curtains. There was music coming from someplace. Cole Porter? No, what tune was that? Maybe Noel Coward. Someone must be playing the radio because the piano had an orchestra behind it. I moved across the empty room. It had such high ceilings. The sofa looked small, fragile. I sat on it anyway. But I didn't belong there. I should go home. But I couldn't move. Major McCann was lying on the floor, in a different suit, a suit without blood. His eyes opened and suddenly, he was standing, in front of a piano, reaching out to me. But I wasn't frightened. I was glad he was there. I smiled at him. He started to say something, but there was knocking, very close, covering his words. I tried to tell whoever it was to stop. I had to hear what he said.

My eyes flew open.

What time was it? I glanced at my watch. Ten till seven. I staggered up and aimed myself at the bungalow's front door, wiping the grit of sleep from my eyes, sure they were puffy and red. My neck felt like it had a collar of cement. I could sure use the coffee. Knowing Anthony, he'd tucked a slice of that pecan pie into the basket anyway.

I unlocked the door and opened it.

The man punched me sharply in the chest with the heel of his hand, knocking me back against the wall. Another man, even larger, followed him in and shut the door.

The first one showed me the butt of the gun under his arm. "We need to go somewhere."

I struggled to breathe and to stay on my feet. He'd caught me right in the diaphragm. He knew what he was doing. I was upright, but practically helpless.

He was broad in the chest and shoulders, with meaty hands, but short in the legs. He had a pitted nose and a face full of rosacea. The other one had small black eyes and a thick brow that loomed over them.

The first one wrapped his hand around my arm.

"No," I managed and yanked away from him. I staggered again, back into the wall. Maybe I could draw this out until the delivery boy arrived. Maybe by then I could manage a scream, and the boy would run for help. They wouldn't shoot him. Would they?

"There are guards," I said, my voice raw.

"We ain't gonna hurt you, you don't make any noise. My boss just wants a word with you."

The other one said, "If we was gonna hurt you, you'd be dead."

"Shut up, Otto, the lady's smart. She's gonna think this through and she's gonna come quiet. Nobody has to get hurt. You talk to my boss, we take you home." He took a step toward me. He smelled of cigars and unaired wool. "You know Willoughby's Drug Store, on the corner, couple blocks from your house? There's a guy there, sitting at the counter, he's reading a newspaper, having a drink. When we get where we're going, I'm gonna call him. And he won't go over and see Juanita. That's her name, right? Juanita. She's a good-looking woman. And he's gonna leave her alone. Why don't you come on with us? See, Otto, I told she was smart."

CHAPTER 13

Otto drove. The other man sat beside me in the backseat, his thick hand ready to grab me if I tried to get out of the locked door.

We drove slowly past the guard's box at the rear gate. The guard sat on a stool, bent over a magazine. He didn't even look up. It didn't do much good to think about how they got in past him. It wasn't going to make any difference to me. I thought about who their boss could be, who would have any reason to just want to talk to me. I wanted to believe I was going to survive the night.

We drove out of Hollywood to 101, and on into the black night. The clouds were thick; there was no moon or stars. Thunder rumbled in the distance, and lightning flashed over the canyons. We passed side roads, any of which would have been good enough to dump a body. We kept going.

At Topanga, Otto turned and in less than a mile, turned again, this time onto a familiar road called Coruna. It climbed, then sharply dipped and twisted, the headlights raking the brown hills spotted with scrub grass, eucalyptus and manzanita. Finally, we came out at the base of a broad crushed-gravel drive lined with softly glowing carriage lamps that led the way to a three-story hacienda.

There were odd things about the house: there were no windows or doors on the side that faced the drive, just a blank wall of shimmering white stucco. And there was a line of cars snaking around the wall's far corner. We didn't stay in the line. We edged smoothly around the corner, and there ahead was the entrance to Ramon Elizondo's nightclub. A tiled roof stretched over the roadway, which was paved underneath the porch so the patent leather shoes and satin slippers didn't get dusty. Uniformed attendants stepped up smartly to open the doors, hand the ladies out, take the keys from the gentlemen, and whisk the car away so the owners could get on with dinner, dancing and gambling.

We kept going, swung around to the back, to the employee parking lot. Otto got out and held the car door for us. When the other man took my arm, I pulled away from him. He shrugged and gestured me ahead. I followed Otto through a back door and up a narrow, harshly lit flight of linoleum-covered steps. At the top, a green-painted swinging door opened onto a long hallway, carpeted in plush mauve and papered in silver stripes. At the other end, a man in evening clothes stood stolidly in front of a set of upholstered doors ready to admit "members" to the casino. On the ground floor, down the sweeping main staircase, the band was playing in the restaurant. Something zippy and lively I didn't recognize. People were having a good time.

Otto knocked on a door directly to my right. A skeletal man with gray hair and gray skin opened it, and we went in. It was a spacious clubroom, with the requisite mahogany paneling and Turkish carpets aged in cigar smoke. There was a baby grand piano tucked into the corner near the bar. Beyond the poker tables, three men sat in soft leather chairs by the stone fireplace. There was a fire laid, but it was for show. It was far too warm to light it. Each chair had its own side table and small, brass-shaded lamp. Each table had a brandy on it.

Two of the three men stood up: Peter and Ramon Elizondo.

"Ah," the third man said, without rising, "our final guest."

Elizondo wore evening clothes, as always perfectly tailored to his still-slim, very masculine physique, although he was now past fifty. He had intense dark eyes, filled with experience, some of it the sort a woman would find attractive. Peter wore the suit he'd put back on that morning in my house. His face was impassive, a look I knew meant bad trouble.

He stepped aside to give me his chair. The skeletal man smoothly, effortlessly lifted a club chair from a poker table and brought it over for Peter. Peter repositioned it before he sat down, a casual movement, but he now had a better view of everyone in the room.

"Are you all right?" Peter asked.

"I'm fine." I didn't think it was a good idea to tell him I'd had the wind knocked out of me.

Elizondo sat back down as well. "This is Mr. Scarza," he said.

Julius "Julie" Scarza, lieutenant to Jack Dragna, the biggest mobster in Los Angeles. Scarza had a large, loose-fleshed face, with thin lips and nasty eyes that protruded slightly behind his thick round glasses. His black hair was precisely parted and oiled back above his long-lobed ears. His pale manicured hands rested on the arms of the chair. They were blotched and red from years of dipping into other people's misery.

"Thank you for coming," he said, without sarcasm. It didn't make me want to slap his face any less. "Ray," he said to Elizondo, "could Eddie use your phone, he needs to make a call." He didn't wait for a reply, but raised his blotched hand to wave Eddie—the man who'd punched me—toward Elizondo's office. "Lenny, a brandy for the lady." Lenny, the gray man, poured one from the bar and held it out to me with his long fingers. I didn't take it. He set it on the table by my chair. After a minute, Eddie came back out of the office and took position behind Scarza's chair.

"There," Scarza said to me. "All taken care of."

I couldn't manage a "thank you," so I simply nodded.

"Mr. Winslow and I've been talking about a case he's working on. Do you know Mala Demara?"

"No," I said.

"Never met her, you're working on her picture?"

"I was hired yesterday, to rewrite the script if she isn't found."

"Or if it ends up she killed somebody. I've heard Mr. Winslow could be a hard man to persuade. What do you think?"

"It depends on whether it's possible for him to do what you want him to."

"That's funny, he said the same thing. You like him?"

"Yes."

"And he likes you, and because you're friends of Ray's, we're all here together, comfortable chairs, some good brandy and we can talk. Go on," he said to Peter.

Peter began to speak, just as if he were reporting to a client. "Her cousin's name is Zorka Karoly, though she goes by Madame. I don't think she knows where Miss Demara is. If she does, she's a good actress. She makes a nice living telling fortunes and running séances, but Miss Demara pulls in three grand a week and gives the cousin connections to the Hollywood crowd. The cousin knows what will happen if Miss Demara becomes a murder suspect."

"Unless the cousin knows Mala's guilty."

"There's a chance Miss Demara's dead."

"Her body'd be in that cabin."

"Not if the killer wanted the cops to think she did it. Do you know whether Mr. Triton was supposed to be with Miss Demara last weekend?"

Scarza didn't answer. Peter went on, "I found out he had a couple of fighters on a card down in San Diego Thursday night. He was there at those fights."

"Could have been. Doesn't mean he wasn't with her Friday."

"Miss Demara left her house Friday morning. He didn't get back to his gym from San Diego till that afternoon. I don't know where she went, but as far as I can tell, she doesn't have a motive. It sounds like Mr. Triton was good to her, played by the studio rules, kept quiet about the two of them."

"They made him watch while she went out with other men."

"Those don't appear to have been romances, only publicity."

"A man doesn't like to see that. If he's a man, he has pride," Scarza said, and I had a sudden vivid picture of what men like him were capable of with women, a picture of being as scared as I was tonight every time the man thought you were looking at some other man the wrong way.

"It's a reason you don't like her," Peter said. "Not a reason for her to kill him."

"Mickey was serious about her, wanted to get married. But she's not going to do that, cross the studio. Maybe she thinks he's too much trouble, but she can't call it off while he's still alive."

"I was hired to find Miss Demara, not to give her an alibi."

"And you knew she might've killed Mickey when you took the job."

"I also thought maybe she didn't. Since then, I found out he was shot in the back of the head. That's not the way men usually die in lovers' quarrels. And even if she ambushed him, women don't usually shoot people in the head."

Scarza said, "That's what we heard too, about the bullet. You suppose we talk to the same cops?" He smiled, his lips pressing tightly against his teeth. "I hear from some of them that a guy got killed last night at the studio and the Feds showed up."

"The dead man was a military consultant on a movie," Peter said.

"Mala Demara's movie. I hear you were there. But the lady

here found the body. Why don't we let the lady talk for a while?"

I said, "What do you want to know?"

"The Feds talk to you?"

"Yes, this morning."

"They ask you about Mickey?"

"No. And they didn't tell me what they were doing there." It was the truth. They certainly weren't at Marathon looking for Nazis, no matter what Agent Bitterston had implied. "I was assigned the bungalow that afternoon. The only thing I did was find the body. I couldn't help them."

He pointed his eyes back at Peter. "And you?"

"The cops asked me why I was there. I told them. I don't know any more than she does."

"Nobody's going to make Mickey go away. You hear anything, you tell me. The Feds ask about him, or you find out anything, you tell me. If you find her, you tell me. If anybody, anybody finds out who killed Mickey, I want to know about it."

"I understand," Peter said.

"Good. Hey, you were right, Ray, he can be reasonable." He splayed his blotched, red hands on the chair arms and pushed himself up.

Elizondo and Peter both stood too.

Eddie handed Scarza his hat, and Otto opened the door, then took a step into the hallway, checking both directions.

Scarza nodded to me. "Ray said you were classy. He was right." He turned and pointed his hat at Elizondo before he put it on. "Thanks, Ray." He went out. Eddie handed over Peter's Colt to Lenny, then followed Scarza out.

Lenny shut the door after them.

Peter punched Elizondo in the face.

The blow knocked him back over the arm of his chair and into the floor.

In a split second, Lenny had the Colt pointed at Peter's head.

121

"No!" Elizondo called out.

And then the room was silent. I couldn't even hear my breathing. I didn't think I was breathing.

Slowly, Elizondo pushed himself up and leaned his back against the side of the chair, one leg extended, the other knee bent. "It's all right, Lenny."

Lenny didn't lower the gun, but he took his finger off the trigger.

From inside his jacket Elizondo drew a long silk handkerchief. The blood from the cut at the edge of his mouth had already splattered his shirtfront. He pressed the handkerchief to the cut.

"Put the gun away," he said.

Lenny complied, slipping it into his jacket pocket, although he wasn't taking his eyes off Peter.

I started breathing again.

Finally, Elizondo grabbed the arm of the chair and hauled himself up. "I didn't know they were bringing her."

"Who told him where she was? Who told him she mattered to me?" Peter took a step toward him.

"Don't touch me again." Elizondo's eyes were rock-hard.

Peter stopped.

Elizondo sat down. Above the handkerchief, I could see his cheek was flushed red and had begun to swell. "Lenny, make sure we're not disturbed, would you please?" Lenny sneered at Peter, but did as he was told, closing the door after him.

Elizondo said, "Julie showed up here today, said he wanted to talk to you. I arranged it. No one said anything about Mrs. Atwill. Mrs. Atwill, why don't you sit down? Please. Let Pete pour you a fresh brandy."

Peter was still breathing hard, his shoulders still rigid, but he went to the bar and poured the brandy. I took it, laying my hand over his as I slid my fingers to the glass. "Are you all right?" he said.

"Yes."

"You sure?"

He stood there, framed against the light of the sconces, handing me a drink, concern in his eyes, the bar and the piano behind him in a quiet room with orchestra music in the distance and the sounds of people having fun, people I couldn't see.

A jolt of memory hit me.

"What?" he said. "What is it? Are you all right? Tell me the truth."

"I just . . . I remembered . . . it's got nothing to with this. I'm all right, really." I dropped my head and sipped. It took a moment to remember how to swallow. Then I said, "I need to talk to Juanita."

"Did they threaten her?"

"They had a man near my house. He'd leave Juanita alone if I came along. I need to call her."

"I'll do it," Peter said. "We have a code I gave her, if I ever called and anything was wrong. I'll know if she's in trouble. I'll tell her you'll be late. I'll get Lou Brandesi to go sit in front of the house till then."

Peter went back to the bar first, scooped ice cubes from the bucket and wrapped them in his handkerchief. On the way into the office, he handed it to Elizondo, who pressed it to his face.

I kept sipping the reassuring warmth of the brandy, and thinking about the hot flash of memory it had triggered. Finally, Elizondo said, "I didn't know."

"I believe you," I said. "Are you badly hurt?"

"I've seen him do worse." He glanced at the office door. "Those men who brought you here, he can't go after them. If he does, I can't help him."

"He won't. It would put me in danger. But he'll find out who told them where I was. He might do something about that if he can."

123

"Of course."

"Mr. Scarza expects him to find Mickey Triton's killer. No matter what he said, that's what he wants. How is Peter supposed to do that? He can't see the evidence, he can't make people talk. He doesn't have any idea why Triton was killed." It was no use pointing any of that out, but I did nonetheless. And other things: "And if he manages to find Mala Demara, he's supposed to just turn her over to Julie Scarza, when she might be innocent."

"Mickey was like a son to Julie."

"That means he can kill innocent people?"

"It means he'll find out who did it. And he wants to make sure no one hides the killer from him."

"But if the killer's never found, is he going to blame Peter?"

I didn't get a chance to continue my useless arguing. Peter came out of the office. "She's fine. Lou's on his way over; she won't know he's there. How's the face?" he asked Elizondo.

"You pulled your punch."

"Not much. What do you know about this, that you can tell me? Scarza knows I've got practically no chance of finding the killer. What else is there? Mrs. Atwill's in this now."

"I regret that." Elizondo got up and went to the bar. He wrung out the handkerchief and folded fresh cubes into it. "Julie knows what the studios can cover up; he's helped them do it. He wants to make sure they don't cover this up."

"Why's he asking about the man who got killed over at the studio last night? The news stories are all treating it like a robbery gone wrong. The cops haven't even released the man's name yet. But he's asking."

"I don't know why."

I said to him, "Mala Demara worked here before she got her contract, didn't she? We saw Lily Graham on the set the other day. Her daughter is Mala's stand-in."

"Janie. She wants to be an actress."

"Lily said Mala met Mickey Triton here."

"The day she auditioned to sing here. Her cousin brought her out. Do you know her cousin, the fortune-teller?"

"I met her yesterday."

"A formidable woman. She brought Mala out here, she's always managed her, even though Mala's got an agent. Mala had an old letter from Marathon, from before the war, promising her another screen test if she fixed her English. That was enough to let them temporarily into the country, but not enough to guarantee the studio would honor that old promise before they had to go back. She got Mala an audition to sing with the band. She wanted movie people to see her, let them know they could sign her. Mala wasn't a great singer, but well, you've seen her. Mickey was hanging out here that afternoon. He took one look at her and came right up out of his chair."

I said, "That's just what Lily said."

"It's true. He stood right up. Love at first sight, I suppose. Unfortunately, I'm afraid I've never had that experience."

"How did she feel about it? Did she think she had to go out with him?"

"Because he was a gangster?" He smiled, at least the uninjured side of his mouth did. "Perhaps it is time I showed you something."

We followed him into the office and through another door into a private apartment. A small sitting room, masculine, impeccable, immaculate. "When they got together, before Mickey got the cabin, they'd come here, in separate cars, park in the back. I'd let them use the apartment. They could have dinner alone, listen to the band, dance. Mickey was a fine dancer."

Through French doors was the bedroom, equally elegant and expensive. On the far side, he opened the door to the dressing room and extended his hand.

"Julie's gone, it's all right. These are my friends."

Out of the darkness, a woman's hand appeared and took his.

Mala Demara stepped out into the light.

CHAPTER 14

My first brief thought when I saw her was that she wasn't as beautiful as I expected. She had remarkable large eyes, brown and luminous. But there was something about her other features—the height of the cheekbones, the strength of the jaw, the width of her mouth and length of her nose—that, lacking the magic of the camera or the spotlight of the orchestra stage, rendered her lovely, but not breathtaking.

I had expected her to be.

And I was ashamed.

Especially as her remarkable eyes were terrified.

"They're friends," Elizondo said again.

I said, "I'm Lauren Atwill. This is Peter Winslow. We're glad you're all right."

"What happened to your face?" she asked Elizondo, hushed, her accent and her distress blurring the words.

"Pete hit me," Elizondo said. "I expect right now he'd like to again. But he and Mrs. Atwill can be trusted absolutely. Why don't we sit down? Lenny's watching the door." Nevertheless, he went back and locked the one between the club room and the office. Mala sat on the edge of the sofa, one foot slightly in front of the other, as if set to run.

She wore an uncomplicated outfit, a narrow black skirt and long-sleeved white silk blouse. Her shoes were plain pumps. There were pearl earrings and a thin silver bracelet.

Elizondo sat at the other end of the sofa. Peter and I took chairs.

"Why would you hit him?" Mala asked Peter.

Elizondo said, "Julie had some men bring Mrs. Atwill here tonight while he talked to Pete. Somebody had told him how important she was to him."

"And you thought it was Ray who told him this? You hit him without asking?"

I said, "It's hard to understand men sometimes. It's a wonder they aren't extinct." She managed a small smile and shifted very slightly back on the sofa. "I'm a writer. I'll be doing any rewrites on your movie. Mr. Bishop and Bill Linden had a falling out, you might have heard."

My chatter didn't have much effect. She began working her right thumb into the palm of her left hand. "I know who you are," she said to Peter. "You are the man the studio hired to find me. I only came here today. Ray was trying to help me. He did not lie to you."

"Not too much anyway," Peter said. "You need to get a lawyer and you need to get out of here. The last place you want the cops to find you is in another man's bedroom."

"I have not slept here," she said. "I did not kill Mickey."

"You knew about the fire. You didn't go home, call the studio, or call your cousin."

She kept working the thumb. "I do not wish to get anyone into trouble."

She said "do," not "did."

I said, "Has your cousin known where you were all this time?"

"No. No, she has done nothing wrong."

"But she knew you were alive," I said. "I met her yesterday. She was quite self-possessed considering what had happened. Why didn't she tell Mr. Winslow?"

"We did not know him. We were afraid."

"Of what?"

"Is it true Mickey was murdered?"

"Yes," Peter said.

"There is no doubt?"

"No. He was shot. Whoever set fire to the cabin was trying to cover that up."

She said, "My cousin did not know where I was. I only told her I was going away for the weekend. I wanted to be alone. There were things I needed to think about. I found a small inn up the coast, a place no one would know me, a place Hollywood people would not go. I wore a scarf on my hair and sunglasses. I just stayed there, and thought about things.

"Then on Monday, I saw the newspapers about the fire. I called Mickey's house, but no one answered. I called Zorka, my cousin. She said it was true, it was Mickey's cabin, and that Mickey was probably dead. Then she said two of Mr. Scarza's men had come to our house, asking to see me. He hates me. I was afraid. She said we should call the studio and they would help. But I was afraid to tell anyone where I was. He has people everywhere he has bought. Especially the police. I know what they are."

Peter didn't reassure her, didn't tell her American policemen weren't like that. Some of them were exactly like that. If they found out Scarza was looking for her, they'd sell her to him in a heartbeat.

She said, "Mickey was dead, and perhaps I was not thinking well. You do not understand what it was like to live in a place where there is war, where there is no order, where the worst people can do whatever they like. But I knew I could not stay hidden. I called her Wednesday, to ask her what to do. She said I had to come home. The studio had hired someone to find me, and if I stayed away, the police would suspect me."

"Why didn't you call the studio?" Peter said.

"Could they protect me from Julie Scarza? Zorka told me to call Ray. He also said I had to come back."

Elizondo said, "I told her I would protect her. Then, an hour after she got here, Julie showed up, out of the blue." He glanced over at her, his hand moving involuntarily toward her arm, then retreating. "He asked me to set up a meeting with you. He didn't mention Mrs. Atwill. I hid Mala. Fortunately, the last place he'd think to look for her would be my closet."

Peter said to her, "The police will want to know why you went away."

"It is nothing to be ashamed of. Mickey wanted to marry me. He did not want to sneak around anymore. I went away to think about it. A few months ago, when he first asked me, I told Mr. Noble, the head of the studio, that we were in love. I said I would hire people to get publicity for Mickey; we could make the fans love him too. He was a boxing champion; he served with honor in the war. But Mr. Noble said if I would not listen to his advice, I did not care about my career. I knew what he meant."

"Yes," I said. "He'd give you second-rate pictures if you didn't come around."

"And now Julie Scarza thinks I would kill Mickey rather than ruin my career. He hated that Mickey loved me. He thought I took away Mickey's manhood. He thinks a woman should always be under the thumb of a man. She is only there for a man to try to take advantage of her. Mr. Darwin was wrong, Mr. Winslow. I have seen it. I know. It is not the best, but the worst who survive."

"I can talk to Scarza," Peter said. "Tell him you'd have come back days ago if his men hadn't scared your cousin."

"Will he believe you?"

"He knows his men scare people, he likes it that way. It would help if I could tell him you have any sort of alibi up at that inn."

"I do not think anyone recognized me. And I do not think anyone could swear they saw me the night of the fire."

"Do you own a gun? How about your cousin?"

"No. Never."

"The first thing you need to do is talk to a lawyer, tell him everything," Peter said. "Then call Sam Ross. He wants to help."

"You must never tell Scarza I was here," she said.

"Ray's a big boy, he knows what he's doing."

"Let's go call the lawyer," Elizondo said, and he and Peter went into the office.

"Why do men do that," she said, "leave the room when there is business, even when the business is about us?"

"They're afraid we'll have an idea better than theirs."

"I am so sorry, what happened to you."

"I'm all right."

"He hit Ray because of you. I mean, because he was afraid for you."

"He thinks I'm a delicate flower and too good for him."

"Mickey is like that." Then she was crying. She dropped her head, her shoulders trembling, her hands motionless in her lap. I had left my handkerchief in my handbag, which was on a chair in Alastair Bishop's bungalow. I went into the dressing room, opened the top drawer of the dresser, the most likely place to find a handkerchief, and slipped one out.

I sat down beside her, not too close, and offered it. She took it, used it, then twisted it in her hands.

"Why would anybody kill him?"

"If he ever mentioned any trouble to you, you should tell the lawyer."

"Sometimes men would try to buy a boxer from him. He used to say they would try to buy a piece of one of his boxers and he would not sell. I think sometimes men asked him to fix a fight, and he did not want to do it. But he never wore a gun,

131

never kept men around to protect him, not like that Scarza. He was not like that. If I tell the lawyer everything, do I have to tell the police?"

"No. Your lawyer will decide what to tell them."

"They cannot make me tell them?"

"No."

"I was going to marry him," she said. "We could have made the public love him too."

"I understand it was love at first sight, at least for him."

"I do not understand. Love when he saw me?"

"I heard that the first time he saw you here, singing, he stood up. Love at first sight we call it."

"I did not meet Mickey here. I met him in London, many years ago when he was there to box. He was the champion then, and was fighting a man who wanted the title."

"I'd forgotten you were in London. Bill Linden told me. He saw your first screen test."

"I was terrible, but he has been kind not to mention that."

"On the contrary, he was quite taken with your talent."

"I could hardly speak English, and I had a little moustache I think." She smiled and suppressed a few sobs. "I was working as a waitress in a bar in London, a bar where many actresses worked, girls who wanted to be actresses. Americans liked to go there. Americans who lived in England. Patriots."

"Expatriates." I explained the difference.

"After he won the fight, he stayed in London for a while. He liked England, and the English liked him, even though he beat their champion. He would come to the bar sometimes. He was nice to me, teased me about my English, did not make fun of me when I told him I had gone to an audition and they said they were going to give me a screen test. And when he came in, none of the men dared to be fresh with the girls. The Americans, some of them, thought they should be able to make passes at us. The owner did nothing. We were girls, and we were pretty, so why not, he said."

"But not Mickey."

"No. He was different."

"So when you saw him here, it was love at second sight."

"Yes. Second sight." She began to cry again, and I sat silently beside her till the men returned.

Elizondo had arranged for Mala to meet a lawyer. He'd get her out the back way, take her there now. She'd stay at the lawyer's house that night. Peter would pick her up in the morning and take her home, where his brother, Johnny, would stay with her.

Then Peter would go see Scarza.

I said good-bye. We left. On the way out, Lenny gave Peter his gun back.

CHAPTER 15

The sky had turned a churning, purpling black. As we twisted up the canyon, the wind shoved the car and screamed in through the seals of the window vents. Peter kept the car steady, but he was deep in thought. I could tell because he drove about half as fast as he usually did.

Finally he spoke. "You might have to go away for a while," he said, "till I can sort this out."

"Are you blaming yourself?"

"I didn't have to take the job."

"For the love of God, Winslow. You can't blame yourself because there are people like Julie Scarza in the world. Could he have had Triton killed for some reason? Is he trying to divert suspicion to Mala?"

"If he wanted to frame her, the cops would have found evidence. And if he's got her framed, why bother to talk to me?"

"But isn't it much more likely some mobster killed him?"

"Let's worry about one thing at a time. Tell me everything that happened today. Who knew or could have known you were going to be in that bungalow tonight, alone?"

I told him every detail I could remember.

Then I said, "I remembered where I met Major McCann. He did lie about never having been in California. I had a dream, I fell asleep in the bungalow. A dream about him. Then back there, when you handed me the drink, with the light, the bar, the piano, I remembered. It was back before the war. At a party, a charity auction with a lot of Hollywood people, at Kitty Dunning's place out in Malibu. I'd had a fight with Franklin that night. We were engaged at the time, and I thought he was paying too much attention to one of the girls serving the drinks. It was a stupid fight, and we said all the predictable things. I was upset and went off to be by myself. I was crying a little. I thought the room was empty at first. But there he was, McCann, over by the bar cart. Most men would have ducked out, but he was kind. He poured me a drink. I told him about the fight. I told him I was a writer. He asked if I was more upset about the fight or about the trite dialogue. He made me laugh. That's why I remembered him. Now, seven years later, he shows up as a consultant on a movie, and four of the people connected to that movie were at the party: Bill, Alastair Bishop, Betty Guinness and Sam Ross."

"That could be coincidence, a Hollywood party."

"Then why did he lie about ever being in California? I recognized him, and that night, someone killed him. Tonight, Julie Scarza wants to know about the killing and if the Feds are asking questions about Mickey Triton. Seven years ago, after that party, two of the guests—who'd come there with Triton—were ambushed in a gang killing. I put it in the report I wrote for you yesterday, but I didn't think it was important then."

Peter said nothing, thinking it over as we dropped into Hollywood. Apparently, we weren't headed for Pasadena.

A half block from Marathon's back gate, Peter's brother Johnny was waiting in his car. As we passed, Johnny eased down the curb and parked behind us when we stopped just short of the back gate. Johnny got out, the wind whipping his raincoat. He held his hat in place.

Thunder rolled angrily toward us. The bruised southern sky vibrated with lightning.

Peter turned to me. "I've got to get to the bottom of this, and there's no other way to play it, not in the time I have. If you come with me, you have to stay out of the way."

"I understand."

"I mean it."

Johnny opened my door for me and handed me out. "It's quiet," he said to his brother. "Hardly any traffic in and out on a Friday night."

I fell in beside Peter's stride. Johnny followed silently.

Half the wrought-iron double gate stood open. We stepped in beneath the peaked tin roof that ran across the drive to the guardhouse. Beyond, the inky road stretched away into the back lot toward the soundstages, lit by hard pools of light.

The guard was alone. He looked up as we approached.

Peter whispered to me, "Is that the man who was on the gate when they brought you out? Be sure."

"Yes. I'm sure."

Johnny scanned for onlookers. "It's clean," he said.

Peter stepped up to the narrow door just as the man cleared it. With his left hand, he grabbed the guard's shirtfront and forced him back inside, into the wall. With his right, he popped him in the windpipe, and let him drop to the newspaper-littered floor, choking, gagging, his eyes spilling water.

Peter crouched and lifted his coat far enough to show his gun.

"You see this lady. You see her?"

The guard's watered eyes shifted over Peter's shoulder to where I stood just outside. "Yeah. Yeah." His breath was like a dog's pant.

"You let two goons in here tonight and they kidnapped her. You let them do it and I want to know why."

"Please, mister, I'm not—"

"Why'd you let them in?"

"They drop the women off, they pick them up."

"Hookers?"

The man nodded.

"Does she look like a hooker to you?" Peter tapped the man's chin with the heel of his hand, bouncing the back of his head off the wall.

The man ducked behind his hands. "I never saw her. They pulled up, said some jane was giving a guy trouble, they had to go in and get her. They drove out."

"Did they ask you where to find her?"

"No."

"They knew where she was?"

"Yeah."

"They come and go when they want, those two?"

"Yeah, but usually later. First time they come so early. That's all I know, all I want to know. I do what I'm told, get a sawbuck now and then."

"Is he still here?"

"What?"

"You know who I mean."

"Mister, I got kids. I got to earn a living."

"You can tell him I beat you up to get inside, but you didn't tell me anything. I already knew what I wanted. You tell him that. Is he still here? Just nod your head if it's yes."

The man tucked his chin once, then again.

Peter stood up. "Where's your map?"

The man pointed to the drawer beneath the counter. Peter snatched out a laminated map of the studio grounds. He glanced at it, then jabbed a point with his finger. "There?" he asked the man.

He nodded.

"Anybody with him you know of?"

He shook his head.

"You sit there, quiet, and nothing happens to you, and nobody knows you told me, understand? Watch him," he said to Johnny.

"You got it."

Peter strode past me and into the lot.

"Where are you going?" I scrambled to catch up.

"Stay with Johnny."

"Peter!"

The sky cracked and in the next second, torrents of rain lashed us, drenching us before we'd gone twenty feet.

"Peter, stop!" The wind shoved me back harshly.

"I mean it, stay out of my way!"

"Stop! Peter! Stop!" Water cascaded off my hat and into my eyes. Viciously I wiped it away. I jumped forward and grabbed his arm. "I don't want you to go to prison."

"I'm going to find out what the hell's going on!"

He slung my arm off and vanished into the marching rain.

My shoes were soaked, my feet slid around in them, I couldn't run. I kicked them off, scooped them up and raced after him in my bare feet.

Ahead, dwarfed by the soundstages, sat a two-story stucco building with a narrow loggia running across the front, draped in white bougainvillea being ripped by the storm.

I caught a glimpse of Peter in the flash of lightning as he disappeared into the black shelter of the loggia. The next second the ancient framing of the front door splintered, but above the howling of the wind, I was the only one who could have heard it. Unless the other person was inside.

By the time I caught up, Peter was halfway down the hallway headed for the only room with a bar of light showing beneath the door.

That door opened and there stood Mack Pace, the chief of studio security, in shirtsleeves. Peter shoved him back into his office, then shoved him again, hard in the chest, hard enough to propel him into his desk. The desk lamp crashed to the floor.

Peter threw off his soaked hat and turned to slam the door. I was standing there. I looked at him, then I stepped inside and did it for him.

Pace scuttled off his desk, his hand stabbing out for a drawer. Peter was faster and kicked him in the side, launching him over his desk chair. Pace hit hard on his buttocks, and tried to scramble up onto all fours. Peter grabbed his shirt collar and belt and flung him head first into the file cabinet.

"Are you crazy?" Pace screamed. He rolled over and scrambled backwards. "You're going to jail!"

"Not yet."

Pace tried to get up again. Peter shoved him back down hard with his foot. Pace crab-walked backward into the wall, a filthy smear from Peter's shoe across his shirtfront. "He's going to jail. You talk to him," he screamed at me. "Or you're both going to jail."

I stood there and said nothing.

A spark of lightning flashed around the curtains and instantly thunder shook the room.

Peter yanked open the desk drawer Pace had reached for, and pulled out a gun. He put it in his pocket. "Get up," he ordered and gave Pace an encouraging kick. "Take a chair."

Pace hauled himself up, wobbled to one of the visitors' chairs and dropped into it. "You have no idea what you're doing. One phone call and—"

Peter grabbed the phone, the whole phone, and threw it at Pace, who flung his arms up just in time. It bounced off his forearms.

"Go ahead, call your boss! Tell him how Julie Scarza's goons came in here and kidnapped Mrs. Atwill because you let them run the place."

"I don't know what you're—"

Peter slapped him.

"I want to beat you unconscious, so don't give me a reason. And if you think Julie Scarza gives a damn what happens to you, he sent his men onto the lot to snatch her, which was as good as telling me he had you in his pocket. He probably figured to let me punch you around so I'd feel better. I don't feel better yet, so you're going to answer some questions. Did you tell Scarza's men where to find her?"

"So you can hit me again?"

"Try me."

His mouth twisted and he spat out: "Okay. He called, said he needed to talk to you. Asked about her, asked what was up with you two. I told him."

"How the hell would you know that?"

"It's in her damned file. I wrote the file. What do you think I am around here, the janitor? He asked me if she was on the lot, I found out, I told him. He said he needed to keep tabs on her, that's all."

"What does Scarza know about the Feds, about the Feds being on the lot? About McCann?"

"I don't know. Nothing from me."

"What did you tell Scarza about McCann?"

"Nothing. Why would I do that? It's got nothing to do with Scarza."

"I know McCann was here undercover. What did you tell Scarza?"

"Nothing. I swear."

I said to Pace, "Call Agent Bitterston."

"I swear I didn't tell Scarza about the Feds."

Peter said, "You got the number. Pick up the phone. Call him."

"Why? What am I going to tell him?"

140

I said, "Tell him that tonight I remembered the first time I met Major McCann."

CHAPTER 16

Bitterston met us at Madison's, across from the studio. He came alone, without his silent sidekick, Agent Larkin.

Anthony had given us a small room off the kitchen, usually reserved for writers' poker games. I apologized for not being in the bungalow when my dinner was delivered, paid for it, and tipped the delivery boy.

Anthony supplied us with a dozen bar towels, then spread a fresh tablecloth over the water rings and cigarette burns, and deposited ashtrays. Even though we were the only people in the room, cigarette smoke seemed to hang in the air. Peter took out a cigarette and added reality to illusion.

In the ladies' room, I removed my ruined hat and used a couple of the towels to squeeze my hair. It hung in wet sticks. Thank God I didn't use false lashes. They'd have been in my eyebrows. I gathered my hair into a drowned knot on my neck and anchored it with a few stray hairpins I found in my handbag, which we'd retrieved, along with the rest of my stuff, from Bishop's bungalow. Powder wasn't going to help a damned bit, but I reapplied the lipstick.

Bitterston hung his dripping raincoat and hat on the rack and took a chair on the opposite side of the round table. Anthony brought in a tray with a bottle of scotch, ice and glasses. A waiter followed with a coffee tray. "If you need anything else, just holler," Anthony said and they left.

Bitterston poured himself a coffee. "Nasty night."

I didn't disagree. Peter poured me a short Scotch. I took a warming mouthful and let it ease into my chest.

"I just saw Mack Pace," Bitterston said to Peter. "He says you're crazy and I shouldn't listen to anything you say. Says you beat him up."

"A little."

"Funny thing, though. He doesn't want you arrested."

"He's got a deal he doesn't want his bosses to know about. He's been letting Julie Scarza run hookers out of the studio after hours. You know Scarza?"

"I've heard of him."

"Maybe more than heard." Peter flicked his cigarette ash into his tray and sat back. "Scarza wanted to talk to me and he wanted Mrs. Atwill around to show me he meant business. Pace told him where to find her and a couple of his goons took her right off the lot. That's why I beat him up. Scarza wanted to talk about his good friend Mickey Triton. Mala Demara was seeing him on the quiet. Scarza said that he thought maybe she killed Triton, and that the studio might want to cover that up."

"And he thought they hired you to do it."

I said, "I know you've asked people about Mr. Winslow. Have you heard anything that would make Julie Scarza think he could be bought to do something like that?"

Bitterston took out a cigarette case, opened it, offered it to me. When I declined, he pulled out a cigarette and lit it from the matchbook by his ashtray. "I heard Mr. Winslow enlisted right after Pearl Harbor, ended up in OCS—Officer Candidate School—then in the Pacific. Purple heart, silver star." He dropped the match into the tray. "Why didn't you stay in?"

"They didn't throw me out, if that's what you mean," Peter said.

"It's a fine record, Captain, that's all I meant. Made up for some of the things I heard from the cops."

"Not from Sergeant Barty," I said.

"Not from the DA either, as it turned out, but Mr. Scarza might have a lower opinion of human nature."

Peter said, "If the studio wanted a frame, they'd tell Pace to do it. They don't know Scarza's got him on a leash. If the studio told Pace, Pace would tell Scarza. So what did Scarza really want? Maybe to find out if Triton's killing had anything to do with the real reason you and Major McCann came to Los Angeles."

They regarded each other through the thin spirals of smoke.

"Tell him," Peter said to me.

I said, "You followed me yesterday. A blue Studebaker followed me out to Malibu and back. It hadn't followed me from my house, so it must have been waiting outside the studio for me to leave. What happened between the time I arrived and left that might interest the FBI? I met Major McCann. I told him I thought I'd seen him before. He lied about never having been in California."

"Where is it you think you saw him?" Bitterston said.

"I know where I saw him. It was seven years ago at a charity auction at Kitty and Tommy Dunning's out in Malibu."

"You didn't say anything about this when I talked to you this morning."

"Because I didn't remember till tonight. Since I saw you yesterday, I found out that two guests—who came with Mickey Triton—were murdered in their car on the way home. Seven years later, Mickey Triton is murdered and Major McCann shows up as a consultant on a movie and four of the people on that movie were at the party: Alastair Bishop, Betty Guinness, Bill Linden and Sam Ross."

"You came out on a night like this to talk to us," Peter said to Bitterston, "and you came alone. I don't think it was because you couldn't find anybody still awake."

"I could have you thrown in jail," Bitterston said. "Some of the local cops would be willing to help with that."

I said, "And I have a lot of money, which I'd spend to get him out. And I'd have to talk to a lot of people while I was doing it."

Bitterston smiled. It wasn't much of a smile, but more than I'd ever seen from him. He pulled his ashtray to him.

Peter said, "It's better if you fill us in, better than letting me stumble around and screw up your investigation. Now that Scarza's threatened Mrs. Atwill, I'm not going away."

"Who did you tell about Major McCann?" Bitterston asked me. "Who knew you thought you recognized him?"

"Alastair Bishop, Betty Guinness, his secretary, Sam Ross, and Morty Engler, the head of publicity, were all there. Some of the crew might have heard as well."

"And then you went right out to Malibu."

"I went to see Bill to tell him I was working on his script. He's a friend, and I wanted to tell him face to face. It had nothing to do with Major McCann."

"Who did you tell out there?"

"I mentioned it to Bill."

"What did he say?"

"Nothing. I said I thought I'd recognized him, that I thought he'd lied about never being in California. That was all. He didn't pursue it."

"How is it you remembered McCann after all these years?"

I told him. Then I said, "He was kind to me. Did I get him killed?"

Bitterston took a long drag on his cigarette and held it over the tray, watching the short glow at its tip for a long time. Then he said, "Back in the mid-thirties, we were working with military intelligence. We knew war was coming in Europe, and America might well end up in it. The War Department needed money to

145

pay for more local agents in Europe, to feed information, set up communication lines, contacts, support anti-Fascists. We helped them arrange to get some, without Congress having to vote on it or know what they were up to. We did it with help from men like Julie Scarza. They hated Mussolini, so they helped us raise the money in Italy.

"There were plenty of people who wanted to get out. They had valuables the government would never let them take. Scarza and the others had connections over there, organizations you might say, men with cash. Those men bought the stuff, jewelry, paintings, gold and silver items. Stuff easily transported out of the country in diplomatic pouches. The military got it out, and we sold it to wealthy Americans, Brits and South Americans over here."

Peter said, "Scarza's friends would pay, what, five cents on the dollar, you'd pay them fifteen and then sell it for fifty."

Bitterston shrugged. "Sometimes more than that. Our local offices knew the art dealers, they'd call their best clients. The jewelers would do the same, sometimes buy the pieces themselves. By the summer of thirty-nine, we were wrapping it up. Germany had invaded Czechoslovakia. We made our last stop out here. We had one of the auction houses approach the Dunnings because they had a reputation for big Hollywood charity parties. We'd set up a charity that was supposed to be helping European refugees, a charity to help funnel the money. We thought an auction could get us better prices out here. Unlike the bluebloods back East, out here you like to show off how much money you have. We wrapped up the operation here, and were going to pay off Scarza for what he'd done for us in Europe."

"How much?" Peter asked.

"Two hundred thousand."

"Two hundred thousand dollars?" I tried not to let my jaw drop.

"From the landing at Salerno to the Italian government's surrender took two weeks, Mrs. Atwill. You think men like Scarza didn't have a hand in that?"

"My brother was in Italy," Peter said. "He was still fighting two years later. Not exactly a cakewalk."

"No, Captain. But it could have been a lot worse."

"Go on," I said to Bitterston. "The auction. Were you there?"

"No. I was in Washington. We had two people at the party, the charity representative and McCann, who was a captain with military intelligence at the time. He brought the two hundred thousand out here. Scarza had an idea. He had an accountant who wanted to take his wife to a Hollywood party. How much do you know about that, what happened to them?" he asked me.

"I know Mickey Triton brought them."

"He was already a guest. He got invited to a lot of parties. He was the welterweight champion back then, headed to England for a fight. Triton brought them along. We would hand over the money to the accountant, along with a few items Scarza had bid on through Triton.

"About one o'clock, McCann escorted the couple out with the briefcase. One of our agents was waiting in a car, along with a bodyguard from Scarza. They all said good night, and Mc-Cann came back inside. Within two miles, a car cut them off. The wife lived long enough to tell the police what happened.

"Two men in masks got out of the car with guns. The agent and the bodyguard started shooting. It was over in ten seconds. Everybody in the car was dead or dying. One of the robbers was dead on the side of the road. The police started looking for his known associates, found one, a man named Ned Gorse, dead, bled to death on the sofa in his living room. The briefcase was on the dining table, empty.

"We got the agent's body out of town. The story made the papers as a mob killing because it was Scarza's accountant. The papers didn't want to embarrass the Dunnings, so nothing was made of where he'd been that night."

I said, "There can't have been many people who knew Scarza's payoff was in the car."

"No. And Gorse had ties to Scarza's gang, running drugs, some loan sharking. We figured one of Scarza's mob was behind it, stealing from his own boss."

Peter said, "Triton?"

"Scarza said he never told Triton about the handoff. He just asked him to take the accountant to the party. He spent a lot of time trying to find out who was behind it. Never did."

"What brought you back out here after all these years?" Peter asked.

"We got a lead."

"That someone at Marathon did it?" I asked.

"Possibly."

"Look," Peter said, impatiently, "you came out here tonight to get some help. Do you want it? Decide whether you trust us or we can go home and dry off."

Bitterston looked at Peter, hard. A lesser man might have been frightened. A lesser woman sure was. Then Bitterston crushed his cigarette. "We'd marked the money. We wanted to see where it went, see if we could learn anything about Scarza's operation from it. It was a good job, nothing easy to spot. You'd have to pass the bills under a special light. After the killings, for almost a year, we had agents in different local offices looking for any sign of it when deposits came in. But it never turned up. Not one bill. Then after Pearl Harbor, we didn't have enough men, just kept one on it, here in Los Angeles. We'd pretty much given up.

"Two weeks ago, a couple of thousand in hundred-dollar bills turned up in deposits from Ramon Elizondo's nightclub. And two twenties came in the next day, part of a deposit from Marathon."

I said, "Lots of Hollywood people go to Elizondo's. Every once in a while, they win."

"All the marked money from Elizondo's was in hundreds, no twenties. Marathon had four of the party's guests working on the same movie. That seemed like a place to start."

Peter said, "I assume you won't be telling Scarza the money was marked."

"Washington won't let us."

I said, "But you could set someone up at the club to check the cash. It's your best chance to find the man responsible for the death of one of your agents."

"I am well aware of that, Mrs. Atwill. Washington won't let us tell him we marked the money. If we put a man in that club, we as good as tell Scarza what we did."

"Because," Peter said, "there's a slight chance you could solve the case, get the money back, give it to him, and continue trying to trace his operation."

"Yes."

"So what is it you want me to do?" Peter asked.

"We need personal bank records. We can't get them without a warrant. What kind of connections do you have at the local banks?"

"Good ones. To get what we want, we prefer bribery to breaking and entering."

"I have a list. We need to see if anyone on it made big deposits of cash recently, whether they have large loans they paid off, anything that looks suspicious. Can you do it?"

"Yes. What kind of gun killed McCann?"

"A Webley, a thirty-two."

149

"English gun," Peter said. "What about Triton?"

"The bullet was useless, melted in the fire."

Peter took the gun from his pocket and slid it across to Bitterston, a .38 Special. "I took this off Pace. You might want to hang onto it. Any possibility the killer was searching Triton's cabin for whatever he was looking for at the bungalow when he killed McCann? Set the fire because he couldn't find it?"

"I'd say no. Triton's house wasn't searched. And nobody tried to burn it down."

"Then the fire was just to try to cover up the killing. An amateur job, shoot a man in the head and then burn the body."

"These men," Bitterston said, "Scarza's men who've been running hookers out of the studio. Could the marked twenties have come from them?"

I said, "The guard on the gate told us they gave him a sawbuck now and then. Not a twenty."

Peter ground out his cigarette. "So you think maybe it wasn't a gangster after all, but one of the party's guests who masterminded that stickup? How could they have known about Scarza's payoff?"

"Maybe they didn't," Bitterston said. "Maybe they weren't after Scarza's money. Maybe just the auction money and got more than they bargained for. The Dunnings cashed all the guests' checks that night, so the charity could have its money right away. They gave the cash to our agent who was playing the part of the charity representative. And he added it to Scarza's payoff in the briefcase. We figured Scarza would be less likely to think about marked money if his accountant saw that fresh auction cash getting tucked into the briefcase with the rest."

I said, "But no guest would have had time to arrange for a stickup."

"I'm afraid the Dunnings weren't discreet. They told plenty of people long before the auction what they were going to do. It was a challenge to the guests. Daring them to bid more than the Dunnings could cover. It worked. We made a lot of money that night."

"You could be right," Peter said. "You said the men in the victims' car opened fire first."

"That's what the wife said, according to the file."

"If the thieves thought they were sticking up gangsters, they would have come out shooting, but they didn't. Can I ask why you sent McCann undercover at the studio when he'd been seen at that party?"

"Only by the Dunnings and a couple of servants. And Mrs. Atwill. He told us about it before we sent him in this time. He couldn't recall her name after all those years, but we figured the odds of ever running into her again were a million to one. And he wanted to go back in. All the men who knew the payoff was happening that night were investigated. They were all exonerated. But all of their careers suffered. McCann had something to prove."

"What was he doing in the bungalow?" I asked.

"Looking for anything Alastair Bishop or Bill Linden had stored out there that might give us a clue they were involved. Safety-deposit-box receipts, bank records, receipts showing they'd sold some of the stuff Scarza bid on, stuff that disappeared with the cash."

"Bill didn't really have anything personal out there."

"Mrs. Atwill, you know you can't tell him anything."

"Yes."

"Sergeant Barty told me you knew how to keep a secret."

He didn't say it, but it was in his eyes: If I didn't do what he said, the FBI would ruin me. Would ruin both of us.

Bitterston slid a folded piece of paper across the table to Peter, along with his card.

"These are the people whose bank-account records we want

to see. Call me in the morning, we'll talk about it."

Peter said, "Whatever I can do, I will, but you don't ask her to do anything for you."

"Except to think about why the money's suddenly turned up after seven years. Sergeant Barty also told me she's good at figuring things out."

Chapter 17

Juanita was fine. Peter's man, Lou Brandesi, was parked in front of the house, making sure.

She was still up, unaware she'd been in any danger, and when she heard the front door, she came out from the back of the house, a cup of Mexican cocoa in her hand, smiling, until she saw what we looked like.

"What happened?" she asked Peter, not without accusation.

I said, "We got caught in the storm. Is there any more of that? It's cold in here."

"Of course," she replied warily and shot a worried glance over her shoulder as she headed back down the hall.

"Look at your hand," I said. The knuckles on Peter's right hand were swollen, skinned and red from when he'd hit Elizondo. "There's merthiolate in the medicine cabinet in my bedroom. Merthiolate, did I say that right? I'm a little tired."

"Where are you going?"

"To the study. I'll go change, dry off, get some cocoa, then I have to get to work."

"What?"

"Bishop is expecting the script-change suggestions in the morning. No sense telling him I got kidnapped, even if Bitterston would let me. He wouldn't care."

"Lauren."

"You should go fix your hand."

"Lauren."

"What?"

"Look at me."

"I am."

"No, you're not. Juanita!"

The urgency brought her racing from the kitchen. Even I could tell something was wrong. I just couldn't figure out what on earth it could be.

"She's going into shock. I need hot-water bottles, all you have."

"And blankets," Juanita said. "Upstairs, in her dressing room."

Peter scooped me into his arms and carried me upstairs, deposited me in the bedroom chair. "Get undressed, now."

He dashed into the dressing room and came out with a small stack of blankets. I never understood why Juanita kept so many.

I tried to remember how my dress fastened. Where were the buttons?

Peter undressed me. He took me right out of my soaked clothes, my dress, slip, underwear. He wrapped a blanket around me and ran back to the dressing room. "Nightgown, where are your nightgowns?"

"The drawer, there's a drawer," I said. I couldn't seem to make much sound.

Nevertheless, he found one. "Put this on."

He ripped the bedclothes back. I was having trouble figuring out how to manage the nightgown and the blanket.

He pulled the blanket away and put me into my nightgown. He carried me to the bed, lay me on the bottom sheet, covered me in a blanket before pulling the bedclothes over me. He piled on blankets.

Juanita appeared with the water bottles, three of them, wrapped in dish towels. Peter lifted the covers and packed them against my chest, my hips, my feet.

"Go find her doctor's number. We might need him."

I tried to protest, but my lips were thick and my teeth chattered. The room seemed oddly quiet, more than quiet. Like it was deaf. Or I was deaf. Which was it?

Peter seemed very far away.

Then suddenly he was lying beside me, on top of the covers, holding me to him, whispering to me. But I couldn't understand the words.

When I woke up, it was just dawn. Sometime during the night, the water bottles had been removed, although I was still covered in blankets. I rolled over. Peter lay beside me, on his side, under the top blanket, wearing the pajamas he kept in the guest room.

He opened his eyes and reached for me, but I was under several more layers. "How are you?" he asked.

"I'm burning up under all this, and I've got a headache."

He threw off his covers, but not mine. While he rummaged around in my medicine cabinet, I peeled back the blankets and sat up, which made the headache worse. He brought out a bottle of aspirin, unscrewed the cap and shook a half dozen tablets into my hand, then poured me a glass of water from the carafe on the night table. I swallowed the tablets, then said, "It's not going to do any good to slip back to the guest room. After you stripped off my clothes, I'm pretty sure Juanita knows what's going on with us, as if she didn't already."

"Lauren—"

"Okay, okay."

"Besides, I have to leave soon. I've got work to do. I've got to get Mala Demara back home, then go see Scarza."

I took his hand. It was no good saying be careful.

"Do you think she did it?" I said instead.

"She goes away the weekend Triton's killed, which takes away any chance her cousin could give her an alibi. And doesn't tell her cousin where she's going. Still it doesn't make much sense that she'd stay away if she did it. It's up to her lawyer now. He'll be with her when the county cops drop by. They probably won't even ask about Thursday night, about McCann. They haven't made a connection between his killing and Triton's."

"Of course, we don't know for sure there is any connection. I have to go back to the studio today."

"No, you have to rest."

"Winslow, I won't be any easier to live with if I get fired off this picture."

"I don't want you alone in there."

"I don't want to be alone. Sam will give me an office in the writers' building, where there are lots of people and a guard in the lobby."

"I want Johnny there, too."

"I can't work with him hanging over my shoulder."

"He goes or you stay here."

"Okay, you're right. Sam will fix it up."

"You know me using the guest room isn't about fooling Juanita. It's about making sure she never has to perjure herself in divorce court."

"I know, but I still was hoping you'd strip my clothes off again."

"Keep thinking about that. It'll give you something to think about instead of the case."

I slept for another couple of hours, then took a long bath, soaking and sipping the strong coffee Juanita brought up, then washed my hair. When I'd got a look at it in the mirror, I wasn't surprised Peter had declined my invitation. My appearance didn't stand up well to kidnapping.

I looped my hair into pin curls. Then I called Alastair Bishop's bungalow. No one answered. It was Saturday, and Bishop would be at home. Betty hadn't come in yet, but she would. Lowly writers and office staff normally had to work half days on

Saturday, but not directors or producers unless they were under the gun to finish a project.

I called Sam Ross at home and asked him to get me an office. I told him Peter wanted Johnny around, although I didn't say why. He said, "Sure thing, sure thing. I'll set something up over at the Tate Building. He can sit in the lobby, if you don't want him in your office."

I hoped he didn't have to call Mack Pace to set any of that up. After last night, I didn't think the head of studio security would be much inclined to help me out with anything. I asked, "Have you talked to Helen? When's she coming home?"

"By next week, she should be through buying out Fifth Avenue. She says she wants to invite you and your boyfriend—sorry, Mr. Winslow—over for dinner before New Year's, what do you say?"

"Fine. That sounds good."

"He called about an hour ago, said he'd have a report for me later. Sounds like maybe he found something."

"I've been told to stay out of this, and I am."

"Yeah, sure."

I rolled out the beauty parlor hair dryer I kept stored in the dressing room. My hair didn't require tortured treatments, thank God, so I didn't need to get it done every week. I sat under the enormous metal hood, ate a bacon-and-egg sandwich, and glanced over the newspaper. Most of the front page was taken up with stories and pictures about the storm, which had dumped two inches of rain, flooded neighborhoods, ripped off roofs and tossed boats around the marinas. But the pictures were all taken at night, so it was hard to tell the extent of the damage. We'd have to wait for the second editions.

There was an "investigation continues" story about Mickey Triton, and since the reporter knew none of what we did, the story was plumped by interviews with Mickey's fighters and the staff of his gym. To read it, you'd never think he'd known a mobster in his life.

The story on Major McCann had been shoved inside, and he was described as someone who'd been visiting the studio. The police were continuing to look into the motive, as his body was discovered in an unoccupied bungalow and he did not appear to have been robbed. Then the reader was reminded about the strikes and the violence at two other studios earlier in the summer—not mentioning, of course, that during the clashes between strikers and non-strikers outside those studios' gates, security staff had been tossing tear gas down on the strikers.

Johnny drove me to the studio, where my car still sat in the visitors' lot. I dropped by Bishop's bungalow, just to make sure I hadn't left anything behind last night when Peter and I retrieved my canvas bag and my handbag with my gun and lock picks inside. Betty still wasn't in. I left her a note, telling her I'd gone over to work in the Tate Building, the switchboard would know the phone number. I locked up after me and dropped the key back through the letter slot in the door.

The man at the lobby desk of the Tate gave me the key to my newly assigned office and told me where to find the typists' room if I needed a script typed. Johnny settled into a chair with a stack of magazines.

My new office, on the fifth floor, had a view of the side of a soundstage, but it had paper, pencils and a typewriter. I unpacked my talismans from the canvas bag: my notebook; fountain pen; silver paperweight; pack of index cards; the empty recipe box to hold them as I made scene notes. I tested the desk lamp. The bottom desk drawer was deep enough for my handbag, but there was no key to lock up the gun inside it. I whipped out one of my lock picks and took care of that in two seconds.

I hung up my suit jacket, and as I started to close the door, I heard voices down at the end of the hallway, coming from Bill's office—that is, his office when he didn't get bungalow privileges.

I found him in much the same position as the one in which I'd first seen him all those years ago, lying on his sofa, one leg resting on its back, a writing tablet on his thigh.

A woman stood in the window, her hips leaning on the cold radiator. She was rail thin, with short dark hair tucked behind her ears and held to her head with cream oil. She wore black pleated slacks, a black-and-silver-patterned waistcoat, a white starched shirt, styled like a man's and tailored to fit her, and a man's tie in black and fuchsia.

She touched her fingertips to her forehead and saluted. "Atwill."

"Hawkins. How have you been? I'm working down the hall."

"I'm avoiding work by talking to Linden, which is almost as big a chore. Now here you are, come to rescue me as I hear you have exciting stories to tell."

CHAPTER 18

Bill threw up his hands. "She didn't get anything from me. Of course, she couldn't because you didn't tell me anything."

I closed the door. "What have you heard?" I asked her.

She said, "That you found the dead man Thursday night. True?"

"True."

"Have a seat. Tell all. Linden, where's the whiskey?"

"Oh, no, thanks," I said.

"It must have been grim, and we'll want the details."

"I'm all right, really."

Bill tossed down the tablet. "Oh, God, she said 'really.' She must be in bad shape. Bottom drawer."

Hawkins pulled out a whiskey bottle and a glass and poured a couple of fingers. She thrust it at me. "So what happened?"

I took the glass and sipped a teaspoon to satisfy them. I told them about finding McCann's body, but not much about anything else.

Hawkins said, "Linden's been well grilled, by the police and FBI. They acted like he'd hidden the plans for the atom bomb in that bungalow."

"Surely no one thinks Bill has military secrets."

"Linden couldn't keep a secret if his life depended on it."

"I haven't told anyone what you got up to at Bunny Morley's last week," he remarked.

"Until now."

"It's all right. Lauren is where gossip goes to die," Bill said. "Don't ever tell her anything you want passed around."

There were footsteps in the hall. Hawkins nipped my glass from my hand, shoved it behind her and slid her rear end onto the desk to hide the bottle. Bill snatched up his tablet and began to write furiously. The door opened without a knock and one of the junior executives stuck his head in.

"This better be important, Mickels," Hawkins said. "You just interrupted the creation of some dazzling dialogue for Alastair Bishop."

"You weren't in your office," Mickels said to Hawkins.

"Linden, I'm not in my office."

"Thank you, Mickels, for pointing that out," Bill said. "Call Bishop or Sam Ross. I know you can't take our word for it, we're only writers, and therefore of no account."

The man eyed me, but no one offered an introduction.

Bill said, "If you don't need Hawkins and don't need me, perhaps you could return to prowling the halls and let us get back to creating."

The man said to Hawkins, "We need the pages by Monday." Then he snapped the door shut.

"Mickels," Bill sighed and tossed the tablet down. "He seeks to increase his importance by discovering problems where none exist. He wants the sofas removed from the offices, says it makes us lazy drunkards. Pour me some of that, will you, Hawkins? What brings you out of Pasadena and into this miserable warren?" he asked me. "It's all right, Hawkins knows I've been booted off the picture."

I said, "I thought it would be easier to work here, then I can just drop the notes off at Bishop's bungalow."

Hawkins said, "Linden can give you a list of words Mala still can't say well. Pronounce well. Jury's still out on whether she can say any of them well."

Bill said, "Hawkins is a snob. She writes drivel, but dismisses anyone forced to act drivel."

I said, "You don't think Mala can act?"

"Better than some," Hawkins allowed, "but that's not saying much. She's not Bergman, that's for sure."

"Well, nobody is."

Bill said, "You'll see, when her English gets better. And with this picture, thanks to me and Lauren, she'll finally have a decent script." He grinned at me. "Hawkins, why don't you write her something? Something she can chew the scenery with, as that is your specialty. Make sure she sheds noble tears. Americans love to see the acting. If it's natural, it just ain't no good."

"She was never natural a day in her life."

"You should have seen her first screen test. Knocked me down."

"Yeah, I've heard that story before. It was you and Dickie Lucas, right? You were probably half knocked down when you got there." She handed Bill his whiskey.

"As you might recall," he said to me, "before the war started, I used my loan-out to Warners to sail to Europe to absorb the ambiance for the script I was going to write for them."

I said, "I recall you sailed off to Europe when everybody was afraid a war was about to start over there."

"I'm not the only one who thought Churchill was just a curmudgeon."

"I also recall Warners got the expense report and declined to pay for any of it."

He shrugged. "It was worth a try. While I was over there, I ran into Dickie Lucas. He was there with a couple of other scouts. They'd held an audition for young women in some of the acting schools over there, and gave screen tests to a few dozen. They were looking for new, beautiful faces. He asked me to watch the reels with him and tell them what I thought. Didn't I tell you this the other day?"

"Not all of it."

"Well, I sat through them, and as Hawkins says, we might have got a bit tight while we were doing it. All the girls were the same. All jabbing the lines earnestly to make it look like they felt something. Then she came on. And it was like she was just talking to you. Said the lines as if she meant them. Crazy how far that goes. The pauses, the gestures, not a phony one in the bunch. I couldn't take my eyes off her. But she had a heavy accent, and I must admit, a bit too much hair in a few places." He waved his fingers at his eyebrows and the area where men have sideburns. "I tried to get Dickie to give her a chance, but he said they weren't looking for someone they'd have to teach English. He did send her a letter saying to get in touch if she got to the States and improved her English. I got hold of her address, wrote her a note, to encourage her. But then the war broke out in Europe, and she ended up getting sent back to Austria. We exchanged a few letters, then we lost touch. I felt bad about that."

"It wasn't your fault," I said. "She must have been glad to see you again."

"She never saw me back then. It was just letters. She's had a rough time, Hawkins; you should behave."

Hawkins rolled her eyes. "If you want to see acting, Atwill, let her cousin read your fortune. I had her do one for me, for the fun of it. If I weren't cursed with natural intelligence, she might have made a believer out of me. She has the talent in the family."

"And the looks," Bill observed.

"I admit Madame Karoly resembles a scowling frog, but if you look closely, you can see vestiges of considerable former appeal. You could almost believe they really were related. Madame from the frog side of the family. Well, I must be off. Much as I hate to admit that Mickels could be right about anything, I do need to work. Thanks for the break. Atwill, good to see you. Try to stay out of trouble—and if you can't, take notes." She saluted me again and sailed out, closing the door behind her.

He said, "She doesn't know anything from me, not about anything you told me the other day. Any word on Mala?"

"I think she might turn up today."

"Good God, he found her?"

"In a manner of speaking."

"Well, that's mysterious." He took a long sip of whiskey. "You didn't come out from Pasadena so you could drop off your notes. The studio has messengers for that."

"I'm not investigating."

"Isn't this the point in those mystery pictures you write where the sleuth goes back to visit all the suspects, and one of them invariably says something that later turns out to be important?"

"I'm not investigating anything."

"In those pictures, doesn't the field of suspects always get narrowed when one of them ends up dead? Fewer suspects and a pivotal clue always found in that death? Let's just hope life doesn't imitate art." He got up, set his empty glass on the desk and claimed mine.

"When are you going to tell Mr. Winslow the truth about you and me?" he said. "Is it worse than what he thinks now?"

"He thinks we once had an affair. You think that's worse than what I did?"

"Lauren . . ."

"I haven't known him that long. I don't know what he would say. You've forgiven me, but—"

"Stop right there! Dear God, you've got that look on your face, like you're about to turn me into one of Hawkins's heroes. Noble, but doomed. Back to your office. Out. Now."

CHAPTER 19

Even though Mala was about to turn up, I had no way of knowing whether she'd be able to shoot the picture. So I worked on my report to Bishop about the three actresses whose reels I'd seen yesterday afternoon—God, was it only yesterday? Not opinions of their acting—that wasn't my job—but about the changes I thought would have to be made, including some examples of proposed dialogue changes. It took me well into the afternoon, interrupted only by my going downstairs to ask Johnny to run over to Madison's to get lunch for me, as well as for himself and the man at the desk. The man was glad to forego his baloney for Madison's roast beef.

About three, I rolled in some fresh paper and started typing rough-idea notes for tweaking the script should Mala remain on the picture, but we had to denude it of anything that might remotely suggest the Triton killing to the audience.

My office had retained its sofa, despite Mickels's efforts, so about four, I lay down to close my eyes for a few minutes before tackling the final draft.

I woke up with Bill standing over me, haloed by the light from the desk lamp. The sun had gone down.

"You're beautiful with your mouth open," he said.

"Shut up." I sniffed a few times and sat up.

"I'm heading out and thought I'd see how you were getting on. Don't take this the wrong way, but you look a bit worn out. Should you be doing all this? You haven't been out of the hospital that long."

"I just need some sleep."

"And maybe some fun. Why don't you go home, take a nap, and come on over tonight? Kitty's throwing her annual Christmas bacchanal. Things won't get started before nine. Invite Mr. Winslow."

"We don't go out in public."

"What?"

"He doesn't want the divorce lawyer to pull out infidelity to try to get Franklin some of my money."

"Frank slept with half of Hollywood. Half the women, anyway."

"Women are supposed to be cowed by just the thought their bedroom lives could become public."

"Thank God I don't know any of them, I'd have no conversation."

"And the truth is, I am."

"You're not getting much fun these days, are you?"

"I'm not sure a party will make up for finding a dead body."

"It couldn't make it worse. Call me if you change your mind."

Bill went home and I finished my draft, then arranged for a messenger to take it to Bishop's house.

I drove home, Johnny following, where he handed me off to another man from the agency, who'd sit in my driveway till I went to bed, then in the living room overnight with magazines, a small radio, and a deck of cards.

"Mr. Winslow called," Juanita said. "He wanted to know if you had plans for tonight. I told him no, you never get to go anywhere." She went back toward the kitchen, calling over her shoulder, "Pork chops, but I hope you're not here to eat them."

Peter answered his office phone, which was unusual, as he was rarely there. His number was normally picked up by one of a team of efficient women charged with taking detailed messages.

After he'd made sure I was okay and his man in place, he said, "Kitty Dunning called the office and invited me out to her Christmas party tonight."

"I think Bill might have put her up to it. He thinks I need to get out more, go places where there's more likely to be fun than felony. But I told him you and I can't go out together."

"Can you get an invitation through Linden?"

"Yes."

"Would you mind going?"

"I guess you don't mean as your date. What's up?"

"I told Bitterston I'd been invited, and he wants to send someone in. Would you let that man be your escort?"

"What good will that do?"

"Bitterston's going back to the beginning, looking at everything all over again, including the house. All this time they assumed whoever masterminded that stickup, whoever ended up with all the money, was one of Scarza's mob stealing from his boss. They never thought about anyone at the party because none of them could have known about the two hundred grand. But maybe the robbers were only after the auction money. That would still have been a lot of cash. The Feds can't walk up to her door and flash their ID and ask to look around. Tonight may be the only chance to get a man inside."

"I cannot tell you how much I'm looking forward to spending the evening watching Kitty flirt with you."

"I'll make it up to you."

"I'm starting a list right now of everything I want."

"I hope there'll be a few things on it you can't put in writing."

I napped, bathed and perfumed myself, then slipped into the evening gown Juanita happily aired and touched up with the iron. I examined the result. Bill had been right: I looked worn out, but only if you knew I didn't normally have bags the size of steamer trunks under my eyes.

I went light on the eye makeup and concentrated on a good lipstick and some impressive jewelry to draw the attention elsewhere. As it was evening and I was over thirty, I should have put my hair up, but given the styling talent Juanita and I possessed, I was much better off just letting it fall in loose waves.

Bitterston's man arrived promptly at nine. His name was Talley. Medium height, medium build, medium scowl. At least Bitterston was smart enough to pick someone older than me and put him in a good tuxedo.

But Talley didn't have much more to say for himself than Bitterston's sidekick Larkin.

Kitty's mansion was a lighthouse, every room shooting light into the night. One of a dozen hired valets met us at the courtyard gate and took Talley's car God knows where. Both sides of the street behind her house were choked with cars.

Once inside, I didn't have to look for Peter, even given the swarm of guests. I had radar where he was concerned and, unlike the real thing, mine was foolproof. Kitty, in a shimmering silver dress, stood on the far side of the ballroom, her arm through his, introducing him around. God, how he must hate being shown off.

"Hey there," said Bill, behind me.

I introduced Talley. Our cover story for Bill was that Talley was one of Peter's men, acting as Peter's "beard" for the night. The cover story for the rest of the guests was that Talley was visiting West Coast friends for the holidays, that he owned an accounting firm in Washington, DC. Since he'd come out with Bitterston from DC, he knew the capital, and apparently something about tax laws. Not that anyone was likely to engage him in conversation about them. Maybe that was the point: pick a cover story that would make him the center of no one's attention.

As I handed my wrap to one of the maids, Bill whispered, "If you and Mr. Winslow want to be alone, the cottage is unlocked, drapes closed, bar stocked. I won't be back before two. Good to meet you," he said louder, to Talley, and strolled off.

Kitty was still introducing Peter. Charlie Dunning, Lord Dunning, her late husband's brother, was acting the host in the entry hall, and giving Peter the occasional sour look. We said hello to him, and I decided to wait till Kitty let go of Peter before saying hello to her. I had business here, and the sooner I got it out of the way, the sooner I could turn my mind to figuring out how to get Peter over to Bill's cottage and start in on that list of things he owed me for doing this.

I took Agent Talley out to the terrace that stretched across the rear of the mansion. Down on the beach, under the full moon and the lights from the house, I could see long, dark body-shapes of seaweed, the only evidence of last night's raging storm. Whatever other flotsam that must have been there— netting, dead birds and bits of broken boats—had been removed.

Even though the temperature in Malibu was much cooler than further inland, we weren't the only guests outside, so I slipped my arm through Talley's and led him to the far end of the terrace, where we wouldn't be overheard. After a minute, Peter joined us. I filled Talley in.

I said, "Seven years ago, down on that beach, there was a bar and some Arabian-style tents with layers of pillows inside. Young actresses dressed as harem girls delivered the drinks. I discovered my fiancé in one of those tents being what I thought was a bit too friendly with one of the girls. We had a fight, and I came up here to cool off. I wanted to be alone, and ended up down here, I think it was in this room, where I ran into Major McCann."

"Do you recall seeing anyone else down there, as you came up from the beach?" Talley asked.

Peter said, "When you saw McCann, he'd just finished putting the payoff briefcase in the car. If the mastermind was a party guest, he had to be in the house, calling the robbers to tell them the money was leaving the house. So if you saw anyone down on that beach on your way up, he can't be the guy we're after."

"I was pretty upset, and it was a long time ago."

Talley glanced in through the French doors. The room was temporarily empty. "Let's go on in."

On the opposite side of the room was an alcove with a grand piano and a small bar. No one needed to go a minute without a drink in this house.

Talley said to me, "I need you to help me get a look at the rest of the house, the layout upstairs, the room where the briefcase was kept, the stairs where McCann brought it down, the door he used to leave. The vantage points from up there where someone might have watched for that briefcase to leave and made a call."

Peter said, "Mrs. Atwill isn't going into bedrooms with you."

"This is Hollywood, Mr. Winslow. Nobody's going to give two cents."

"Mr. Talley," I said. "If you want my help, it might be best not to imply it's the sort of thing I do all the time."

"That's not what I meant."

"I'm sure Mr. Winslow can help you find a way to examine the house without me and without getting yourself caught doing it."

"When we're done inside," Peter said to Talley, "I suggest we go have a smoke, take a walk around the grounds. There's something I want to show you."

"Okay." Talley went out, avoiding looking at me.

Peter turned to me. "I'm sorry to get you into this."

"For heaven's sake, I'm not that delicate a flower."

"We should be done in an hour at the most. I'll meet you back in here."

"Meet me in Bill's cottage. He offered it to us. It's open. And he promised not to come back till two. I'll be there at eleven-thirty."

"Winslow? You coming?" Talley called.

I was on my own. I roamed back through the main hall and into the ballroom, pausing here and there to speak to a few casual acquaintances, but Bill had been scooped up by a bunch of young people. Despite his age, he was popular with them. They liked to borrow the clever things he said and claim them as their own at the next party.

Boy, I was in a bad mood.

Time for some fresh air.

It wasn't much better outside. The terrace was full of couples who could spend time in public together and not worry whether people knew they liked each other.

I decided to take myself down to the beach.

Carrying my evening slippers in one hand and the hem of my gown in the other, I picked my way barefoot down the weathered wooden stairs that ran from the edge of the terrace to the beach. I knew nothing about the tide, but I thought it must have been out for a while: the sand was cold and damp, yet hard enough to walk on comfortably.

A few strollers kept well above the lapping foam. Only one man stood at its edge, still in his shoes, smoking and staring out at the hard glisten on the water.

I claimed a spot several yards away and took a few breaths of the damp night. I had an hour. An hour before I would get to see Peter in the cottage.

"Hullo, it's Mrs. Atwill, isn't it? Sorry to disturb. If you'd rather I disappeared, please say so, I won't mind."

"That's all right," I said. "Lord Dunning, right? We met here the other day."

"Lord Dunning? Not Charlie? You might have to produce your passport, my dear girl. Are you sure you're an American? Don't get me wrong, I like Americans."

"But we are instantly intimate."

"Tough on us Brits. We invented stuffy and we're rather attached to it. Are you sure I'm not disturbing?"

"Not at all. It's a bit lonely out here, suddenly."

"I needed a breather. Kitty does like big parties."

"I don't know how she manages it."

"She likes crowds. Tommy did too, my brother, late brother, died in the war, at Dunkirk, you know, her husband. I'm not that good at it. Never quite got the hang of small talk."

"I understand you sometimes teach actors how to be British."

"There, you see, that's what I mean. You start off, ask me something about myself. I should have asked you. I should have had some idea of chitchat before I staggered over here. Sorry, I'm a bit drunk."

"I've found that by asking other people about themselves, you don't usually have to make much real conversation, just ask questions and listen."

"And look interested. Perhaps that's the part I could never achieve. Perhaps I'm not shy. I'm a rude, self-centered bore."

I laughed. "Will you be staying long among the barbarians?"

"There's not much left calling me back to England, I'm afraid."

"I hear things are very difficult."

"Well, at least in England, you can find food. It's not worth eating—English cuisine and all—but you can find it. I'm here to cast my fortune with the colonists."

"Kitty must have some very good connections. Not that I meant . . . I didn't mean—"

"Of course not. But I suppose that's what they all think. The sotted, besotted little brother. Sorry, I am drunk. Please forgive."

"I won't say a word. I'm familiar with besotted."

"Kitty's got herself a muscle man she picked up somewhere."

"Don't worry about him. He's not Kitty's, not going to be. I can guarantee you that."

"Excuse me," said a deep, soft, mellifluous voice. Kitty's butler stood on the sand, his dress shoes in his hand, the socks rolled neatly inside, his trouser legs folded up precisely. "I am sorry to intrude, ma'am, sir. Mrs. Dunning would like to speak with you, ma'am, if it is quite convenient."

Oh, for the love of God. Agent Talley must have got himself caught where he didn't belong. I was about to be thrown out by my hostess.

CHAPTER 20

At the base of the wooden steps, the butler graciously gestured me ahead, and I waited halfway up while, with dignity, he rolled down his trouser legs and reapplied his socks and shoes. Then I followed his soft steps through the party, which, with the liberal application of liquor, had grown loud and determined in the way parties do when people want others to see what a great time they're having.

We went upstairs, around the gallery and down toward Kitty's suite, the one Bill and I had invaded two days ago. The butler tapped twice softly, opened the door to Kitty's sitting room. The room was lit only by candles and small lamps draped with gossamer cloth. Large, vibrantly colored pillows lay strewn across the floor. An Arabian night come to California. The butler entered and held the door for me. I went in. He went out.

Talley wasn't there. Neither was Peter.

But Mala Demara was. She wore a gown of deep lavender with cathedral sleeves, the tips of which tapered down her graceful hands. I recalled that not long ago, and possibly still in parts of Europe, purple and lavender were associated with mourning.

"Lauren!" Kitty Dunning said and took both my hands in hers. "Oh my God, that necklace! How beautiful! I didn't know you were coming."

"Bill sort of asked me at the last minute."

"That's just like him. Madame spotted you downstairs."

I hadn't seen Madame Karoly, planted in a winged chair,

wearing a velvet dress of deep purple with a heavy, sequined evening coat.

I said to Kitty, "I'm sorry I didn't say hello earlier."

"Oh, never mind that. Sit down, sit down. What can I get you? Champagne?"

"Sure." I wiggled in among the pillows on the sofa.

Kitty poured a glass from the standing bucket by the hearth, handed it over. She said to Madame, "What about this ring?"

Madame examined the gold pyramid with a circle of diamonds at its base on Kitty's right hand, a bit chunky for Kitty's thin hand, but impressive. "Give it to me," Madame said.

Kitty slipped it off and set it in Madame's extended left palm. Madame brought her hand to her chest, and lay her right on it. She closed her eyes. "No," she said finally. "Trouble, much trouble. I would not wear for a party."

"Well," Kitty said, and giggled, "I didn't know Grandma ever got into trouble. Why don't you let Madame check your necklace?"

"I've had it for years, and never had anything bad happen yet while I was wearing it." Except of course the man who gave it to me proved not to be the love of my life. But to please the hostess, who after all was being gracious to someone she didn't invite, I started to unclip the necklace. Madame held up her hand.

"No, only if you wish."

I left it on my neck.

"Does aura change?" I asked her.

"Of people, yes. Sometimes things, depending on the person who has worn it, what has happened to them."

"Well, I have to go," Kitty said, and put the ring back into an ebony jewelry case on the mantle, a case that appeared to have only rows of velvet-covered ring holders, and they were full. "If you need anything, just pull the cord. I'll be back in a bit. Have to go back to my party." She kissed Mala on the cheek and sailed out.

"Do not worry," Mala said as soon as the door closed. "I did not tell her anything of what happened last night. She thinks I only asked to see you to talk about the movie, to take my mind off other things. How are you? What a horrible ordeal it must have been for you."

"And you, since Saturday."

"Monday," Madame corrected. "She did not know poor Mickey was dead until Monday."

"Of course, that's what I meant."

Mala said, "I wanted to tell you how sorry I am about last night."

"Mr. Scarza's to blame for last night," I said. "It's not my business, I know, but are you sure it's wise to be seen at a party? If the police find out, it might be misinterpreted, I mean, this soon after Mickey's death."

"I am not going down to the party. Kitty insisted that I get out of my house. There are a few people here, a few who knew about Mickey and me. She will bring them up later. She is a good friend."

"How did you meet her?"

"At the club, when I was singing. Zorka made me audition. She knew Hollywood people would see me there. Fortunately, they did not care that I cannot sing very well. I met Mickey there."

"I thought you said you met him in England."

Madame said dismissively, "That was not meeting, that was her serving drinks in a bar and pretending to tell fortunes."

"But he was nice to me," Mala said. "I remembered that."

"You told fortunes?"

"Not like Zorka can. But the owner liked me to do it. He told me I was only allowed to tell them good things. I am ashamed, but they would tip me more."

"The gift runs in the family, then," I said.

Madame said, "It is true, we have—we had—a family with such gifts, some more than others. They are all gone now. Two wars in twenty years. We picked first the Kaiser, and who would not? The French think they are still the country of Napoleon, and cry how they are betrayed when they show how incompetent they are. So we lost everything after the first war, when the Austrian and Hungarian empire broke up. Then we chose to fight Hitler, and the family was thrown into prisons and worse. Then we choose democracy, and the communists overran us. There is no one left."

"Please," Mala said, "Lauren has not caused any of our calamity. And America has been good to us."

There was a knock on the door, and Kitty stuck her head in. "Mr. Bishop would like to say hello."

Bishop?

He swept in, as much as a man of his size could sweep. Following was Betty Guinness, wearing an elegant aqua-green gown with elbow-length sleeves.

"My dear," he said and bowed over Mala's extended hand. "I heard this afternoon from Sam Ross that you had returned. I was sorry to learn you were alone when you heard the terrible news about Mr. Triton."

"We're so glad to see you again," Betty said and it didn't quite stick in her throat. I remembered the nasty little crack she'd made in the screening room about Mala's acting talent.

"You are very kind," Mala said. "You know Lauren—may I call you Lauren?—and my cousin."

"Madame Karoly." He bowed over her hand too.

"Mr. Bishop, is so good to see you." The accent was maybe twice as thick as a minute ago. "You are looking—what do you say—masterful this evening."

"Ah, Madame, come to lie to me some more?"

Madame chuckled and smiled without showing her teeth. "I am never lying to you, Mr. Bishop. You must believe in good fortune when it presents itself."

He turned to me. "I received your notes today. I think our script would benefit from the changes you suggested for Miss Demara. Betty will call you. We'll talk Monday."

"Of course." That was it from him for me. We were rewriting assuming Mala would be in the role.

Kitty gestured another couple into the room, warm concern in their eyes.

Madame rose. "If you will excuse me. You will have so much to talk about." She came over to the sofa to retrieve her evening bag from the side table. "Champagne gives me headache," she said to me. "Let us go find whiskey. Mr. Bishop, please to take my chair."

When we were out in the hall, I said, "I didn't know Mr. Bishop was a friend of Mala's."

"He is friend of whoever is friend of Mrs. Dunning."

"He's chasing Kitty?" My voice jumped up an octave.

"He is chasing money. But he does not regard actresses seriously, so he is harmless to Mala. I did not think you wished to be in room with him."

"And I think you wanted to talk to me."

"Do you mind if we go downstairs and sit? I cannot stand in these foul shoes."

The buffet and the orchestra's dance music had pulled the guests to the other end of the house. The resulting privacy in the music room had attracted two couples. When we opened the door, they climbed off the sofas, laughing, gave us cheery little waves, and hurried out the French doors, readjusting their clothes. Madame went directly to the bar and poured us each a stiff whiskey, no ice.

We sat by the fireplace. A fire had been lit against the night-ocean chill.

I recalled what Hawkins had said that afternoon about how, if one looked closely, there were vestiges of good looks. Her face was wide and rather puffy—she was cursed with all her extra weight showing in her face. Under the heavy makeup, the skin was rather rough, perhaps from years of undernourishment followed by recent overindulgence. Still I thought with a bit more skin care, a less matronly arrangement of her hair and the liberal use of hair-removal wax, she could be an attractive woman. She certainly didn't have a starlet's figure, but it wasn't matronly either if you looked past the clothes.

She said, "Mr. Winslow is here. And he is not a man who would come to this sort of party unless there was reason. He is not interested in Mrs. Dunning. And it is not to see you. This he could do privately. Why is he in this house?"

"I don't know the reason for everything Mr. Winslow does."

"I think you know this one. The police came to see us today. They called first. In this country, they call first, if you have money. Mala has a lawyer, and so we all were waiting for them. They asked questions about where Mala was last week. Each day where she was, not just when poor Mickey died. Why would it matter where she was the rest of the week? One of the detectives was from the Los Angeles police, not the county. I saw it on his badge when he showed it to the lawyer. A man was killed at the studio on Thursday night, in a bungalow that belongs to Mr. Bishop. What does this have to do with Mickey, this other man who died?"

"I can't tell you that."

"But you know."

"Yes."

"We are not citizens. If the police say anything against us, they can send us back."

"But you're here legally."

"We have Austrian passports, but what does that mean? We are guests. I trust you, and also Mr. Winslow. But, how do you say it, at the end of the day? At the end of the day, I do not know how much power you, or Kitty Dunning or even the studio would have to help us."

"They want to find who committed these crimes. They're not interested in convicting just anybody."

"Please forgive me, but you have not lived our lives these last years. Do you know Mr. Pace?"

"Mack Pace, the head of Marathon security? Yes."

"You have an enemy there."

"How do you know that?"

"Because this afternoon he asked to be my client. He has heard about me from others at the studio. He asked if my special ability could find out things about you and Mr. Winslow."

"He and Mr. Winslow got into an argument."

"An argument that left Mr. Pace with the face he had this afternoon?"

"Yes."

"I told him no, this is not how I use my gift. But he might look elsewhere, for those who will."

"I'm not afraid of what he'd find."

"If I believed that to be true, I would not have told you this."

"Madame, I've noticed your grammar has improved since we met."

"My English is as good as it needs to be. Mrs. Atwill, there is always something to fear in one's past. Americans want to forget the past. All is the future. A new start. I think this is a very great mistake. You have been good to Mala, and so to me. And tonight when you heard the story of my lost family, I know that it did not even occur to you to wonder how we could have come to such an end. How, with our gifts, we could not see our future and so avoid it."

"I can't imagine anyone being cruel enough to think such a thing."

"Then you have never met a Nazi. It is not as people imagine it, this gift. It is not a gift that lays out the future clearly. What would life be if we knew all that was coming? We would go mad."

The hallway door flew open, and several gleeful partygoers stumbled in, headed for the piano. A young man slid deftly onto the bench and began playing with talent that almost matched his energy. His friends began singing along, with less talent.

"I should go back up," she said and rose. "There is something you fear from your past, something about Mr. Linden and Mr. Winslow. Whatever it is, I think it is not of your own doing."

"You would be wrong, I'm afraid."

"I am not in the habit of telling people only what they want to hear."

Madame said good night and left, nearly knocked aside in the doorway by a second wave of partiers dashing in.

They began to sing Christmas songs. I left my whiskey, went out onto the terrace, watched the moonlight shimmer on the water, and heard a dozen off-key songs as I made a mental Christmas list. Which was better than thinking about what Madame had said.

I couldn't decide what to get Peter. I thought about a new watch, except that if I gave him one that was too expensive, he might feel like a kept man. And if it was not expensive, he might feel like I thought too much about the class gulf between us.

I glanced at the grandfather clock inside: eleven-fifteen. In fifteen minutes I was meeting Peter in the cottage. I'd rather be waiting for him there than here.

A few guests were sitting in the rear garden, a few more strolled the lawn on the second tier in front of Bill's cottage.

They paid no attention to me, so I used the front door, which was, as promised, unlocked. The bar, likewise as promised, was well stocked. I hadn't touched my whiskey and very little of the champagne. A stout gin and tonic seemed just about perfect right now. I got some ice from the tiny compartment in the refrigerator. On the kitchen counter under a damp cloth, Bill had laid out sandwiches and pastries he must have cadged from the main house.

I put a sandwich on a napkin and went back to the living room and lit the fire laid in the grate. Then I sat down, nibbling the sandwich and watching the flames.

This thing I fear from my past, she said. Cripes, I didn't even believe in spiritualists and second sight.

The mantle clock chimed the half hour. As the final chime faded, there was a short rap on the front door and Peter came in.

With Talley.

"The bar's over there," I said, "and food in the kitchen."

"No, thanks," Talley said. "I'm leaving. Mr. Winslow said he'd take you on home. I, uh, I just wanted to say thanks for your help, and that I didn't mean any disrespect earlier. I shouldn't have asked you to go upstairs."

"Thank you, Mr. Talley. Your apology is accepted."

He nodded, and left.

I said, "Did you make him say that?"

"I'm sorry I got you into this. Do you have your things? Come on, I'll take you home."

"No."

"What?"

"I'm not going yet."

"We can't stay here, there are people all over."

"Well, I don't really care."

"How much have you had to drink?"

"Two sips of champagne and half of this gin. You always say you shouldn't get me into things, but then you do. I wonder why that is."

"I think we should go."

"You can't go on treating me like this."

"I said I was sorry."

"Oh, God, Peter, that's not what I meant. Half the time you treat me like someone with a brain and guts, and then you act like I'm some hothouse flower who'd be ruined by any brush with real life. Why do you act like I'm too good for you?"

"Lauren—"

"I won't do it. I won't go on with you thinking I'm some damn princess. And that I'm still in love with Bill Linden. Sit down. For God's sake, sit down. I've decided to tell you this, and it's not easy. So please, just let me do it."

Slowly, he sat down across from me. I tried, but I couldn't look at him. "You know I don't get along with my parents. If you didn't before, you did when you called them from New York. I was dying and they didn't come."

"It's your business, Lauren. You don't have to tell me."

"I do. Let me do it. My father's a successful man, a professor, historian, writer, quite famous in some circles. My mother's the perfect academic wife, beautiful, charming, dedicated to her husband. She was not dedicated to me. I don't say that to blame her. Or my father. There was another child, a son, his name was Marty, named after my father. He died when he was three. I was born six months later. I don't think they were ready for another child in their grief. Some people think you can replace children, but you can't. And I must have seemed like a changeling to them. By all accounts, Marty was a magically sweet child. I was shy, awkward, plain, and as I grew older it was clear I had none of the talents or interests they had.

"My mother was Bennett Lauren's sister. And by the time I

was twelve, my uncle was a very rich man. He was generous with my parents. And that money meant a life of more luxury than even a successful academic could afford. An impressive house, money to travel, to do his research, to entertain important people, to live a satisfying life of an intellectual of means.

"My parents thought my uncle encouraged me too much, encouraged me to have ideas that weren't proper for a young girl who'd have to please a husband someday, especially a girl cursed with being tall and not blessed with beauty. Please don't protest. I'm not overly modest about my looks. I'm an attractive woman, by any but Hollywood standards, but I was not a pretty child.

"I wanted very much to have a career. My parents felt a career for a woman was fine, as long as it could be fit in between the hours of taking care of the husband, the children, the entertaining, the running of the household, and the hiring of the servants. But my uncle never cared about any of that. And they didn't want to discourage his interest in me. He had married young, been divorced, and had no children.

"He sent me to Vassar because I wanted to write, and it would give me a better shot at New York magazines and publishers. My parents wouldn't have spent that kind of money when a California college could provide all the marriageable education I needed. Then when I realized I probably wasn't cut out for magazine writing, he got me a job at Marathon.

"That's where I met Bill. He was good-looking, smart, funny, and talented. He took me under his wing and out to parties. I thought we'd be the perfect match, living an exciting, creative life, in the world I still believed Hollywood was back then. Then one day I introduced him to my uncle.

"In our worldly sophistication back at Vassar, we knew about such things. I might have even suspected my uncle had what in our sophistication we referred to as 'the problem.' But not Bill. I never guessed Bill. I was in love with him.

"For five years, they were together, discreetly of course. Only five years. Then Uncle Bennett was diagnosed with cancer, untreatable, virulent, he was dead in six months. And for those six months, Bill never left him, to hell with discretion. He nursed him, cared for him, would go God knows where in the middle of the night and buy morphine from criminals because the doctors wouldn't give my uncle enough.

"My parents came to visit, but it was too unsettling for them, and they hated Bill. The obituaries said family had been with him at the end, but it was only me and Bill. And then just Bill, sitting vigil that long night with the body, in grief I had no power to ease.

"I was left a small fortune. My parents were left a trust fund to support them the rest of their lives. The remainder of my uncle's personal fortune had gone to charities. To Bill, he'd made substantial gifts of money, stock and some pieces from his art collection when he found out he was sick. But nothing in his will. Nothing public.

"The day the will was probated, I got a call from my mother. Bill had taken advantage of a vulnerable older man, she said. She and my father would never have been left with so little had Bill not exercised undue influence. He had taken their inheritance from them, the money they'd come to expect, had planned for. She was Bennett's sister. It wasn't right.

"And so I went to Bill and here in this room, I told him I'd give him some of the money I'd been left, and he could give back what my uncle had given him. I told him he didn't want his private life or my uncle's made public, not outside of Hollywood. Why didn't he just give it back, and everything would be all right? I sat here and told him to give back all the things my uncle wanted him to have. And he got up, walked to the door and asked me to leave.

"After Bill threw me out, I called my father. He said not to worry, he had a lawyer. I needed to make a deposition. So I did. I answered all the lawyer's questions, telling him as much as I knew about their private lives and about my uncle's circumspect life before he met Bill, about his generous treatment of me, the expectations he'd raised in my parents about my future and theirs, and that before Bill came into my uncle's life, there had been no rift between them and my uncle. The stenographer took it all down, even the things the lawyer told me he'd learned about Bill, about affairs and night clubs for men and the things that went on there. He had seduced my uncle, he said, it had to be undue influence. What my uncle had given Bill was worth more than he had given me, his own niece. He said I'd been a big help toward getting my parents their inheritance back. Bill Linden would be sorry he ever tried to steal from Bennett Lauren's family. So, I betrayed a friend and I betrayed the man who'd been the dearest person in my life. Maybe you should think about that before you decide I'm too good for you."

I got up and hurried away, into the kitchen and used one of the kitchen towels to dry my eyes. The living room was silent.

"Use this," Peter said then, standing in the door.

I took his handkerchief. "The damn things we women carry around aren't much good in a crisis."

"They're only for delicate flowers."

"Don't you dare make fun of me."

"I'm not. It was a rotten thing to do, you're right. You sold off a friend and you sold off your uncle to get your parents to like you. And maybe because you were still mad at Linden for not falling in love with you. Come on back, have a seat."

He made me a fresh gin and tonic, and brought in the plate of sandwiches. He'd poured the drink with a light hand. No sense tempting me to get even more maudlin.

He said, "Eat something." He handed me a couple of
sandwiches on a napkin. I did as I was told. Then he said, "And
maybe you haven't told me about any of this before because
you were afraid what I'd say. About your uncle. About Linden."

I answered yes by crying a little more.

He sat down. "You're not expecting me to confess every rotten thing I've ever done, are you?"

"No, not even one."

"We'd be here a while."

"I wouldn't mind that part, I mean being here." I wiped the
new tears away with his handkerchief.

"You've had a hell of a week," he said.

"I won't argue, for once in my life."

I finished the second sandwich, and Peter got up and turned
on the radio. The station had gone off the air; it was past
midnight. He dialed around until he found a station, probably
out of Mexico, with an orchestra playing.

He held out his hand, then pulled me into his arms. I laid my
head on his shoulder. He pressed his cheek against my hair.

He said, "So tell me the rest. Linden is speaking to you, and
your parents aren't."

"I went back to sign the statement. It was right there in front
of me, everything I'd said, shaped just the way the lawyer
wanted it. He handed me the pen. I just sat there, with it hanging over the page. Finally I said, 'I can't sign it.' The lawyer
said, 'I know he was a friend.' I said, 'I'm not refusing to sign it
because he's a friend. I can't sign it because it's not the truth.'
He wasn't happy, but he said it didn't matter. They could still
call me as a witness, bring in the stenographer's notes. If I
didn't sign, it was much more likely my uncle's life would end
up in court.

"I went home and called the president of my uncle's company
and told him what my parents were planning. Someone called

my father—I don't know who—and pointed out that even to threaten such a lawsuit could start gossip, such gossip would injure the company and its ability to continue its generous contributions to the university at which my father taught, and the endowments for research he had enjoyed. My father knew who'd called the company. He dropped the suit. I gave them some of my money. They never acknowledged it. We haven't spoken since."

"So stubbornness runs in your family."

"I come by mine honestly, as you see. Did you learn anything out there tonight prowling around with Talley?"

He laughed. "Once you get your teeth into something, you don't let go, do you?"

"Not often."

"Well, if whoever planned that robbery was a party guest, he needed a place where he could see the briefcase as it was leaving, see what car it was put into, and be close to a phone to call the robbers. The way the property slopes to the water, you can't see the back gate from the house, not from anywhere that's close to a phone. You'd have to be in the chauffeur's rooms over the garage. Or upstairs in this house."

"Bill isn't involved in this."

"I didn't say he was, but he was living here then, and he doesn't lock his doors."

"It could have been the chauffeur."

"Yes. It could have been anyone who'd been out here often enough to know the layout. The Dunnings did a lot of entertaining. Nothing we saw gave us any ideas who it might be." He lifted his cheek from my hair. "Did you go into the study?"

"What?" I raised my head. He was staring beyond me into Bill's office. "I came in the front door."

"Did you touch anything in there?"

"No."

"Somebody's been in the house."

CHAPTER 21

"Get in the kitchen."

I backed into the room, and placed my hand on the knife block. Peter, without any sort of weapon, edged into the study, then upstairs. But no one was hiding in the house.

I was relieved, then furious. "You and Talley searched Bill's house?"

"Calm down. Talley was going to take a look whether I was with him or not. I thought it was a good idea to watch him while he did it. That drawer wasn't shut all the way, now it is. That box, the one with the desk lamp on it, that's been moved. When did you get here?"

"Eleven-twenty maybe."

"We left just before eleven."

"Maybe it was a thief."

"Thieves are after cash or jewelry, and they start with the bedrooms if they know what they're doing. Linden's still got a couple of hundred upstairs in his cufflink box sitting right on top of the dresser."

He moved around the study, examining—without touching—the desk, the shelves, the closed drapes over the French doors, which hung from rods above the lintels. "They left through the patio door. The drapes have been moved."

"You do this a lot, do you, breaking and entering?"

"The first thing you look for is another way out in case you need it, and you figure out if you can use it without leaving a trace. Anybody you can give an alibi to?"

"No." I told him what I'd done between the time he left me in the music room and I'd arrived at the cottage. I was alone after eleven o'clock."

"I have to call Bitterston."

Bitterston had put Talley up for the night at a hotel only a mile away, so Talley got back in twenty minutes. He'd been shaving before bed when he got the call. A strip along his jaw was smooth and clean.

Talley looked around and in all the places he'd searched before, downstairs and up. He was even more precise than Peter. I wondered if the Feds' training included classes in secretly searching people's homes.

He said, "Whoever it was, they didn't have much time. For all they knew, Linden could come back any minute. So what they went for might give us a clue. They searched at least a couple of the drawers upstairs and all of the drawers down here. They also searched that wooden box under the lamp and the leather box in the bookshelf. They went into the file cabinet. The top drawers are all scripts. The bottom ones are personal files, bank records, taxes, legal correspondence. It looks like they spent most of their time in here."

I said, "You have to tell Bill. He could be in danger."

"We don't know this is connected to McCann's killing," Talley said.

"The hell we don't."

Peter stepped between us. "Agent Talley answers to Bitterston, so it's not up to him. And Bitterston has to look at all the possibilities. One is that Linden might have had some part in all this, the stickup and the killings. The other is that, even if he's innocent, if you tell him, he could say something to the wrong person. Can we trust Linden to keep his mouth shut? Call Bitterston," he said to Talley.

"Look," said Talley, "you don't give the orders."

"You're right," Peter said.

"Okay, then." Talley picked up the phone.

After he filled Bitterston in, Talley handed me the phone. Bitterston pointed out that Bill lived in a neighborhood with a guarded gate, and on an estate with plenty of servants around. The intruder had taken advantage of the party. The place was otherwise very difficult to get into.

I agreed to wait forty-eight hours. Nevertheless, I wished Bill would start locking his doors.

Peter drove me home, but he didn't stay the night. He wanted me to sleep. So I got to stare at the ceiling for an hour with nothing to show for it. Finally, though, given what I'd been through the last week, my body overpowered my brain.

I slept till noon, awakened by the phone. It wasn't Bitterston. It was Peter, telling me he was leaving town.

His boss was sending him to San Francisco. The agency had been hired to make sure a reluctant witness made it down to Los Angeles to testify in a lawsuit.

The Feds had taken Peter into their confidence, but not onto their payroll. He couldn't tell his boss, and he couldn't refuse a job.

He wasn't working for the studio anymore: Mala Demara had reappeared.

He said he'd only be gone for a few days.

"There's something I'd like you to do," he said. "Take a look at copies of the bank-account records I got for Bitterston yesterday."

"How did you get bank records on a Saturday?"

"That's the best time. Saturdays, at every bank, an assistant manager has to be there. They have to work half days while their bosses are out on the golf course. After the tellers go home, there's nobody to ask them why they're letting somebody take pictures of bank records. Look, I need to get moving; it's a long drive. I'll send a copy of the file over. See if anything gives you an idea."

"What do I do if I don't hear from Bitterston about whether he's going to tell Bill?"

"I'll be back Wednesday night. I'll come by your house, about ten. Can you sit on it till then? You notice I'm not telling you what to do."

"Thanks. The one time I wish you would."

Lou Brandesi, a rock-hard, hound-faced man, one of Peter's regulars, brought over the copies of the bank records and an appetite that always lifted Juanita's spirits. While Lou ate lunch in the kitchen, I took a tray into my study and went through the file.

Except for Mala and her cousin, Madame Karoly, the records went back to 1939, when the stickup and murders had occurred after the Dunnings' charity auction. Even though neither woman had been in the country back then, Bitterston had still asked for their records, perhaps to see if he could connect the marked bills that had appeared two weeks ago in Marathon Studios' bank deposits to either woman through money passed from Mickey Triton.

Mala Demara: She was frugal with her newly acquired money, her living expenses reasonable for a movie star. Of course, she might have debts that wouldn't show up here. Her salary was maybe half what she was worth.

Madame Karoly: She was doing well off the spiritualist business. Not nearly as well as her cousin off movies, but well enough. And this was only the money she chose to deposit. I'd seen Kitty slip her cash for the séance, so who knew how much she made that she'd never pay taxes on. However, she was wise enough to show the government a public record of a good income.

Mickey Triton: His account had fluctuated wildly. Before the war, he was flush, a boxing champ, then a gym owner. Then for a couple of years, very little coming in—the years he'd been in the army, I assumed. Now he appeared to be making a nice living off his gym and his fighters and whatever he was doing for Julie Scarza. It was impossible to tell, of course, the true nature of his finances from a bank account, but he had plenty of cash.

Alastair Bishop: From his paycheck deposits—and quickly calculating what his having to pay 50–70% in income tax over those years would mean—it appeared that he had started at Marathon making about six thousand a week under his contract, and his weekly salary had climbed to ten thousand. But his balance was as thin as Depression soup. He spent everything he made. Of course, he could have healthy investments somewhere, but if he did, he wasn't drawing on them to fatten the bank account. He had three overdrafts in the last four months.

Betty Guinness: For a secretary of a top director, she was not paid particularly well. Judging by the regular deposits of one hundred fifty dollars, that was her current weekly salary. The only additional income over the last seven years had been monthly cash deposits—now amounting to a thousand—which seemed to coincide with withdrawals from Bishop's account.

Kitty Dunning: She had plenty. And she spent plenty. It was hard to imagine how anyone could have that much money to go through with tax rates over 80% for her, but she did. The deposits at the first of every month, which I assumed were from her investments and trust funds, had grown smaller over the last seven years with the war-time tax increases. Her spending had grown larger.

Charlie Dunning: Kitty's brother-in-law was busted. He had a small account that never strayed above three thousand. When it dropped below five hundred, there'd be a deposit, and for a while, smaller withdrawals. But as soon as he was flush, he'd nearly drain the account. Still, he'd been busted for all seven years, and the marked money had only turned up in the last few months.

Sam Ross: Now I knew how he and Helen afforded the houses, the cars, her two-week shopping trips to New York. He made a lot of money at Marathon. And had for many years. But his expenses were sizeable. And I didn't see any indication that they were saving much for the day he didn't work in Hollywood anymore.

Bill Linden: He had about five thousand in his checking account, an amount kept constant by regular deposits that must have been his paychecks. And from time to time, he would slide money over from a tidy savings account. He was certainly not living within his Marathon income.

CHAPTER 22

Monday morning, as I entered the lobby of the Tate, the writers' building, the guard gave me a warning jerk of his head. A man in a light-brown suit sat in one of the armchairs behind a newspaper. The newspaper came down, revealing heavy brows, stormy jowls and hard blue eyes.

"Sergeant Barty," I said, "how are you?"

He folded the newspaper methodically, set it in the magazine rack beside the chair, and removed the matchstick he'd been chewing on. He stood up. "Can we talk?"

"Of course."

"I mean if I ask you some questions, is there any chance you'll tell me the truth?"

"Why don't you come upstairs?"

One of the elevators slid open and a maid rolled out the coffee wagon, on her way back to the studio commissary after her coffee-break rounds. I bought a cup from her and managed not to spill too much into the saucer as the elevator shuddered its way to my floor. The operator pulled back the gate and we got out.

Barty closed my office door and hooked his hat on the rack. I sat down behind my desk and wiped my saucer with the paper napkin the maid had given me, knowing as she did the vagaries of the Tate's elevators.

He took one of the visitors' chairs. I sipped.

"Where's Pete?" he asked.

"In San Francisco on business."

"What business?"

"Nothing to do with your case."

"I don't like coincidence, especially when I find Pete Winslow hanging around in it. You might have heard, Mickey Triton got himself bumped off out in the county last week. Three days later I get a case out at Marathon, a Major McCann gets himself shot in a bungalow used by the director and the writer of Mala Demara's new picture. And then I find out Miss Demara and Triton were seeing each other on the real quiet."

I said nothing.

"I called up the county boys, and it turns out they didn't know he was playing around with her. They don't like co-incidence either, so they let me go with them when they talked to her on Saturday, so we could ask about where she was when Major McCann died, not just Triton."

"Ah," I said. "I saw her cousin at a party Saturday night. She told me about it. She noticed on your badge that you were from the LA police."

"She also tell you why Miss Demara's got a lawyer?"

"It's a murder and she's a foreigner."

"This morning I got a call from the county boys. They found another bullet. It looks like Triton was shot again after he hit the floor. Bullet went straight through him, through the floorboard and into the ground underneath the cabin, so this bullet didn't melt, didn't get mashed by the bone like the other one. A thirty-two, from a Webley. Same caliber, same make as what killed Major McCann. That probably doesn't surprise you much."

"You need to talk to Agent Bitterston."

"He's going to tell me he's chasing Nazis."

"He doesn't know about the second bullet. Without that, he wasn't sure there was a connection between the killings."

"But you were."

"I can have all kinds of opinions. I don't have to prove anything in court."

I set down my cup and told him, briefly, about my kidnapping Friday night, about the threats from Julie Scarza, about finding Mala. Everything up to and including Peter smacking Mack Pace around for letting Scarza's men get to me. "We met Agent Bitterston over at Madison's. He told us some things about what he's really up to, what McCann was up to. Tell him about that bullet. He wants to find Major McCann's killer very badly."

"Just not bad enough to trust the cops."

"I understand Julie Scarza might have a few of them on his payroll. The FBI doesn't want everything getting back to him."

"What's McCann's killing got to do with Scarza?"

"It's about something that happened a long time ago."

"Maybe I should go talk to Mr. Pace. He neglected to mention that Scarza's boys are getting free passes in and out of here at night, maybe the night McCann died."

"Please talk to Agent Bitterston before you do anything else."

"If he won't level with me, I'm coming back to see you, and I expect to hear the whole story."

"I understand."

He retrieved his hat and strode out, leaving the door open. The elevator groaned its way up, then down.

I swiveled my chair and stared out at the side of the soundstage across the street. I didn't have a number for Peter in San Francisco. The best I could do would be to leave a message at his office that he wouldn't pick up until tonight.

With the discovery of the second bullet, it was now certain the same person who killed Triton had killed McCann. Was it also the person who'd directed the theft of that money seven years ago and caused the deaths of so many others? The day I recognized McCann—the man sent onto the lot to investigate that case—he dies. Unlike Sergeant Barty, I believed in coincidence, but I didn't believe in this one.

If all the crimes were indeed committed by the same person, did that eliminate any suspects?

Kitty Dunning and Charlie Dunning were the most obvious ones to have been involved in the theft. They were in the best position to know that the auction cash was in that briefcase. And would know the best places in the house to watch for it leaving. They both had Hollywood friends, but had either one been on the Marathon lot when McCann died?

Madame Karoly had been on the lot, in an appointment with Alastair Bishop. But she hadn't been in this country seven years ago.

Mala Demara had no alibi for either Triton or McCann's killing, and might well have been able to figure out how to sneak onto the lot Thursday night. But like Madame, she had not been in the country when the money was taken.

Alastair Bishop had been a guest at the auction seven years ago and had been on the lot Thursday. According to bank records, he liked to spend everything he made. Perhaps he had hidden the stolen cash somewhere safe, for retirement, but was drawing on it now because he was tapped out and was chasing Kitty Dunning.

Betty Guinness. Could she have been so enthralled with Bishop all those years ago she'd allow herself to be talked into participating in the robbery? Given her ability to organize, she might have even planned it. Perhaps it was guilt and not affection that held them together.

And then there was Bill. He'd probably been on the lot Thursday. He'd told me out in Malibu that he was going to his office that afternoon to work for a while. He'd been at the auction. His cottage was a perfect place to have watched for the money to leave. And he hadn't been rich seven years ago.

I found Bill alone in his office, lounging on his sofa.

I said, "I was wondering if you could give me that list of words Hawkins said Mala has trouble pronouncing. Bishop's asked me to start with changes to the script assuming she'll be shooting it."

"Hawkins was mostly kidding. But Mala's not too good with a 'w.' Don't string too many of those together. Vindow vashers vatch vomen."

He uncurled himself. "I got some things for you." He opened the top drawer of his file cabinet, and pulled out a stack of scripts and a manila envelope.

He tossed the scripts on his desk. "When I started working on this one, I dug these up from the writers on her first two pictures. I used them to see what sort of syntax works best for her. And they'll give you an idea of what they had to change for the Hays Office. The censors treat foreign actresses differently than Americans."

"And you paid no attention to that."

He chuckled. "They always take something out. You know that. It's their job. So I put in some stuff I don't mind losing. The envelope's got some letters in it, the letters she wrote me after her first screen test, the one I saw in London. Would you take a look? I read over them yesterday. Mickey Triton's name is in one of them. See what you think. See if I should give them to her, or if it would just make her sadder."

He threw himself back on the sofa. I pushed the scripts back and sat down on the edge of his desk. "Is Bishop chasing Kitty Dunning? He came up to visit Mala in Kitty's suite Saturday night, and he's no great friend of Mala's."

"He's taken Kitty out a few times, but I thought it was because she wanted to go places she couldn't take her latest younger-man mistake. Of course, she might have held back on me. She knows I loathe him."

"He came to the party with Betty. Would he take her out in public to the house of a woman he's trying to sleep with?"

"I think we have Alastair Bishop in a nutshell."

"Has Kitty ever visited him on the lot, do you know?"

"I avoid him when I don't have to work with him. I've seen her around the lot before. She likes to hang out with actresses."

"How about Charlie?"

"Once in a while. I told you he makes some money teaching actors how to be British, does some dialect coaching. Why? Has this got something to do with McCann?"

"I don't know. Oh, I meant to tell you. When I was in your cottage Saturday night, I noticed one of the desk drawers was open. I hope none of the guests wandered in and stole anything."

"There's nothing in the study worth stealing, not even a new idea. I won't ask you if you and Mr. Winslow enjoyed your evening. It's not a good sign if you were looking at my drawers, so to speak."

"I told him the truth. Everything."

"Did you now? Well, well. You don't look like there were serious repercussions."

"No. You were right, as usual. You're a philosopher."

"I'm a hack. But I know enough about secrets to know what they can make you do trying to keep them. Worse than the secret most of the time. Dear God, what if it's true about Kitty and Bishop? Could you imagine, Alastair Bishop living next door to me? There'd be a murder done for sure. What's wrong? Did I say something?"

I got up and shut the door.

"Talley, the man I was with Saturday night, wasn't a beard for Peter. He's an FBI agent. He was there to look around Kitty's house, the grounds. I can't tell you why. But he searched your cottage. I had no idea he was going to do it. Neither did

Peter. But Peter stayed with him, to keep an eye on him. Peter noticed some things, like that drawer being open. Then when he came back later, to be with me, the drawer was closed. Somebody else had been in the house."

He sat up. "Good Christ."

"You can't tell anybody about this. Anybody, no matter how much you trust them. We have no idea who did it."

"What the hell is going on?"

"Someone searched your house, and someone searched your bungalow."

"It wasn't my bungalow."

"You were the last person to use it."

"I don't have the slightest damned idea what they could have been looking for. I didn't move my life into it. What the hell were the Feds doing looking around Kitty's house? Do they think she's got something to do with Major McCann's killing?"

"No," I lied. "You can't tell her, you can't tell anybody. Whoever searched your cottage doesn't know the Feds know about it. It's a clue, not much of one, I admit. Can you look around your study, your house, see if anything's missing, anything at all?"

"You've seen my study. The crown jewels could be in there, I couldn't find them. How would I know if anything's missing?"

"The intruder searched the desk drawers, the leather box on your shelf, the carved wooden box under the desk lamp, and the files in the bottom drawer of the cabinet. What's in those?"

"Nothing. Old papers, notebooks, bankbooks, stuff I throw in there. This is crazy."

"I'd rather you not be out there alone at night. We could get one of Peter's men to stay with you."

"Like a babysitter?"

I heard my office phone ringing and dashed down to grab it.

"Where are you?" Betty Guinness demanded.

Since she'd called me, I figured she already knew the answer to that.

"You had a meeting with Mr. Bishop at ten," she said.

I said pleasantly, "Saturday night he said you would call me and set a time. He must have forgotten to tell you. I'll come right over."

"You are late," Bishop announced, "and so you have missed most of what Mr. Pace had to say."

Mack Pace sat on the sofa, his legs crossed, looking at me like, if it were up to him, I'd be late for everything forever. The marks Peter had left on him were fading.

Sam Ross sat in the other armchair. Morty Engler, from publicity, had the other end of the sofa. Gallantly, he stood up and despite my protest gave me his seat. I sat down next to Pace.

Morty pulled a hard chair over from the dining table.

"Betty, bring more tea and get her a cup," Bishop commanded. She picked up the teapot from the tray and went out. She looked grim and unhappy, dark shadows beneath her eyes. I didn't think it was because I was late. "Mr. Pace was just telling us he has learned that the police have no reason to suspect Miss Demara in Mr. Triton's death, but that he has been quite unable to learn anything from the FBI about the killing of poor Major McCann."

Pace said, "I said we're working on that. These men are from Washington. Our contacts are the local agents, and Bitterston's men aren't telling them much. Maybe you can help," he said to me. His mouth twisted like he'd tasted something nasty. "One of the detectives investigating the major's killing came back on the lot this morning. He went straight over to see you. Then he left. What did he want?"

I said, "He knows Mala and Mickey Triton were having an affair."

"Where did he get that?"

"I have no idea. But as Mr. Bishop can attest, there were several people at Kitty Sharp's party Saturday dropping by upstairs to tell Mala how sorry they were. Apparently, their affair wasn't that big a secret."

"What did he want from you?"

"He's going to question everyone again. He started with me, because I found the body. He believes there could be a connection between the murders. He'd be a fool to rule that out. He's going to get answers. He won't give up. This isn't something that can be swept under the carpet."

Pace said, "Nobody's trying to sweep this anywhere."

"I hope not. The studio could be ruined."

"We don't need you to lecture us on how to handle this."

Sam said, "Everybody calm down. Mack, you, me, Morty all need to go have a talk. I'll call you later, Alastair."

Betty stepped aside for them, then brought in the fresh pot of tea and my cup.

Bishop said, "Did you hear, Betty? It would appear we now need alibis for two murders. I admit I cannot provide one for either night. However, if these murders were committed by the same person, then Mala can no longer be a suspect. She was not on the lot Thursday night."

I said, "There's no guarantee someone didn't sneak in."

"What, climbed the wall?" Bishop said.

"I'm only saying the police won't eliminate anyone easily."

"You seem very friendly with them," Betty said archly.

"I am. Anything you'd like to get off your chest?"

"What?"

"Quiet, Betty," Bishop said. "Lauren makes friends quickly. You saw her with Mala Saturday night. We thought they hadn't even met, and there she is in a room with Mala's closest friends. However, she's made no friend of Mr. Pace. I wonder why." He stood and said to me, "Perhaps you will decide to tell me what you did to him. But we must get to work now. I have seen your report on the script revisions. Acting is a bag of tricks, most of it. You give it too much credit, you and Mr. Linden both. He thinks he is some sort of expert on the subject. But at least you understand the bag of tricks. We will begin shooting tomorrow. We will begin shooting Miss Demara's scenes in a week. Betty, make a note to remind the makeup people that Miss Demara will need a bit of wax before we shoot. She has grown a considerable amount of hair on her temple since the last time I saw her. And remind me to suggest once again she consider electrolysis.

"Bring your cup," he said to me. "Let's go into my office and get to work. We have received the changes that will be required by the Hays Office. They were not pleased with that scene Mr. Linden put in the bedroom."

"I didn't think they would be."

"And do you have a solution?"

"We could play it in the living room, but with the bedroom door open, just the corner of the bed visible, with a soft key light on the coverlet."

"Excellent. Come along. You can watch us and see if you believe we have secrets. Betty, be careful what you say to her."

CHAPTER 23

Bitterston phoned that evening to say he'd leveled with Sergeant Barty about what McCann had really been up to, at least to the extent that I wouldn't have to worry about another visit from the Los Angeles police. He also asked me to continue to keep it a secret from Bill that somebody had searched his cottage during Kitty's party. I let him think he convinced me. I didn't think it was a good idea to tell him I'd already told Bill.

He didn't bother to ask if I'd seen copies of the bank-account records. He assumed I had. He wanted to know if I'd had any ideas. I said no. I didn't say that revising a script was taking up all my time, being as it was, after all, my job, and I wasn't, after all, a detective.

I was feeling grumpy. And not without reason, I assured myself.

These were people who had created a phony charity and secretly funneled money they raised into Europe to buy military intelligence. And they couldn't among them figure out how to get one private detective on their payroll and out of San Francisco and back to Los Angeles.

On Tuesday Bishop began rehearsing and shooting, but scenes that did not include Mala and wouldn't require revision. I sat in my canvas chair through the morning and contributed nothing, so I pulled out the packet of Mala's letters Bill had given me.

There were only five, over a span of eight months, the first from London in August of 1939, the others from Linz, Austria.

I set them in my lap and slipped the onion-skin pages of the first letter from its envelope. The creases were a bit powdery with age.

It thanked Bill for his letter of encouragement after her screen test. Mala was polite, even a bit stilted. Perhaps it was her English. Perhaps she thought Bill was trying to sleep with her. I was struck that she didn't attempt to elicit any further assistance from him. Most ambitious young women who'd been noticed by a man from Hollywood would have. Mostly, she talked about acting.

I also continue to study. I study Mr. Stanislavski, and my teachers make us work very hard to be, as you say, natural. I was very glad that you saw this in me. I would tell my teachers, but they do not encourage us to go for film auditions. They do not like films. They say the ideas are cheap. I do not tell them how much I love films, especially American films. This will be my secret.

I have received the letter from Marathon Studios and Mr. Lucas, and it has promised me another screen test if I can make my English better and improve some parts of my appearance. I am keeping safe this letter. I believe you have had a hand in this, and I am more grateful than I can express.

This felt too much like prying. I scanned the rest. I was after all only looking for Mickey Triton's name. Bill wanted my opinion on whether he should give the letters to Mala, whether they would make her feel worse or better.

I tucked that letter back into its envelope and opened the next. After war was declared, in September, Mala had been sent back to Austria, her passport revoked along with those of thousands of other Austrians, and Germans and Italians. She was living with an aunt and uncle, as her parents were dead.

Nevertheless, she remained optimistic.

We do not think anyone wishes to go to war, not after what we suf-

fered only so few years ago.

But then there hadn't been much fighting yet. Germany wouldn't invade Belgium until May of 1940.

Part of her optimism seemed to come from having been reunited with her cousin Zorka. There was a small photo of the two of them, smiling, squinting a bit into the sunshine, their arms linked. Madame was as thin as Mala back then, and smiled with her teeth showing.

My cousin Zorka's English is better than mine and she teaches me. I know the words, but I do not have her gift for hearing how to say the words. And so I must work harder. It is not popular to take English lessons now, and I could not afford them anyway. I have found acting lessons, although they do not teach Mr. Stanislavski. With Zorka here, I am bolder and believe that we can come to America one day. Zorka says that we shall save our money and go to America and we will both be gold diggers. She tells me this is a joke. I hope she is correct.

The third letter was mostly about what she was learning in acting class, and her regret that American films had disappeared from theaters. Zorka had decided to attend some classes as well, although she did not have Mala's zeal for it. Mala was distressed to hear rumors that anyone without Austrian or German passports would be asked to leave Austria. She and Zorka had Austrian passports, but most of the rest of her family had Hungarian ones.

I opened the fourth.

Thank you very much for your kind offer to help me when I am in America. I have shown your letter to Zorka, and we have wept a little together. I only say this to show you how happy we are. Please I hope it does not embarrass you. With your help and the letter from the studio about my screen test, I feel we will not have to be gold diggers. I was glad to hear this was a joke, and made you laugh.

We are already saving money for this trip. Zorka and I are now telling fortunes, as I did in London. Our family has many people who possess this gift. People here are very superstitious and want to have their fortunes told, and the government has made all the gypsies leave. I am glad to report that so far they have not asked any of our family to go back to Hungary. But I am no longer as hopeful as they that we can avoid a war.

I found Mickey Triton toward the end of the final letter.

Zorka has told me to ask if you know a man named Mickey Triton. I told her I met him in London at the bar where I worked. He is a champion of boxing, and they even know who he is here in Linz. I told her he said when I come to America I should look him up. I think that is what you say. Look him up. But he is famous and I do not think he could have meant it. Zorka says perhaps he did. I think this is forward of us. But if you know him, would you please give him my kind regards.

The letter was dated April 20, 1940. On May 10, Germany invaded Belgium, and the war had truly begun.

After that, letters would have been difficult to send from both Austria and the U.S.

I sat there and thought for a while about how her life had changed in the intervening years. So much tragedy, the family she talked about wiped out except for her cousin. I tucked the letters back into my handbag. I thought she would want to see her family talked about again, even if they were all gone now. She'd enjoy seeing Madame Zorka's suggestion they would be gold diggers in America. And she'd want to see how shy she was about Mickey Triton.

I'd keep them with me and give them to her the first time I saw her.

At lunch I went to get my gun cleaned and checked. I didn't call the Paxton Agency to send a man to escort me, despite my promise to Peter not to leave the lot without an escort. I didn't want anyone to tell Peter I was now carrying a gun.

Cobby Knox was a cowboy, not only in the movies but also in life. He'd wrangled cattle from the time he was twelve, first on ranches in New Mexico when it was still a territory, then in Wyoming. He came out to Los Angeles in the early days of films, lured as so many cowboys had been, by the possibility of making good money as their ranges began to disappear. He rode, roped, and gave lessons to actors in both.

He avoided the fate of men like Wyatt Earp, who came to turn their stories into gold and ended up destitute. Cobby was young enough to make money, and smart enough to save it, and bought himself a business selling guns, rifles, saddles and other riding gear. In the Depression, he'd added a pawn shop in the store next door.

I had always taken my gun to Cobby for cleaning and inspection, although never as often as I should. From time to time, although not recently, he'd also given me shooting lessons, starting when I was in high school. My uncle was a collector of both handguns and rifles, which was why I knew something about them, and Cobby had maintained his guns. My parents had even approved of the lessons. Skeet shooting, as long as I never got good enough to beat a rich man at it, was something a lady could learn to do.

I never told them about the handgun practice.

Since I'd last been there, Cobby had added a new neon sign, complete with cowboy hat, and repainted the entire storefront. The windows gleamed and the saddles on display in them shone.

The bell above the door announced my entrance. It was a loud bell. A man with guns on the premises would want to know when someone walked in.

At the front, Cobby sold boots: cowboy, riding and hunting boots; the walls were lined floor to ceiling with shelves of the boxes. Short rows of wooden chairs stood on either side for customers, and salesmen's stools with ramps in front on which the customer's foot was placed to be measured and fitted.

Beyond were rows of saddles, Western in the front, English further back. The store smelled of heavily waxed old wood, oil and leather.

I told the clerk I was looking for Cobby, and he pointed me through the wide arch that led into the gun shop—where there was no shop door to the sidewalk. Horizontal racks of rifles and shotguns hung along both long walls, with shelves of ammunition beneath. Behind the long glass display case of handguns stood Cobby Knox.

Contrary to movie-fed images, cowboys generally aren't tall in the saddle. Or on the ground. Nor are they a beefy breed. They're generally small, quick, and light on a horse's back. Cobby's face was spectacularly creased by the sun and framed by a sturdy supply of white hair. Age and the dryness of his skin gave his flesh a hard patina. He offered his large-knuckled hand and I dared to shake it, risking my tarsal bones.

I complimented him on his new sign and the paint job. He grunted. "Have to do it, don't want to look like the old buzzard I am. So what can I do for you today?"

I handed over my gun.

He slipped it from the chamois bag, deftly popped out the cylinder and double-checked the gun was empty. "Nothing in here but dust. You haven't been practicing."

"Not in a while."

"Shouldn't take long, you want to wait. Or you can go on, do your errands."

"I don't mind waiting."

From the shelves behind the display counter, he pulled out a wooden box containing gun oil, clean white cloths and new brushes with stiff felt bristles. He hitched himself on a stool and started to work.

I said, "I need to ask you something. If I gave you a list of people, could you tell me if any of them bought a Webley from you, a thirty-two?"

He took the question in stride. He poured a bit of oil into a shallow glass dish, dipped the brush tip and smoothed it into the barrel. "This Webley, what did it do?"

"Something bad."

"Cops were here last Friday, asked me about a thirty-two Webley. Would that be the same gun?"

"Yes, probably so."

"Course, they had a warrant." He dipped again and moved the brush in and out of the barrel. "I sold quite a few Webleys before the war, but they're English guns, so I didn't have many the last few years. I couldn't tell them everybody I ever sold one to, but I had some sales slips going back before the war, six years or so. Hetty says I'm a pack rat."

"Do you remember if you ever sold a Webley to any of these people?"

I laid a list on the counter. He glanced at it. Then he went back to working, cleaning the cylinder.

"The police had a list too. A lot more names than that."

Sergeant Barty no doubt had included everybody who might have been on the Marathon lot the night McCann was killed.

"Were any of these on their list, do you recall?"

"Yep, all of them. But I didn't sell a Webley to any of them. In fact, nobody on their list either, not what I found in my records." He began to clean the cylinder.

"Can you tell me if any of them bought any sort of gun recently?"

His sharp eyes examined me. "One of the cops asked me that too, big fellow."

"Lots of eyebrows? Sergeant Barty."

"I didn't ask them why."

"If the person they're looking for used the Webley, he'd get rid of it and might want to replace it."

"I had to say no. None of them on that list of yours. A couple of folks on their list bought guns, but nothing recent. Men got their army pistols and all now from the war. Not going to sell that many guns if the army's giving them away. Why you want this cleaned now? If you need some protection, I can fix you up with somebody."

"Thanks, I'm fine."

"Well, you probably know enough not to shoot a toe off pulling it out of your purse, but you ought to get some practice. There's plenty of places out in the canyons, glad to take you."

"I'll let you know."

"Need ammunitions for this?"

"Yes, thanks."

"Load it?"

"If you would."

He got down a box of cartridges from a shelf behind him, then dabbed oil lightly over the gun and began rubbing it gently with the cloth.

I said, "My uncle. He left his guns to friends and other collectors."

"Left a few to me."

"Did he own a thirty-two Webley?"

"It's not a gun to collect, but I couldn't say for sure if he ever owned one. It's been a while."

"Well, thank you."

"Not sure it's much to thank me for, 'cause you're still thinking somebody you know's a killer."

CHAPTER 24

I remained on the set through the afternoon, in case Bishop needed a quick adjustment of dialogue or it became apparent we'd need changes down the road and I could take notes.

By the time we wrapped up the day, and I pulled myself out of my canvas chair, it was past five and dark outside.

The temperature had dropped ten degrees since lunch, the first chill of approaching winter we'd had. Of course a first chill in Los Angeles meant you just needed a light coat. I'd left mine in my office and headed over to the Tate Building to pick it up and call Peter's agency to send out the man who would follow me home.

Workers had begun to leave their offices, flowing toward the parking lots. Some carried packages, Christmas shopping done during their lunch hours.

The night guard in the Tate lobby nodded, then tucked his chin back over his comic book. The PBX operator had already gone home, her board dark. If any calls came in now, the guard would put them through. The elevator operator hauled his protesting machine to the fifth floor, while reminding me that he left at six o'clock and I'd have to call the guard if I wanted to leave after that, unless I wanted to take the stairs.

Marathon appeared to be saving money on light bulbs. The overhead fixtures hadn't been turned on yet. The only light was cast from the glow of desk lamps through the pebbled glass of a few office doors. Typewriters clattered behind those doors as well. But Bill's door was closed, his office dark.

I opened my unlocked door and fumbled for the light switch.

Something moved in the dark to my left, a shape suddenly rising toward me. I slapped at the wall, found the switch, and raised my handbag like a club, completely forgetting I had a gun in it that might have been of more use.

"Atwill," Hawkins said genially, sitting up on my sofa and stretching. "Sorry to scare you. Didn't know you'd be around. Hope you don't mind."

"Not at all." I set the handbag down on the desk, reminding myself it was time to take the gun out of its chamois bag, if I intended to go armed.

Hawkins wore her customary slacks and vest today. The crisp shirt beneath sported a flowing ascot clasped with a carved white brooch.

She said, "That ferret Mickels was snooping around, making sure everybody's still hard at work till six the week before Christmas. I can't think with him lurking in my doorway." She lay back down with a sigh. "Atwill, I believe the assembly line will be the death of creativity. These middle-class sons of industrial managers are convinced that if a man isn't moving, he isn't working."

"Would you like a drink?"

"Hell, yes. What have you got?"

"Nothing, but there's whiskey in Bill's desk."

"So there is. But he's gone and the door is locked. He told Mickels to his face he had to get home before dark, said he promised someone he would. It might even be true. I hope so. I mean, there's someone."

"Yes." We looked at each other, both of us who loved him. "Let's go get drunk."

"The door's locked."

"There are ways around that."

I dropped my handbag into the desk drawer, but not before digging past the gun to pull out my lock picks. Hawkins was suitably impressed by my skills.

It felt wonderfully wicked, drinking someone else's booze, uninvited, in someone else's office. We relocked Bill's door, turned off the light, left only the glow of the moonlight through the windows. Hawkins lounged on the sofa; I threw myself back in Bill's desk chair, kicked off my shoes, and planted my feet on his desk.

Through the first round, I told her how my first day on the set with Bishop had gone. She offered her opinion that he'd be docile enough with me, since he couldn't try to steal writing credit from someone who wasn't getting writing credit.

Through the next round, she told me about the movie she was working on, and her constant struggles with Mickels. "He can't imagine anyone coming up with a new idea while flat on their back. Doesn't bode well for Mrs. Mickels."

We drained our glasses and I poured some more. Bill kept very good whiskey.

I said, "What shall we toast? Not the modern world, feeling as you do about the middle-class sons of industrial managers."

"As a matter of fact, I have very little against the modern world," she protested. "Can't abide these women who sigh about the good old days. As if the good old days were anything like what they see in the movies. Mind you I write those movies, so I must accept a share of the blame. But good God, do they really want to go back to whalebone and waiting for your parents to tell you who to marry?"

"To the modern world, then."

We raised our glasses and drank some more.

I said, "That's a lovely brooch, by the way. Does the modern world say 'brooch' anymore?" After two large glasses of whiskey, I was having trouble saying the word at all.

"Thanks. It was my grandmother's. It's ivory. Sort of old-fashioned today, but I'm an old-fashioned girl."

"Everyone says so."

She laughed, a half dozen hearty barks. "How's the investigation going, that body you found?"

"I don't know. The police don't talk to me."

"Drink up, Atwill. In whiskey, veritas."

I was fairly easy to persuade in my condition. "Well, if I had to guess, I'd say the police don't have many leads; otherwise they'd have pulled someone in for more questioning by now. Whoever shot Major McCann will have got rid of the gun if they have half a brain." Of course, the killer hadn't got rid of the Webley after shooting Mickey Triton with it. Surely they would now though, after a second killing. Toss it in some garbage can, or drop it off a pier. I gestured with my glass. "So. Their suspects are limited to absolutely anyone on the lot that night or anyone who could have sneaked onto the lot that night."

"We know that dead guy had something to do with the Feds. I'd hate to think he was in that bungalow looking for something on Linden. Things are so crazy these days."

"What in Bill's past could the Feds possibly be looking for?"

"Linden has expressed an unpopular political opinion or two in his time. I think he used to hang around with the commie crowd, back when he was writing books. But then haven't we all? I mean, haven't we all done things we might regret now? None of us has a golden past. More guilt than gilt. God, that was awful."

"Yes, it was."

"And would only work on the printed page."

"And not very well at that."

"Mickels may be right about the pernsh—pernich—pernicious influence of drink. Too bad, as I hate to think he might be right about—shh!"

Footsteps thumped our way. Knuckles rapped on the glass of a door down the hall. The door opened. "Hawkins?"

The door closed again. The footsteps continued our way, and he knuckled our door, tried the knob. We didn't move. He retreated, then there was rapping on another door—the one to my office, I thought. It opened, closed. Then after a few moments, the elevator arrived and shuddered its way down.

She said, "I'm surprised he didn't go search the ladies' room. Well, my stuff's still in my office, so he knows I haven't gone home. I'd better go brush the whiskey off my breath before he comes back. I have to finish some notes anyway. Thanks for Linden's whiskey."

"Any time." I got up, opened the door, peered out in case Mickels had not taken the elevator after all. I saw no one. Hawkins slipped past me, saluted, and walked in a more-or-less-straight line into her office and shut the door.

I sat back down to finish my whiskey. Then I remembered I had to drive home. I'd spent such a long time being driven around by others, I'd forgotten my Lincoln was waiting for me.

What the hell. When I was ready to go, if I wasn't capable of driving, I'd let the man from Peter's agency drive me home, drive me back in the morning. Pick up the car then. What the hell.

I sat there in the moonlight and gazed out at the scattering of stars above the soundstage across the street. I hadn't lied to Hawkins too much. I really didn't know what the police were up to. But I was fairly certain that unless they and the Feds got very lucky they'd never find the killer. Washington wasn't going to give Bitterston permission to take Elizondo into his confidence and put someone in that casino to look for the marked money being spent out there and the person who spent it. They were never going to risk the mob finding out they'd marked the money they'd paid Scarza, or rather the money they were supposed to pay Scarza before it got stolen.

The Feds had their own secrets to keep.

Like Hawkins said, no one has a golden past.

More guilt than gilt.

Someone indicted for stealing gold would be gilty as charged.

I'd had far too much to drink.

I set down my glass, and suddenly, there it was again, the thought that had been niggling around at the back of my mind since Friday. Something that had been stuck there, in my unconscious.

I doubted I could focus my mind any better tonight, drunk, but I gave it a shot.

It had been the morning after I'd found Major McCann dead. I'd gone into my study after breakfast, after reading the story about Mickey Triton's body having been identified. I was gathering my talismans, everything I needed to help me settle into an unfamiliar office. Then I had dug out my lock picks so I could lock and unlock desk drawers that were missing keys. Then I'd opened my safe and moved the jewelry boxes out of the way, found my gun. Checked the gun, planned to get it cleaned, then I'd put my jewelry boxes back in place, closed the safe. Looked at my new painting, at how the lighting didn't do it justice and planned to take care of that.

I was thinking it needed light. More precisely, the right kind of light. Too much light would betray the artist's intention as much as too little.

Too little would make the golden pentimento even more difficult to see. Too much would render the gold more prominent, or more attractive than the artist had intended.

Both would be lies.

Lies about the meaning of the past.

A lie about the past.

A golden lie.

That was it. I sat straight up. A golden lie.

And very possibly a guilty one.

I jumped up, staggering, catching myself on the desk. What time was it? What time? Ten till six. Ten till six. I had time. Maybe.

I dumped the whiskey bottle into the bottom drawer, ran to the ladies' room and rinsed out our glasses, shook them, then dropped them in with the bottle, still wet. I whipped the lock pick from my pocket, relocked Bill's door, dashed to my office, unlocked the desk, grabbed my handbag, kicked the drawer shut, snatched my coat from the rack, yanked the door shut and dashed to the elevator. I rang. Waited. Nothing. I rang again. The operator couldn't have left yet. Where was the door to the stairs?

Then I heard the elevator groan to life.

I barely let the operator get the gate open before I dashed out, across the lobby and into the street, taking a few precious seconds to remind my whiskey-soaked brain which way to go. Left? Left.

It was only a half a block away, convenient for writers. The place was supposed to close at six, but what if they left early the week before Christmas?

I hit the swinging doors to the studio's reference department at five till six.

"We're closing," the woman behind the counter announced primly. "If you have a request, fill this out, we'll call you in the morning."

"I'm working on a script for Alastair Bishop," I said, gulping air.

"We'll call you in the morning."

"One thing, just one thing, please. I need to find out when someone died."

"We can do that tomorrow. We have reference books for the

deaths of famous people; we can also—"

"I don't know the name."

"Then how do you expect us to find the date?"

I grabbed a pencil from her cup and wrote out the title on the slip of paper she'd thrust at me. "I think that's it. Do you have that book?"

"I think you mean Burke's, not Burt's."

"Did I write Burt's? Sorry. Yes, that's it. Do you have it?"

"Of course."

"Please. Please, I need two minutes."

The next morning as soon as the local FBI office opened, I was standing in front of the reception desk.

The woman behind the desk asked me to please have a seat, and she'd see if she could find the Agent Bitterston I had asked for. I handed her the folded sheet of paper I'd taken out before I left my car: I didn't want to risk anyone catching a glimpse of the gun in my handbag.

"Tell him it's Lauren Atwill," I said, "and show him this."

She took the paper from me in the way she must have taken every piece of paper handed her by every kook and crackpot in Southern California. She laid it on the desk. I took a seat while she relayed my name to the switchboard operator, who plucked a cord from the base of her board and plugged it into someone's extension. She whispered into her headset. Eventually through the doorway behind the receptionist appeared the cleanest-cut young man I'd ever seen short of a movie screen. She handed him the note, and he disappeared back through the door. All I caught was a glimpse of a linoleum hallway.

Within sixty seconds the door flew open and Bitterston stood there, his eyes furious. "Get in here."

He kept one short, angry step behind me until we were inside his temporary office. Then he slammed the door.

"Where did you get that?" He marched around his desk, snatched up my now-unfolded sketch and thrust it out at me. "Where did you get this?"

"I drew it, from memory. Why didn't you tell us this was how you paid off Scarza?"

"What are you talking about? I told you. Friday night, at that bar, I told you there were other things in that briefcase besides money."

"Things that Scarza bid on, you didn't say what."

"What the hell did you think I meant, the *Mona Lisa?*"

"I thought you meant art, yes, small pieces of art, not that. Is that one of them? One of the things?"

"Where did you see it?"

"A week ago. The day Major McCann died."

"Where, for God's sake?"

"In the hands of Kitty Dunning."

He was suddenly rock-still, then slowly he let out his breath. "Sit down."

I did. He did. I told him my story.

I described the day Bill and I interrupted Kitty's session with Madame Karoly, and how Kitty had asked Madame to check the "aura" of a bracelet she wanted to wear. A gold cuff bracelet of art-deco design with raised stars charged with diamonds.

Bitterston flipped open a manila folder on his desk. He pulled out a black-and-white photo from a small stack. I assumed these were pictures culled from the photos they'd taken of all the jewelry they'd sold off in their fund-raising mission. This folder contained the pieces that had gone into that briefcase and disappeared.

"Is that it?" he asked and handed it to me. "Be sure. There could be plenty of other bracelets like that around."

"Not belonging to a woman who was dead before it was made. Kitty said the bracelet belonged to her husband's grandmother. It's not the sort of thing you'd expect to see on the arm of an old woman from the stuffy British aristocracy, but I had no reason to doubt her at the time, not consciously anyway." I told him briefly—and without including that I'd been drunk—how I'd realized last night what had been bothering me.

"Her late husband, Tommy Dunning, was an earl. Last night, I looked up his family in *Burke's Peerage* in the reference department over at the studio. They keep books like that, in case we need to look up character names to make sure we're not slandering a real nobleman in a script. Both of Tommy Dunning's grandmothers died before 1920. The bracelet's art deco. It's highly unlikely it was made while they were still alive."

"You're sure it's the same bracelet."

"As sure as I can be." I handed back the photo. "There was a ring, too. I saw it at the Christmas party when she asked Madame to check it. Pyramid-shaped, with diamonds at the base."

He pulled another picture out and slid it to me.

"It could be. I didn't get as good a look. She put it away in a ring box, full of rings."

"Would you recognize that box?"

"Probably. It was ebony, with gold piping, red velvet inside."

"What did she do with the bracelet?"

"She took it into her bedroom. I don't know where she put it."

"Did you see any other jewelry that looked like these?" He spread photos of five other pieces on the desktop. I hadn't seen any of them at Kitty's. He sat back, closed his eyes briefly, long years of questions answered.

I said, "The day I saw the bracelet, she slipped some bills into Madame Karoly's hand, to pay for the séance. It explains how those marked twenties ended up in a deposit from

Marathon a few weeks ago. Madame visits clients at the studio. She spent them there, or got the cashier to break them."

"Maybe after all these years, Mrs. Dunning doesn't feel so guilty," he said. "And she's got that character Madame Karoly to reassure her there aren't any ghosts of murdered people around to haunt her if she starts spending the money and wearing the jewelry."

"Mickey Triton must have found out somehow," I said. "Maybe something Kitty said to Madame Karoly, and it somehow got to him and tipped him off where Julie Scarza's money has been all this time. Talk to Alastair Bishop again. He's been chasing Kitty. She might have dropped by to see him the day McCann was killed. I left her house about three. She had plenty of time to get into town."

"We'll see if his memory improves when he finds out she's a killer. I'm getting the head of the local office in here, and Agents Larkin and Talley. You and I are going over all this again. And again. Then we get a stenographer. We'll need your statement to get a search warrant. When we go out there to her place, you'll have to come along. We don't know what that ring box looks like and we could end up with the wrong box and no ring. We need to find as many of those pieces as we can."

Bitterston laid his forearms on his desk. "I know it was hard on you, not telling your friend Linden that somebody searched his place, but this is why I couldn't let you tell him. It turns out it's a friend of his. What if you'd told him and he let something slip to her? She might have hidden all the evidence, destroyed it."

I nodded, my face hot, sick at my stomach. There was no use confessing I'd told Bill. I could only hope he'd kept his promise not to mention it. To anyone.

Chapter 25

I called Bishop's bungalow and told Betty I was laid up, maybe with the flu. I'd let her know if I'd be well enough to come in tomorrow. Next, I called Juanita and told her to lie and say I was in bed asleep if anyone called.

Then I spent a couple of hours making my statement.

The head of the local office knew a judge who'd be more impressed by the Feds than by Kitty's family money, and Bitterston got his warrant. By two o'clock I was in the backseat of the Studebaker, in a caravan of sedans and Los Angeles Police Department patrol cars. The theft had occurred in Malibu, but jurisdiction didn't matter much with the Feds in charge.

At the colony entrance, Bitterston showed ID to the guard, and left one of his men there to keep the guard away from the telephone. The broad gate at the rear of Kitty's estate was wide open, so the agents and officers streamed through, past the astonished chauffeur, who was washing the Packard. Two officers secured the garages; another one locked the gate.

Because Bill's cottage belonged to Kitty, it could be searched without another warrant. Agents Larkin and Talley headed in that direction with a couple of local agents and a locksmith.

Within a minute of passing through the back gate, Bitterston was ringing the mansion's doorbell.

The butler pronounced himself unfamiliar with search warrants, and expressed his opinion that we should come back when Mrs. Dunning was at home. Bitterston spent five more seconds explaining that the butler's opinion didn't matter much before he led us into the house.

Agents and officers peeled off quickly to gather the servants and keep them in one place.

"They have work to do," the butler protested.

"As do we, sir."

"This is not Germany!"

"Which is why we have a warrant. I have a copy if you'd like to read it." Bitterston headed for the main stairs, the butler struggling to remain dignified while scrambling after him. Sergeant Barty and I followed, trailed by a half dozen men.

In Kitty's sitting room, we found her maid, tidying up. The butler ordered her to check Mrs. Dunning's appointment book, discover where her mistress had gone and find her immediately. And to call Mrs. Dunning's lawyer.

The effort was unnecessary. Before the woman picked up the phone, Kitty arrived from the hairdresser's, freshly coiffed and furious.

"What the hell is going on?"

Bitterston held out his identification and told her who he was. He offered the warrant. She snapped it from his hand.

"You will not touch anything till my lawyer gets here and reads this thing. You will wait outside my house."

"You're welcome to watch if you like, ma'am. He can too when he gets here, but we're going to carry on."

"What the hell are you looking for?"

"Stolen property."

Then she saw me. "What is she doing here? Is she claiming I stole something?"

"No, ma'am."

"Is it about Charlie?" she asked me. "Do you think he took something? He's harmless, really he is. We don't need to do this. We can work it out."

"Nobody's stolen from me," I said.

One of the men stuck his head in from the bedroom. "Sir."

"Who is that?" she demanded. "Are there men in my bedroom?"

Bitterston, Sergeant Barty and I followed the man, with Kitty stalking alongside, through the bedroom into the dressing room. Closets lined three walls; a row of dressers, the other. One of the closets stood open, revealing shelves of jewelry boxes and a small standing safe. "Would you open that please, ma'am?" Bitterston said.

"I will not. That's private. Not till my lawyer gets here."

"Then we'll start with the boxes. Ma'am, you'll have to stand out of the way."

"I'm watching everything you do."

The agent pulled out the first jewelry box, handed it to Bitterston, who set it on one of the dressers and opened it. After all these years, he had the stolen pieces memorized: he didn't need pictures. Nothing in the first box resembled them. He continued. The fourth box was carved teak, the size of a thick book. Inside lay the gold cuff bracelet.

"Ma'am, is this yours?"

"Of course it is."

"We'll need some proof of that."

"How am I supposed to get proof? It belonged to my husband's family."

"Did he tell you that?"

"My husband is dead; he was killed in the war."

"Did he tell you this bracelet belonged to his family?"

"How am I supposed to remember who told me?"

"I believe you told Mrs. Atwill it belonged to his grandmother. You specifically said his grandmother the day you asked Madame Karoly to check its aura."

"What does it matter?"

"You've been seeing Madame Karoly for some time. Why were you only now asking her to check the aura if this bracelet had been in the family for years?"

"That's a stupid question, and none of your business. I'm waiting for my lawyer."

The agent handed Bitterston another box, a shallow ring box, ebony with gold piping. He glanced at me, and I nodded, before he opened it. The box was full of jeweled rings, in three rows. In the top row, a golden pyramid with a base of diamonds. "And this?" Bitterston asked, pointing to it.

"Why do you think these were stolen?" she demanded, but now her voice was shaking and it wasn't in anger.

"Because they were."

The agents pulled out the other boxes and they found all the pieces that had disappeared the night of the auction. Kitty grew paler with each discovery and gradually fell silent, pressed against the doorframe, her arms locked across her chest.

"Ma'am," Bitterston said, "I'm going to ask you again to open the safe. If you make us drill it open, it won't look any better for you."

She stood there, shoved against the door. Bitterston signaled a man inside, and within five minutes he'd drilled the safe open. Inside was a black valise, like an oversized doctor's bag. Bitterston hauled it up onto the dresser. It was locked.

He turned to Kitty. Her lips had gone white.

"Ma'am, do you have the key?"

"I'm not talking to you. Stay away from me."

"I'll do it," I said. I pulled out my picks and took care of it.

There was money. A lot of money. Used bills, stacks of them, mostly in hundreds, held together with simple rubber bands.

"My husband died in the war," Kitty said. "He was a hero. He died for his country. He was forty years old. He didn't have to enlist. But he went back after . . ."

"After what, ma'am?" Bitterston asked.

Kitty pitched forward. Sergeant Barty could move fast for a big man. He caught her before she hit the floor.

Barty carried her into another bedroom. He'd had the presence of mind to bring along a policewoman, who stayed, along with the maid, and watched Kitty. When revived, she refused to talk, waiting for her doctor and her lawyer.

The search continued. Now, they were looking for the .32 Webley that killed McCann and Mickey Triton.

Bitterston had to get the grounds searched before dark. There would be nobody to take me home for a couple of hours. I sat out on the terrace for half that. Bill did not come home. I decided to take a walk.

In one of the downstairs bathrooms, I removed my stockings. My gun was still in its chamois bag, so I took it out and used the bag to protect the nylons.

I told the agent in the foyer where I was going, and he checked with Bitterston, who had no objections.

I left my shoes on the terrace and picked my way barefoot down the weathered sea steps to the beach.

The horizon was a soft pink ribbon as the sun began to set. I stood for a while, watching the winter evening, my feet in warm sand, then walked along the foaming edge of the ocean, past the silent mansions, the only movement in them the rhythm of lights being turned on. Nobody in those houses had any idea the life of one of their neighbors had just been ruined. And nobody knew the woman down there on the beach had caused it.

Finally, the air and sand began to chill. I turned and went back.

I found Charlie Dunning sitting on the sea steps with a glass in his hand. Something on the rocks.

"Oh, hello," he said, managing a disarming smile though he

was clearly surprised to see me. "Bill ring you up? I'm afraid they won't let you through. FBI all over the place. Have a seat," he said and scooted over for me. "Did you walk all the way up from the sea road? You are a determined girl."

"Have you seen Bill? Is he here?"

"He's putting his house back in order. He gave me a drink." Charlie lifted the glass. "Did he tell you they broke his lock?"

"But they had a locksmith."

"Not a very good one, it seems. They won't tell me what they want. I thought the FBI chased bank robbers and chaps too fond of Russia. They can't think Kitty's a spy." He set his glass down and pulled out a handkerchief. He wiped his hands. His fingertips were soiled in black ink. "I can't wash this off. Did Bill tell you they got fingerprints from all of us?"

"No."

"They said they had to know whether the prints in the house belonged to people who lived here, or strangers, that it would mean something. I didn't quite understand what." He picked up his drink again. "I could nip over and get you a bit of something, while you wait, tell Bill you've arrived."

"I'm fine, thank you."

He kept looking at me, with his bright friendly eyes, a frown gradually forming between them. "What are you doing here?" he said finally.

"I'm sorry?"

"Dear girl, I just realized. Bill hasn't been home a half hour, and he didn't know anything was wrong till he got here. He might have rung you, but you wouldn't have had time to drive out from town."

"I came here with them, with the FBI."

"Why? Why on earth? What are they doing here?"

"I really can't talk about it. It's got something to do with stolen property. Nothing stolen from me."

"I don't think the FBI raids the homes of people like Kitty just because she might have accidentally bought something that was stolen."

"No."

"They think she stole something herself? What?"

"Some jewelry."

"They think she's buying jewelry from thieves? Why would they think she'd do that?"

"There were some things they found. They might be the ones that were stolen."

"Then they'd knock on her front door and ask her. They wouldn't ransack her house and dig up the damn flowerpots."

"I can't talk about this, Charlie. I'm sorry. I just can't."

"Kitty wouldn't steal. What are they doing here?" He flung his drink down and began rubbing his hands hard. "Damn," he said miserably, "this is never going to come off."

I turned and stared out over the water, a sinking sickness in my stomach.

"My brother was a war hero," he said. "He died at Dunkirk, you know. This town is full of Englishmen who wouldn't fight. But he went. He did his duty. I stayed dry on an escort ship."

"Please, Charlie, don't say anything else." Carefully, I picked up my handbag, pulled it into my lap. Felt the gun inside against my hip. I tried to stand, but my legs were like water.

"What do they think she stole?"

"There's a bracelet, a ring."

"They can't tarnish his name. They can't blame her."

"Charlie."

"They took our fingerprints."

"There will be prints, other than hers. Where they shouldn't be. On the inside of the bag."

"The bag."

"A valise. A black valise. There will be fingerprints."

231

"She found it."

"Yes."

"It shouldn't have been in Tommy's things. I shouldn't have done that."

"Charlie."

"All these years."

For another minute, we were silent. He continued to smooth the handkerchief over his soiled hands. "Well," he said finally, "I suppose I should go have a talk with someone."

"The agent in charge is named Bitterston. You should talk to Kitty's lawyer, Charlie."

"You don't think Tommy could have known, do you? He couldn't have known what I did."

"No. I'm sure he didn't know."

CHAPTER 26

I spent the next day in bed. One can only run on nerves for so long. I didn't call Bishop. I assumed Kitty would have told him by now that I had not been laid up with the flu, but instead had been busy ruining lives.

No one phoned all day. I longed for Peter, but he wasn't due home till tomorrow night. He wouldn't call before that. He was busy, and the story probably wouldn't even make the papers by then. The FBI would keep it quiet as long as they could. There was no sense leaving a message for him with his agency. I couldn't leave any details.

In the evening, I got a call from Bitterston instead. He drove out to Pasadena and spent two hours on the sofa in my study, drinking Scotch and filling me in.

Charlie confessed. He swore Kitty had nothing to do with any of it. He admitted hiring those two men to stick up the car and steal what he thought was just the auction money. One of them, Ned Gorse, had sold him cocaine from time to time, sometimes a bit of heroin. Charlie owed him money. He knew his brother and Kitty were planning to cash the auction guests' checks, and he knew about the man upstairs with the briefcase, the man he thought worked for the charity.

No one was supposed to get hurt. It was a stickup. The occupants of the car were supposed to be from a charity, and they weren't going to cause trouble.

When Charlie saw the people with the briefcase leave the

auction party, he'd called Gorse, who was waiting in the lobby of one of the hotels across the highway from the Malibu Colony. Gorse and his henchman followed the car, passed it. At the first red light they came to, they got out, guns drawn. It had all gone horribly wrong.

Early the next morning, Charlie heard the story on the radio about the dead people in the car. He went to Gorse's house, where they were to meet to split the money, and found him bleeding to death on the sofa, homemade bandages of sheets soaked through.

He said Charlie had to find a doctor, one who wouldn't talk, and get him out of town. It was Scarza's men in that car, he said. Charlie knew the man was not going to make it, and in any event, he didn't know any doctors who wouldn't report gunshot wounds. And if they did, he would be implicated, of course. Gorse had hidden the case, but Charlie found it. Opened it. Transferred all the money into a valise he had brought with him, and left. Left Gorse to die.

Charlie had put the money in the attic, locked inside a trunk, beneath stacks of abandoned clothes. He and Tommy had gone off to war, and only Charlie had come back. He couldn't stand to think about the money, touch it. He left it where it was. Kitty, going through some of Tommy's old things, must have found it.

Even with Charlie's confession, the Feds were going to have to explain his crime in court, or at least in court documents. So they'd come up with a story. A federal agent, working under-cover, had been transporting known mobsters from a charity auction at which they had been guests and had purchased some items of jewelry. Also in the possession of these mobsters was a large amount of cash, assumed to be from illegal activities. Both the jewelry and the cash had been stolen in a deadly robbery that had left the agent dead. The cash was recently discovered in the possession of Charles Dunning.

It wouldn't hold up to the scrutiny of a trial. But since he had confessed, he could plead guilty and they wouldn't have to talk overmuch about the shady details.

But they wouldn't get justice for their colleague, Major McCann.

The FBI hadn't found the .32 Webley, nor any other evidence that Charlie Dunning had killed McCann and Triton. And no evidence that he—or Kitty—was involved in the burning of Triton's cabin. None of Charlie's or Kitty's clothes had shown any trace of gasoline or other flammable liquids. The Feds still hadn't found anyone who could place either of them on the Marathon lot the day McCann died.

Bitterston still needed answers. He still needed ideas. But my brain had no more ideas left in it.

There was a message waiting for me the next morning at the lobby desk of the Tate Building. There was no need for me to come to the set. I should work on the script revisions and send them over to Bishop.

I locked up my handbag and went down to see Bill.

His door was closed. I knocked. "It's Lauren."

He called me inside.

"How is she?" I asked as I shut the door behind me.

"Heartbroken." He leaned back in his chair. "Sit down. I don't blame you."

"She does. And I think she told Bishop. I've been told not to bother coming to the set."

"She keeps calling Charlie's lawyer, telling him Charlie doesn't have to lie for her—she didn't do anything. She thought the money was probably something Tommy had been hiding from the tax authorities in England. She didn't do anything, and neither did Tommy as it turned out, so Charlie doesn't have to be so damned noble."

"I'm so sorry."

"They say he hired those men to steal charity money, and they got the wrong car. It was a mob car with mob money in it."

"Yes, I've heard that."

"I can't believe he'd try to steal money from a charity."

"They found his prints on the money in that bag."

"But he's lived in that house off and on for years. He could have come across that bag in the attic where Kitty found it. He could have opened it, put it back, decided not to ask questions."

"He hired those men. It doesn't matter why. He hired them and they killed people, including a woman and a federal agent."

There was a sharp tap on the door and immediately Mickels stuck his head in.

Bill jumped up. "Get the hell out of here! If you set one foot in this room, I'll kill you, I swear to God!"

Mickels leaped back. Bill slammed the door.

I waited.

Finally, he let out a long breath, leaned back against the wall, crossed his arms. The lines around his eyes were very deep.

I said, "I'm sure they thought it would be a walk in the park. Stick up some charity people who wouldn't put up a fuss—nobody would get hurt. But of course, they weren't charity people. After the killings, Charlie couldn't bring himself to spend the money, but he couldn't quite bring himself to get rid of it either."

"Why did he search my house?"

"He must have discovered the valise he'd hidden was gone. Kitty hadn't said anything to him about finding money, and none of the servants had quit abruptly to retire. You pretty much had the run of the place, so it might very well have been you. He needed to look for anything that indicated you'd made large cash deposits to your bank accounts. That file cabinet in your study had your bank records in it."

"But he could have searched my house anytime. Why the party?"

"You got thrown off the picture. You were home a lot more. And it's possible he did search it more than once, kept at it, hoping something would turn up, maybe a stack of bills wrapped in rubber bands. He searched the places he could get to. Your home, your bungalow. He couldn't search this office, because of the guard downstairs. He ran into Major McCann and panicked."

"What about Kitty? What will they do to her?"

"I don't know. The police will have to look at it for a while."

"She says she's been trying to contact Tommy through Madame Karoly to see if he would tell her anything about it."

"If only she'd told Charlie, McCann would still be alive. She must feel awful now, knowing that."

"She feels awful because she's in love with Charlie."

"I'm so sorry."

"I don't blame you," Bill said.

"I think you're trying not to. Can I drop by later?"

"Maybe tomorrow. Not at the house. You can't come visit me at home, you know."

"No." Not unless Kitty invited me, which seemed highly unlikely to ever happen. "Are you getting any sleep?"

"Not much. Kitty's had me up at the house half the night. But Mala and Madame are coming over today to stay through the weekend. I can get some sleep, clean up the mess the police left."

"I hear they broke your lock."

"The whole front door. I need to get it fixed, but there doesn't seem to be any need to lock anything now."

"Bill—"

"I'll get over this," he said.

I touched him lightly on the arm and left. He closed the door.

I'd said nothing to Bill about the murder of Mickey Triton. I'd already surmised that Kitty was trying to reach her late husband through Madame to ask about the valise. And that Madame must have innocently said something to Mala. And Mala to Mickey. And Mickey Triton had somehow figured out who stole Scarza's money. And Charlie shot him for it.

I didn't want to talk about it with Bill. I couldn't burden him with that, because if I did, he might start thinking what I was. What I had been thinking since Bitterston left my house last night.

The government didn't want to talk publicly about what they'd been up to all those years ago, paying off a mobster. Now, with Charlie's confession, they could stay out of court and they could get justice for McCann. All they had to do was tell Julie Scarza that Charlie Dunning killed Mickey. He wouldn't last a week in jail.

My phone was ringing as I reached my office door.

A woman from Peter's office wanted to know what time I'd be leaving. One of the men would be in the neighborhood in the late afternoon, and could simply swing by to escort me home. I said six. She said fine, he'd wait in the lobby.

I wasn't particularly looking forward to an evening at home with my thoughts.

I was grateful for something to do this afternoon that would distract me. I pulled out the censor's notes and looked over them.

The Hays Office had ordered the word "lousy" be removed, along with a couple of other bits of slang the censors considered crude. I often wondered if the censors yanked from movies whatever slang their high schoolers happened to have brought home, terrified America's children would want to hang out with jazz musicians.

I had to rework the embassy party. The censor was adamant that Mala's character not be seen near alcohol. She was a foreigner, and in the script a married woman, they pointed out, and she was tempted by the hero. The morality of this woman was already in dispute. The censors were willing to compromise as long as we removed all other signs of temptation and loose ways. I suppose we were lucky they hadn't demanded she be a widow, which would require we rewrite the entire script.

Generally, it was enough to agree that a "nice" woman wouldn't hold a drink in a film. Permission for a nice woman to actually hold a drink was pretty rare. She could sit at a table— almost never at a bar—with a drink in front of her. She might be allowed to stand near a bar, as long as there was a suitable man with her. A "bad" girl could sit at a bar, but, even then, she rarely held the drink.

Women were almost never allowed to actually put a glass containing alcohol to their lips.

Large portions of the country were "dry," and the censors were very sensitive to how those customers felt about alcohol. Sometimes this resulted in party scenes in which absolutely no one was allowed even to hold a glass. Waiters would pass through with drinks on trays, but no one ever took one.

All the guests seemed perfectly happy to just stand around and talk, empty-handed. In my experience, most people couldn't get through a party unless they were stiff.

Well, I wasn't about to write one of those scenes. I'd have to refigure the embassy party into something that would allow for a bit more reality.

Next up, the censor objected to the investigator hero's clandestine search of the heroine's flat. They would permit the opening of a closet door as long as he touched nothing. Under no circumstances could he open the drawers of her dresser, as he would naturally be looking at her undergarments, even if the audience never saw them.

Cripes. What sort of hero—no matter that he'd fallen for the heroine—would conduct a serious search by just glancing into a closet? No investigator I knew.

All right, we'd start the scene with his closing the closet door, as if the search of that room were complete, maybe have him first reposition a hatbox on a shelf with precision. Surely they'd allow him to touch her hatbox. Then he'd go into the sitting room and search her desk. There, beneath a packet of letters, he'd find a handkerchief, a small, feminine, lace handkerchief. I was sure the actor and Alastair Bishop could find something to do with it that would look smitten, but not smutty.

Take that, censor.

I worked on that scene and made a valiant stab at reworking the embassy party through the afternoon. The sun went down, and offices began to empty. Men lifted their fingers from their typewriters, pushed back their chairs, grabbed coats and hats, and shut their doors, calling out hearty good-byes to colleagues who, through perseverance or fear of their bosses, were still at their desks.

My phone rang, the guard calling to say my escort home had arrived, a bit early. He'd wait in the lobby.

I said I was ready to go. It would do me good to take a break and put fresh eyes on the revisions at home after dinner. And Peter would come home tonight. I needed to talk to him badly about my fears the FBI was going to let Scarza avenge McCann for them by telling him Charlie had killed Mickey Triton.

I folded the half dozen script pages into my handbag, which was getting to be rather full. I shared the elevator with men shrugging on their coats, lighting their end-of-day cigarettes, talking about holiday plans, heading to their houses, their wives, their children, to the precious pressures of domestic life.

The guard said my escort was outside, getting some air, having a smoke. I shoved open the door, stepped onto the sidewalk, looked around. Someone moved to my right.

Eddie, Julie Scarza's meaty thug who'd punched and kidnapped me, slipped from the shadows and planted himself in front of the door.

CHAPTER 27

He showed me his hands. "Nobody's going to get hurt. Look around, there's a lot of people. I'm just here to deliver an invitation."

"I'm not going anywhere with you."

I didn't see any sense in pulling out my gun. It was buried under script pages. Besides, he'd have a sixth sense for guns, certainly for when somebody was reaching for one. By the time I fumbled it out of my handbag, he'd have taken it away from me.

And, as he said, there were plenty of people around. And a guard thirty feet away.

"I'm not going anywhere with you."

"Mr. Scarza's across the street, in the restaurant across the street. Lots of people over there too. He'd like to talk to you."

"If he wants to talk, he can come over here."

"He's asking you for a favor. And if you give him this favor, he would owe you one. He would owe Mr. Winslow one. Maybe Mr. Winslow's the kind of guy who could use a favor from Mr. Scarza someday."

I went with him.

"I'm going to have to take the handbag," Eddie said as we crossed the street." He looked inside, put my gun in his pocket and returned the purse. "You'll get it back."

Scarza had a booth in the back room at Madison's, in the far, dark corner, but there were plenty of people in there, jovially ordering a round of after-work cocktails before they responded to the scent from the grill and moved on to steaks. Scarza was alone, but Eddie's partner Otto sat at the table next to the booth, watching whatever moved.

Scarza wore a shark-gray suit with a string-thin pinstripe. The pale-gray tie had tiny yellow squares and a tie tack with a marquise-cut diamond. His pale, red-blotched hands were folded patiently in front of him. He had the good sense not to offer me one to shake.

"Please sit down." His fingers, just the fingers, gestured toward the seat across from him. I slipped into the booth. Eddie sat down at the table with Otto.

"Where's Mr. Winslow?" Scarza asked me, in his strangled rasp of a voice.

"In San Francisco, working."

The waiter brought over a glass, ice and a sealed bottle of whiskey.

"Want something to drink?" Scarza said.

"No, thank you."

Scarza moved his fingers again, and the waiter went away.

"I appreciate you accepting the invitation."

"Eddie didn't hit me while he was delivering it like he did last time."

Scarza gave me that flat smile, his fat lips stretched over his teeth. "I've heard you're the one who found my money."

"Yes. And the FBI trusts me not to tell anyone else it belonged to you. I believe Agent Bitterston would have spoken to you about that." And warned you to leave Peter and me alone.

"That bother you, it's my money?"

"It's got nothing to do with me. You performed a service for your country, and they paid you."

Scarza wrapped his hand around the bottle's neck, snapped

the seal, wrung the cap off, and poured himself an inch of whiskey.

"You got moxey." He took a heavy sip, then wiped his lips with the back of his index finger. "So, this character who ended up with my money."

"He didn't kill the people in that car."

"He killed this McCann, who was working for the Feds. I hear this McCann was killed with the same gun that killed Mickey."

"They were killed with the same gun, yes."

"Why'd he do it?"

"It's useless for me to speculate. Just because I come up with a reason doesn't mean it's true."

"You don't think he did it?"

"It doesn't matter what I think. It's what we know."

"You sound like a cop. Better than a cop. You don't ask to get paid for your opinion."

I believed Charlie must have done it, killed both men. But the thought of turning him over to Scarza's revenge, helpless in a prison cell, made me sick.

I said, "If he killed Mickey, it was because Mickey found out he had the money. Could Mickey have found out and not told you?"

"If Mala was mixed up in it. This dame that had it, she's a friend of Mala's."

"Mrs. Dunning didn't tell anyone she had it."

"She says."

"I know you don't like Mala, but Mickey loved her and she loved him."

"She tell you that?"

"She did."

"She's an actress."

"She wasn't in this country seven years ago. She can't have

been involved in the robbery. If Mickey found out anyone else had your money, even suspected someone had it, he would have told you."

"He would have looked into it, maybe, and this guy shot him."

"How could Mickey have traced that money to Charlie Dunning?"

Scarza's small unhappy eyes stared deep into me. "Then why'd he get killed?"

"I don't know."

"If you figure it out, I want to know. I would owe you a favor for the rest of my life."

"I wouldn't do it for that."

"I know," he said softly. "I'm just saying."

"Good night, Mr. Scarza." I slid out of the booth.

Eddie followed me out. On the sidewalk, I opened my handbag and he put my gun back into it.

"I'm sorry I had to hit you the other night," he said.

Then he went back inside.

Adrenaline surged through me. My body vibrated, my hands shook, my legs barely carried me to my car. I slammed the door, jammed the key into the ignition and roared the engine up.

Someone had told Scarza, told him I had a regular escort home, and what time I usually left. It was the only way he could have set me up with that phony call, the woman pretending to be from Peter's office. I was sure it was Mack Pace, trying to prove he wasn't afraid of Peter. Or proving he was afraid of Julie Scarza.

I had to calm down before Peter came home, before I saw him. Because right now I'd be perfectly happy to tell him he could put Mack Pace's head through a brick wall.

I needed to get out of here. I needed to drive, drive a long way, somewhere with fewer cars and stoplights. Somewhere without holiday crowds wishing each other the joy of the season while people were dead and other lives had been destroyed.

I headed for Santa Monica. By the time I reached Highway One, it was just past seven. Peter said he'd be at my house about ten. I had plenty of time.

I rolled down the window and let the wind whip my hair and buffet my body. The chill ocean air stung my cheeks, watered my eyes. I wiped them and kept driving.

Sitting in that booth, across from that repellent man, I realized I hadn't thought too much about why Mickey Triton died. He hung out with gangsters, was friends with a gangster. I hadn't cared about him. I cared about McCann and whether I'd been in any way responsible for his getting killed.

But, in that booth, scrambling for reasons to keep Scarza from exacting his own kind of revenge, I also realized I had no idea why Charlie would have killed Mickey Triton. Shot him in the back of the head, then again through the body when he lay on the floor. And then set fire to his house, burned his body to try to cover it all up.

I had made a vague assumption that Triton found out somehow that Charlie had Scarza's money, that Kitty had let slip something during a séance, and the information had somehow got back to Triton.

But Kitty was being very, very cautious about her discovery. She lied to Madame about where the jewelry came from. And although she was trying to reach her dead husband through Madame to ask him about the valise, would she be likely to blurt out that she'd found two hundred thousand dollars in her attic? Would she be less circumspect about that than she was about a bracelet?

And the more I thought about it, I was sure Charlie hadn't even known the valise with the money had been found. When I first sat down beside him on the beach steps, he truly had no idea why the FBI was there. He was not pretending. It was only as we talked that he realized what had happened.

Was it possible Mickey's death and Major McCann's had nothing whatsoever to do with the theft of the money? We had all assumed the crimes were connected because some of the marked money had turned up at Marathon. And the day a federal agent came to investigate, he was killed.

But if Charlie didn't kill those two men, then he also didn't search the bungalow or Bill's house. Whatever the searcher was looking for, it wasn't related to the money.

I couldn't drive like this. I yanked the car into the gravel lot of a seafood joint, bumping hard over the tire ruts left by years of customers, past the rows of cars, and parked at the far end, my headlights beaming into the high yellow grass.

I dug into my handbag, past my folded script pages, my notebook, my gun, my lock picks and everything else in there. I pulled out my handkerchief, wiped away the water the wind had forced from my eyes. Cleared my eyes. Tried to clear my mind.

Start over, start from the beginning.

Mickey was the first to die, and the killing was intentional.

The killer had burned the cabin to try to cover up the crime, even though it was a clumsy job. An amateur job, Peter had called it. It wouldn't conceal the bullet hole in the skull. And if the killer had just walked away, the murder might have been put down to some mobster, a shot to the back of the head.

What was the killer trying to cover up?

McCann's killing had almost certainly not been planned.

The killer was searching the bungalow assigned to Bill, and was surprised there.

Later, Bill's cottage was searched.

Bill had something the killer wanted.

But Bill didn't know Mickey Triton.

Whatever the killer was searching for in the bungalow, it was dangerous to the killer. So dangerous he killed McCann rather than face questions about what he'd been doing there.

Yet McCann had not thought the killer dangerous. He hadn't drawn his gun.

Was it someone who belonged there?

Someone who looked harmless?

Someone McCann trusted?

What could be so dangerous it was worth taking another life?

Dear God.

I flipped the ceiling light on, dug furiously once again into my handbag, past the script, the notebook, the gun. And found the reason.

CHAPTER 28

I had to find a pay phone. But who would I call? The local police? They didn't know me from Adam, weren't about to send squad cars out because I told them to. Sergeant Barty? Bitterston? Even if I could find them, they were too far away.

I fishtailed across the gravel and bounced out of the parking lot onto the highway. I floored the accelerator. How far was it? A mile. Two?

The highway was two lanes. I had to weave into oncoming traffic to pass, had to wait for an opportunity, cursing the holiday traffic I hadn't counted on. Cursing the red lights I had to stop for. I couldn't afford to run any of them, couldn't afford to get pulled over.

Two miles took an eternity.

There it was, the Malibu Colony. I flung the car across the highway to the gate. The guardhouse. The guard. He was on the phone.

I slammed on the brakes and screamed at him. "Call the police! Send them to Kitty Dunning's! Tell them to use sirens!"

The receiver still in his hand, he took a step toward the car, frowning, official.

He was going to stop me, make me explain.

"Call the police! Send them to the Dunnings!"

I rammed the gas pedal into the floor, skidded around the corner and into the narrow lane behind the houses.

Kitty's back gate was open. I roared into the courtyard, hit the brakes, and jerked to a stop. I threw myself over the seat back and snatched up the flashlight on the floor behind me. I pulled out my gun.

There was no sign of the chauffeur, of any sort of help. The garage was dark, the courtyard silent. But it was not empty. There was a Buick convertible next to Kitty's Packard.

I didn't scream for help. The chauffeur was probably down in the main house, having dinner. Even if someone came, they'd only slow me down, get in my way, ask me what the hell I was doing.

I dashed across the courtyard and down the steps to the second tier. There were hard shadows across the lawn, across Bill's house. But there were no outside lights on. The cottage was dark. The curtains drawn. No sign of lamplight around them. But Bill was supposed to be home. He said he was spending the evening at home.

The front lock was broken; the FBI had broken it. I could storm right in. But the killer could be in there, and I'd have no idea where.

I'd be an easy target.

I lay on the doorbell, rang it over and over and over. I screamed, "Bill, open the door! Bill, the police are coming! Bill, open the door!"

I released the bell and dashed for the corner.

I'd been right. The killer was inside. Before I got there, I heard the patio door open, then someone moving, heels lightly scuffing on the paving stones, moving fast for the shelter of the trees that lined the property, the dark and invisibility.

I stepped around, leveled the flashlight, snapped it on. "Stop right there!"

The light struck the figure in the back. Still, it kept moving, hunched forward, a coat over the head, racing toward escape.

"I've got a gun and I'll use it! I know who you are! Stop!" I raised my gun and fired into the air.

I'd forgot how much recoil a gun had. It threw my arm back, staggered me. I almost lost my balance.

"Stop! Madame, stop!"

She stopped. She straightened her back and turned toward me, slowly, precisely, regally, her coat slipping back down to her shoulders.

"Where's Bill?" I demanded. "Where is he?"

"Why do you have a gun? Why are you shooting at me?"

"Where's Bill?"

"With Mrs. Dunning, in the house. Your hand is shaking. I think you do not know how to use that gun."

I pointed it directly at her face. "You want to bet your life on it?"

There was shouting from the garden below and the sound of feet scrambling up the stone steps.

"Over here!" I called to them. "It's Lauren Atwill!"

Bill and the chauffeur dashed toward us, the chauffeur still with a dinner napkin tucked into the collar of his uniform. They both stopped dead when they saw my gun.

"Jesus, Lauren!" Bill said.

Mala and Kitty raced up after, followed by the butler and some other household staff. I wasn't sure how many. I was watching Madame.

"What's going on?" Kitty cried. "Oh, God!" She grabbed Mala and pulled her back.

"What are you doing?" Mala strained to get away from Kitty. "Please, please put that down."

Madame said, "I am out walking and then she is screaming at me and pointing a gun."

"She's been searching Bill's house." I jerked my head toward the patio door, but it was closed. "The police are on the way. Bill, call the FBI. There's a card in my wallet. Bitterston's

251

number's on it. Call him."

"Where's your purse?"

Damn, it was in the car. "No, don't leave. You," I said to the chauffeur. "Go get the purse, in the front seat of the Lincoln. Bring it here."

Nobody moved.

"All right, all right. I'll put the gun down. But only if I know she doesn't have one. Bill. Do not get between us. Please go over to her. Go over to her, and see what she has in her coat pockets. See if she has a gun."

"Okay. Everybody stay calm. I'm going over there." He edged across, keeping well out of my line of fire. He came up beside Madame.

"Kitty, are you letting her do this?" Madame said.

"Kitty," I said, "the police think Charlie killed that man at the studio. But he didn't. Bill, check her pockets."

"No," Madame said. "This is wrong."

"Then we just stand here and wait for the police, and I keep this gun right where it is."

"Why on earth do you think she has a gun?" Mala said.

"Prove me wrong, Madame."

Bill took another step and Madame stiffened, took a half step back. He caught her elbow gently, and slid his hand into the capacious pocket of her coat. Nothing. He stepped behind her and did the same with the other.

He came out with a gun. Instinctively, he retreated, keeping it out of her reach.

"Is it a Webley?" I asked. "A thirty-two?"

"I don't know anything about guns."

"I do," the chauffeur volunteered. Holding it gingerly in front of him, Bill brought the gun back over and showed it to the young man. "Yes," the chauffeur said, "it's a Webley."

"A thirty-two?"

"Yes, ma'am."

"What the hell is going on?" Bill asked me.

"Major McCann was killed with a thirty-two-caliber Webley."

"She is not making sense," Madame declared.

I said, "Hang on to that, Bill. We'll just wait for the police." I lowered the gun, but kept it close to me.

Madame said, "I find this gun while I am walking, just now and am bringing it to Kitty."

"She found it, she found it," Mala pleaded. "She does not own a gun."

"The FBI searched this whole place the other day, both houses, the garages, the grounds, and they didn't find a gun," I said to the chauffeur. "Would you go into my car now? Please bring me my handbag. We need to call the FBI, too. Major McCann was working for them. They need to know the gun has been found. Would you please get my purse, and would you write down the license number of Madame's car while you're out there?"

He glanced at Kitty, who nodded cautiously, and then he strode off across the lawn, the napkin still in his uniform.

"I will not stay for this," Madame declared.

"Then leave, and I'll tell them whatever I want. The police will have your license number, they'll pick you up. Why don't we send these people back to the house?" I suggested to Kitty. "We'll wait for the police in the cottage."

Mala said, "I am not leaving her with you."

"Of course not. You and Kitty are welcome to stay." How absurd it sounded, like I was inviting them to tea.

The butler said, "I would wish to wait with your ladyship."

"Thank you," Kitty said, "but please see to the staff."

"Very well, ma'am." He bowed and reluctantly departed, shepherding the nervous, whispering staff back to the house. He went down the steps, watching me over his shoulder.

The chauffeur returned with my handbag and the license number written on a sheet from the slim notebook he kept inside his jacket. The napkin was gone.

I gave Bill the flashlight and took the handbag. I sent the chauffeur back, to watch for the police at the gate.

"It shouldn't be long. Let's go inside," I said. The rest of us went into Bill's cottage through his broken front door.

I directed Madame to the leather chair by the fire. I gave her the best seat. It was also the one furthest from the kitchen and its block of knives. I closed the kitchen door.

Mala and Kitty sat on the sofa. Bill pulled two of the dining chairs around to complete the circle. He set the chairs down where Madame wasn't too close to the guns we each held.

I got out Bitterston's card and called the number from the study. I explained things briefly. The FBI operator promised to find him.

As I came out of the study, there was a knock on the door. I thought the police were rather polite in Malibu. The door opened. The butler appeared.

"Ma'am," he said to Kitty, "we have received a call from the guard at the colony gate. He asked if there was a problem, that a woman had run through the gate and said something about your house. I'm afraid he waited to ask before calling the police, but I have instructed him to do so now."

"Thank you," Kitty said.

He bowed and left.

She said, "We get people who drink too much and play stupid pranks."

The guard had been circumspect, afraid it was some drunk's idea of a joke, afraid to call the police to Kitty's again after what had happened the other day.

"Ten minutes," I said. "It shouldn't be more than that."

Mala looked at me as I sat down. "Why are you doing this?

You were so nice to us. You and Mr. Winslow."

"Let's wait for the police."

"To tell them what? That you have such a crazy idea?"

"Mala," Bill said quietly, "she had the gun in her pocket."

"She found it! Did you not listen to her? And how can you say it killed anyone?"

I said, "Maybe it's not the same gun. The police will find out."

"By that time," Madame said, "you will have ruined her. It will be in the papers. No matter what the truth is, it will ruin her."

"Don't blame me for what you've done to your cousin." I held her eyes, pushing the full meaning of how much I knew. "For everything you've done to your cousin."

Her eyes, a luminous deep brown, with their heavy shadowing beneath, bore into mine. And then as if a veil had passed over them, all emotion disappeared.

"I am leaving." She stood up. "Unless you plan to shoot me."

"No!" Mala cried as she jumped up and grabbed her cousin's arm. "Please!"

Madame looked at me. "And will you tell her all the truth?"

"That can't be helped, not now. But I won't tell all of it to the police. And nobody in this room will either."

"She must not be ruined. She has done nothing."

"I will do what I can," I said.

"What are you doing?" Mala threw her arms around her cousin. "Please do not go."

Madame held her close, kissed her hair. "My cousin, my friend. You must rely on your other friends now."

"What are you talking about? Please. I know you did not do anything. I do not care what happens to me. Do not do this for me."

"I am not. You will understand that soon. Mr. Linden. Please."

Bill handed me the Webley, got up and with difficulty drew the protesting Mala away from her, into his arms. Held her while she wept and reached for Madame and begged her not to go.

"I once told you," Madame said to me, "that we cannot see all that will come. If we did, we would go mad."

"I'm sorry. I wish this had been different."

"I believe you do."

And she walked out of the cottage.

"What the hell have you done?" Kitty demanded of me.

"You don't really believe she just found that gun, lying around on the ground. Bill, sit her down." He settled Mala gently into the leather chair. He poured a brandy from the bar cart and handed it to her. "Go on, take some." Obediently, she did. He pulled over the ottoman and sat at her feet.

Kitty said, "Are you saying she was trying to blame me or Charlie or Bill?"

"Not Bill. She still had the gun with her. She was searching the cottage again. She wasn't planting the gun. I don't think she'd hurt Bill, not if she could help it."

I went into the study and put the guns away in the file cabinet, in different drawers. When the police arrived, I didn't want them to get confused by the presence of two guns, and think they had to confiscate mine. I locked both drawers and slipped the key into my pocket.

I came back to the living room. I couldn't sit. My nerves were on fire with a raw, painful electricity in my upper arms and thighs. "We thought the cases were connected, Major Mc-Cann's murder, the killings after the auction party, the theft of the money. McCann came to Marathon to investigate all that, and the day he arrived he was murdered. But there was no connection. It was sheer coincidence.

"He went to that bungalow looking for sales receipts, deposit slips, correspondence, anything that might indicate either Bill or Alastair Bishop had ever been in possession of any of the stolen jewelry or large sums of money that couldn't be explained. He heard someone breaking in the back door. He hid in the bathroom. Madame came in and began to search as well.

"McCann stepped out to ask her what she was doing. He didn't pull his gun. He had no idea she was dangerous. But she couldn't afford to answer questions, let anybody know she'd been there, let anybody see the gun in her purse."

"What the hell was she looking for?" Kitty asked.

I picked up my handbag and pulled out the packet of letters. "These. Letters Mala Demara wrote to Bill before the war. He'd seen her first screen test over in London, and thought she was wonderful. He wrote to her, encouraged her. For a while she wrote back, then the war made it impossible. The letters are from a girl who wanted nothing more than to act. A girl with dreams and ambition and talent. She writes about her cousin Zorka Karoly, and their plans to come to America. She even writes a bit about Mickey Triton, whom she met briefly in London and who was nice to her. Who said to look him up when she got to the States. There's even a picture of the cousins." I slipped it out and handed it to her. "Quite clearly Mala and Zorka."

"So?" Kitty said.

"In the end, it's what you won't find in the letters. Mala Demara's handwriting or Mala Demara's fingerprints."

Mala pulled herself back into the chair, suddenly small and frail, weeping quietly.

"This is not Mala," I said. "This is Zorka Karoly."

Bill said, "She can't be. I saw her. I saw Mala."

"A long time ago, and only on screen. And you were drunk. You mostly remembered she was a wonderful actress. She was pretty, dark-haired, large brown eyes, lovely figure. You never actually met her. And you always knew she was older than she claimed to be. It was Madame you saw. She's the real Mala Demara. All those years in the war, whatever she'd gone through, the deprivation, the loss of her family, had robbed her of whatever youthful beauty she had. She had gained weight. She drank too much. And so she made herself look even older than she was. The heavy makeup, the clothes, the hairstyle, the untended hairline. And yet, if you looked closely, you could see that she was actually an attractive woman. She changed herself to conform to her clients' idea of what a spiritualist should look like. But she also wanted to make sure that anyone who'd ever seen her would not look beneath the image. Just as the studio crafted the image of Mala Demara, she crafted one for Madame Karoly.

"But she didn't fool Mickey Triton. Or at least Mickey realized the woman he saw auditioning to sing at Elizondo's was not the Mala Demara he met in London. He stood up when he saw her. Of course, everybody thought he was smitten. But he stood up because it wasn't Mala.

"He fell in love with the new Mala, kept her secret, kept away men who claimed to know her, even beat up some of them to keep them away, on the off chance one of them actually did know the real Mala.

"But Mickey got tired of being a back-street romance. He wanted marriage. And Mala did too. Then Bill told Mala that he'd found the letters she'd written to him, but he got booted off the picture before he gave them to her. The cousins could hardly demand them. They couldn't make them seem important. But Madame knew she had to get them back. She didn't remember precisely what she'd said in them. What if there was something that gave it all away and eventually Bill realized the truth? If he breathed a word, it would be disastrous. They had only got into the country because Marathon had once offered

Mala Demara another screen test. To get into the States, they needed to switch identities, in their passports. One word and they might both be thrown back into Europe.

"Mickey was a more serious problem. He wanted to marry the woman who claimed to be Mala Demara. He wasn't the sort to let his wife have a serious career. But that career was all Madame had. Living the life of a star through her cousin, guiding her, advising her, teaching her how to act the parts as she would have done them. It was all she had.

"So she killed him. She did it when her cousin was out of town, presuming her cousin would have an alibi. The killing would be blamed on the sort of men Mickey knew. She burned the cabin not to conceal the murder, but so no one would find any evidence her cousin had ever been there. Then she planned to get the letters back. They'd be safe.

"But Scarza's thugs came around their house, looking for Mala. Madame hadn't realized how much Scarza hated the woman Mickey loved. She told Mala, who was terrified and refused to come home. It was now more important than ever that no trace of their identity switch remain.

"After her appointment with Bishop on Thursday, she went to the bungalow Bill had been using, just to look for the letters, and there—by pure coincidence—was Major McCann. She panicked. She couldn't risk him finding the gun in her purse. She shot him with the same gun she used to kill Mickey."

"No, no," Mala whispered.

"The police are going to be here soon. Kitty, take her back to the house."

"I cannot let you say those things," Mala said, sobbing.

"Kitty, please. Take her to your room, keep her there. Agent Bitterston will be here soon. Please do this. For her. Call her lawyer, and say nothing to the police till he gets here. Don't let her tell them the truth about who she is. There might still be a way to keep that secret."

Kitty and Bill helped Mala to the house. I called Juanita. Peter would be there soon, I said. Ask him to wait for me. Tell him the killer had been found, and I was fine. But I might be a while. I didn't say where I was. He'd come out here. It wouldn't do any good.

Bill returned as the police rolled into the courtyard. I told him not to mention the letters to anyone. I had removed the Webley from the file cabinet by then and laid it on the dining table. I told the police what the gun had done. They got on their radio to call for the detectives investigating the Mickey Triton killing. It would take a while to get them—they'd be at home now.

Bitterston arrived a couple of minutes before the detectives. He showed his identification, and the officers gave us enough time alone for me to tell him everything quickly. When the detectives appeared, he spoke to them. I'd been working with the FBI, he said, and all he could tell them now was that the gun had been recovered in Madame's possession, and there were witnesses. Madame Karoly had motive for killing Mr. Triton and they might want to get a warrant to search her house for any evidence she had started the fire. She depended on Mala for her career as a spiritualist, and Mala had decided to marry Mr. Triton. The FBI wasn't yet sure why she had killed the man at Marathon Studios, but they were investigating and would debrief the detectives as soon as they could.

After the detectives verified my story about where the gun had been found, they had little choice but to release me into Bitterston's custody.

Peter was waiting in my study.

We told him what had happened. It was apparent that everyone's secrets were about to come out. I didn't care whether the world discovered the FBI had been in league with the mob.

But I cared very much about Mala suffering any more than she already had, and about this bringing devastating publicity down on Sam Ross and the studio.

Peter poured himself a bourbon, unbuttoned his coat, sat down and looked at Bitterston, "How many federal laws are you willing to break to keep your secrets?"

Chapter 29

The police and FBI wired pictures of Madame Karoly and sketches of what she'd look like without her heavy-makeup disguise to all the border checkpoints. They also watched the ports, the train and bus stations. They didn't find her.

Bitterston briefed the detectives with the story Peter helped him invent: Madame had been jealous of Mickey. Mala was going to marry him and was considering leaving her career. It would have been devastating for Madame's business. She killed him and burned the cabin to try to cover up the crime. They had no idea why she had gone to the Marathon Studios bungalow. Major McCann had been involved in a case that had nothing to do with her. Whatever she was there for—perhaps to leave the gun in a clumsy, desperate attempt to cast blame elsewhere—the major had confronted her, and she must have panicked and killed him.

It wasn't the tightest of stories—Sergeant Barty in particular was dubious—but they had two killings they could mark solved. Their bosses said leave it alone.

The studio delayed filming, and the publicity department rolled into action. Morty Engler began to weave his magic, casting Mala as the victim—and placing considerable distance between her and the cousin she had loved. Alastair Bishop affirmed publicly that he'd seen signs of this jealousy in Madame Karoly, and had advised Mala to break with her cousin. But Mala was a kind, loyal girl. He regretted that he did not see how dangerous the woman had become. He was a good liar.

Peter called in the favor Julie Scarza had promised us if we found Triton's killer. Mala was innocent, Peter said. She'd loved Mickey and he wouldn't want her destroyed by this. Scarza turned out to be, at least as far as favors were concerned, a man of his word.

Scarza made another deal with the federal government. He would tell them where a drug shipment was landing, and in exchange they'd get Mala Demara a passport with her real name on it. The drug agents would make headlines. People would get promoted, citizens would remain confident their protectors were doing their jobs. Scarza's men of course would be warned and get away before they could be picked up.

Bitterston went back to Washington, his case wrapped up, his secrets safe.

Peter took Christmas week off—his boss could like it or not—and stayed with me.

Helen returned from New York and took care of me, too. She got me out of the house, took me shopping for Christmas. I bought Peter a new fedora. It seemed like the sort of thing a private detective ought to have. She and Sam invited us over for a quiet dinner. Sam offered me the job of working with Bill to rewrite the script. It was going to need a lot of work now. Bishop had agreed to let Bill come back, if he promised to keep his mouth in check.

The body of the real Mala Demara was found on a Monterey beach on New Year's Day, dressed in a fur coat and a white satin gown. A bottle of champagne and a crystal glass beside her. A gun near her hand.

She'd died from a single gunshot to the head.

There was a small, private memorial service for Madame, arranged by some of her loyal clients.

Her cousin, the actress Mala Demara, did not attend.
I was not invited.

ABOUT THE AUTHOR

Sheila York spent much of her childhood in Germany, the daughter of an army officer, and later studied abroad as an exchange student in England and France. After postgraduate studies in psychology, she took a sharp turn and enjoyed a long career as a radio disk jockey—with assignments in New York and Los Angeles, where her stories take place—before combining her love of movies and history into writing. She serves as treasurer of the New York regional chapter of the Mystery Writers of America, and lives in Bloomfield, New Jersey, with her husband, David F. Nighbert.